Kate Fortune's Journal Entry

Heavens me! My long-lost son, Brandon, has a grown daughter! Of course, no one in the Fortune family knew about Angelica until a blackmailer began threatening to murder the young woman and frame poor Brandon for this unspeakable crime. How ever can I help Brandon out of this mess?

Flynt Corrigan is the only person I can trust with this delicate business. I know, without a doubt in my mind, that Angelica is innocent. So I've just sent Flynt down to Birmingham with Brandon to protect the newest Fortune and to introduce Angelica to her father. Of course, even I never thought anything might develop between Flynt and Angelica. But it has. And now, with a little nudging from me, Angelica will not only know the love of the Fortune family but also discover true love with Flynt.

Dear Reader,

I was delighted to be asked to write a book in the Fortune's Children: The Brides series, because I was already familiar with the Fortune family. I'd previously written *Stand-In Bride* for the original Fortune's Children series and a short story in *A Fortune's Children Christmas*.

The Brides miniseries introduces Kate's brother-in-law Caleb's grandchildren, but my book, *The Hoodwinked Bride*, brings back some characters from the original series. This intrigued me, because I'd always wondered, What happened when Brandon was returned to his family after he'd been missing for all those years? A little back story is probably in order here: shortly after birth, Brandon Fortune had been given away (but was presumed to have been kidnapped) by his father to demented movie queen Monica Malone. At the end of the series, Brandon learned his true identity, and this long-lost child—now an adult who'd been brought up as a spoiled Hollywood kid—came back to be with the Fortunes. Except we never saw those scenes!

Brandon wasn't quite hero material, but it seems he has a daughter he didn't know about. Angelica, living with her mother, who is Brandon's first love, is found and is fascinated by Flynt Corrigan, the investigator her grandmother Kate hired. I hope you enjoy reading about them being "hoodwinked" into a wedding and a happy ending.

Sincerely,

Barbara Boswell

A FORTUNE'S CHILDREN™
Wedding

BARBARA BOSWELL
The Hoodwinked Bride

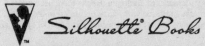

Published by Silhouette Books
America's Publisher of Contemporary Romance

If you purchased this book without a cover you should be aware that this book is stolen property. It was reported as "unsold and destroyed" to the publisher, and neither the author nor the publisher has received any payment for this "stripped book."

SILHOUETTE BOOKS

A FORTUNE'S CHILDREN WEDDING: THE HOODWINKED BRIDE

Copyright © 1999 by Harlequin Books S.A.

ISBN 0-373-38900-0

Special thanks and acknowledgment are given to Barbara Boswell for her contribution to the Fortune's Children series.

All rights reserved. Except for use in any review, the reproduction or utilization of this work in whole or in part in any form by any electronic, mechanical or other means, now known or hereafter invented, including xerography, photocopying and recording, or in any information storage or retrieval system, is forbidden without the written permission of the editorial office, Silhouette Books, 233 Broadway, New York, NY 10279 U.S.A.

All characters in this book have no existence outside the imagination of the author and have no relation whatsoever to anyone bearing the same name or names. They are not even distantly inspired by any individual known or unknown to the author, and all incidents are pure invention.

This edition published by arrangement with Harlequin Books S.A.

® and TM are trademarks of Harlequin Books S.A., used under license. Trademarks indicated with ® are registered in the United States Patent and Trademark Office, the Canadian Trade Marks Office and in other countries.

Visit Silhouette Books at www.eHarlequin.com

Printed in U.S.A.

Fortune Family Tree

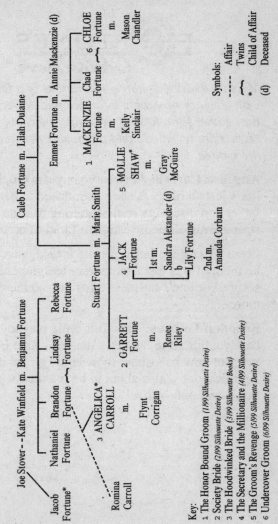

Joe Stover - - Kate Winfield m. Benjamin Fortune

Caleb Fortune m. Lilah Dulaine

Jacob Fortune*

Nathaniel Fortune

Brandon Fortune ⟨ Lindsay Fortune

Rebecca Fortune

3 ANGELICA* CARROLL
m.
Flynt Corrigan

Romina Carroll

Stuart Fortune m. Marie Smith

2 GARRETT Fortune
m.
Renee Riley

4 JACK Fortune

1st m.
Sandra Alexander (d)
b
Lily Fortune

2nd m.
Amanda Corbain

Emmet Fortune m. Annie Mackenzie (d)

1 MACKENZIE Fortune
m.
Kelly Sinclair

Chad Fortune ⟨ 6 CHLOE Fortune
m.
Mason Chandler

5 MOLLIE SHAW*
m.
Gray McGuire

Symbols:
- - - - Affair
⟨ Twins
* Child of Affair
(d) Deceased

Key:
1 The Honor Bound Groom (1/99 Silhouette Desire)
2 Society Bride (2/99 Silhouette Desire)
3 The Hoodwinked Bride (3/99 Silhouette Books)
4 The Secretary and the Millionaire (4/99 Silhouette Desire)
5 The Groom's Revenge (5/99 Silhouette Desire)
6 Undercover Groom (6/99 Silhouette Desire)

FORTUNE'S
Children™

Meet the Fortunes—three generations of a family with a legacy of wealth, influence and power. As they gather for a host of weddings, shocking family secrets are revealed...and passionate new romances are ignited.

Angelica Carroll: At twenty-six years old, her life's just starting, as she's introduced to her real father and discovers soul-shattering passion in the strong arms of the investigator hired to protect her.

Flynt Corrigan: Jaded private investigator. What he thought was just a temporary assignment to secure Fortune's business turns into so much more....

Brandon Fortune: This California playboy has barely adjusted to the news that he's Kate Fortune's son, but now he's about to meet his *grown* daughter. And Brandon's also about to be reunited with his first—and only—love!

Prologue

"I've located your missing granddaughter, Kate,"
Flynt Corrigan addressed the Fortune matriarch before
turning to her son Brandon. "We've found your daughter, Brandon."

"Nice work, Corrigan." Sterling Foster, Kate's attor-
ney husband, nodded approvingly at Flynt, then laid a
supportive hand on her shoulder. "Another grandchild!
Congratulations, Kate, my dear. Oh, and, er, congratulations to you, too, Brandon," he added quickly.

Flynt studied Brandon Fortune, assessing his reaction
to newly discovered fatherhood. Once he'd confirmed
the news, Flynt had come to the Fortune family's estate.
Kate had brought everyone into the study to hear his
findings.

"So it's really true?" Brandon was clearly stunned.
He sank into a chair and ran his hand through his overly
long blond hair. His skin, tough and leathery from too

much California sun and surf, had turned ashen beneath his perpetual tan. "All of it, Flynt? The daughter? The threats? It's all true?"

Flynt felt a surge of sympathy for the man. Brandon Malone Fortune, third son of Kate and Ben Fortune who'd built the multi-international Fortune Corporation and founded a dynasty, had led a very strange life indeed. Learning that he was a father at this late date—*and* the victim of a blackmail threat—was another startling chapter in it.

"It's all true, Brandon," Flynt assured him.

"Brandon has a daughter! How wonderful!" Kate Fortune was smiling. Even though she'd only learned about this possibility a few days ago, she clearly didn't mind the revelation. "Except for the threats, of course." Her smile faded. "Who could have sent that note to poor Brandon? It's beyond cruel—first informing him that he is the father of a daughter and then threatening to kill that daughter and frame Brandon for the murder unless the Fortune family pays."

"Terrible," Sterling muttered, heading over to the bar in the study. "My poor Kate."

Flynt glanced at Brandon, who still seemed to be in a state of shock. Sterling handed his stepson a shot of brandy, which Brandon drained in one gulp.

"I'm a father," mumbled Brandon.

Flynt took his cue to proceed with the information he'd gathered. "Your daughter's name is Angelica Carroll, Brandon, and she is—"

"Carroll?" Brandon sat straight up in the chair. "Romina?" He jumped to his feet. "But I haven't seen Romina Carroll in years. *Years!*"

"Romina Carroll is the mother of your daughter, Brandon," said Flynt. He was more than a little surprised that Brandon remembered Romina Carroll at all, given that it had been decades since the two had been together. And from his own investigation, Flynt had learned that Brandon's list of female companions down through the years had been—well, numerous was one word that came to mind, which was something of a diplomatic understatement.

"You remember this Romina Carroll, Brandon?" Sterling Foster seemed to be speaking Flynt's own thoughts aloud. Flynt met the older man's wry gaze with his own.

"Of course I remember Romina!" Brandon began to frantically pace the room. "She was my high school girlfriend! Well, she didn't go to Beverly Hills High School with me, she lived in East L.A. We met on the boardwalk in Venice Beach one day when we'd both ditched school. It was like love at first sight for us and we—we were each other's firsts, you know? You just don't forget that! We went together for two years, longer than I've ever been with any other girl."

He slumped back down onto the sofa, scowling. "Romina dumped me when she was sixteen and I was seventeen. I took it hard, and after that I never saw her again. Now, you're saying she was—she was—" He couldn't seem to get out the word.

"Pregnant," Flynt said it for him. "With your daughter, Angelica, who is now twenty-six years old." He reached into the file he was holding and retrieved a photograph. "Here's a picture of Angelica, taken by one of my investigators. It was shot with a long-distance lens so the quality isn't very good…'' Before handing it over to Brandon, Flynt couldn't resist taking another look at it himself.

Though it was grainy and not too clear, Flynt had spent an inordinate amount of time studying that photograph. He wasn't sure why. She was pretty, that was quite evident despite the somewhat blurred black-and-white telephoto shot, but he'd never been the type to drool over pictures of pretty girls. Not that he was drooling over Angelica Carroll, Flynt promptly assured himself.

He was intrigued by the concept of her. That had to be it, Flynt decided. As a former FBI agent, he had naturally slipped back into full Bureau training mode, which required an eye for detail in a case. His eyes had certainly detailed Angelica Carroll, he acknowledged a bit sheepishly.

So he provided himself with another rationale. In his current role as president and founder of Security Management Services—SMS to the industry—he knew it would be good business to commit to memory everything to do with this case, because it involved the Fortunes, one of the most prominent and successful families in the country. Therefore, he had seared Angelica Carroll's face into his memory, along with the facts he'd learned about her.

''Angelica is unmarried, has no children and works as a nurse-midwife at MetroHealth, a university-related hospital in Birmingham, Alabama.'' Flynt recited the facts.

Brandon raised his eyes from the photo. ''What about Romina?''

"Romina lives in Birmingham, too. She has three other children, all younger than Angelica. As for the threatening note you received—"

"Do you think it's possible that Angelica herself might have sent Brandon the threat, Flynt?" asked Sterling. "Or perhaps the mother, Romina, sent it in a bid to cash in on the, uh, Fortune connection?"

"I don't know," admitted Flynt. "There is that possibility, of course. I haven't met either of them. I thought I'd give you this information first and let you decide what to do with it before I proceeded any further."

"Brandon must meet his child," Kate decreed. "And if Angelica or her mother sent that awful blackmail threat—well, we shall deal with that misguided bid for attention later."

"Kate, I consider a blackmail attempt to be a criminal action, not simply a misguided bid for attention," countered Flynt. Breaking the law was a personal affront to him.

Kate shrugged. "I propose that Brandon go to Birmingham immediately to meet his daughter, and that you go along with him, Flynt. For protection as well as for moral support."

She stood beside her son and fondly ruffled his stiff, dry hair. It was a maternal gesture, one that she'd been unable to make when Brandon had been a child because she hadn't known him as a child. She hadn't known him until he had come back into her life some nine years ago because he had been taken from her as an infant. Pain shot through her, as it always did when she thought of the terrible fate that had befallen Brandon—and herself.

For years she had lived with the horror; her newborn

baby boy had been kidnapped and despite a ransom payment, had never been recovered. And then nine years ago, the truth—and Brandon—had surfaced, breaking Kate's heart all over again. Brandon hadn't been kidnapped at all. He had been secretly given away to the legendary movie star Monica Malone by Ben Fortune, Kate's first husband and Brandon's father at the end of their tempestuous affair. Obtaining Brandon had seemingly satisfied Monica's obsession to have a child by Ben. And Ben had never considered it necessary to mention the affair or the kidnap hoax or the baby boy to Kate ever again.

Brandon had been raised as a spoiled, yet emotionally neglected, Hollywood kid by the narcissistic movie siren. And though Kate had been overjoyed to have Brandon back, his upbringing had resulted in traits that annoyed or infuriated other members of the Fortune family whenever he visited from California. He had yet to be fully accepted by his siblings and his numerous adult nieces and nephews.

"Bad karma, huh, Mom?" Brandon stared up at her, seeming to read her thoughts. "I mean, Monica blackmailed Ben into handing me over to her and now here's my own kid and more blackmail. I wonder what gives? What do you think, Flynt?"

Flynt was not one to delve into the arcane mysteries of karma. Now that he'd located Brandon's daughter, which had been a personal request from his friend Gabe Devereax, husband of Kate's youngest daughter, Rebecca, his mind was back on the business of running SMS. "I'm sorry, Kate, but I won't be able to go to

Birmingham with Brandon. That really isn't the sort of work that—''

''I believe your company has handled some computer surveillance for the Fortune Corporation in the past,'' interjected Kate. ''But your firm does more than investigate electronic espionage, doesn't it?''

''SMS provides a full range of services,'' Flynt said eagerly. His company was his pride and joy. ''We're very well regarded in all branches of the security field.''

''Well, I have every confidence that we can arrive at an agreement that would be mutually advantageous to your company and ours, Flynt.'' Kate easily resumed the executive mantle she'd worn for so many years. ''One involving the full range of security services provided by SMS.''

''Kate, are you attempting to bribe Corrigan with a comprehensive contract for his Security Management Services?'' quizzed Sterling. He didn't appear to be averse to said bribe, however.

''My offer is to turn over *all* corporate security matters for the Fortune Corporation worldwide to SMS,'' Kate said, spelling out the terms. ''I'll run it by Michael and Caroline—those are my grandchildren who are the company's chief executives,'' she added to Flynt in an aside, ''but I'm certain they'll agree.''

The offer—okay, so it really was a bribe—swirled in Flynt's head. What an opportunity! The Fortune Corporation would be the most lucrative, prestigious account in his fast-growing business.

''Let me get this straight.'' Flynt was pleased to hear how steady his voice sounded, as if he fielded fantastic offers like this every day. ''SMS gets to handle all the

Fortune Corporation's security if I go to Birmingham with Brandon and set up a meeting between him and his daughter?''

Which meant that Brandon wouldn't be the only one to meet Angelica Carroll. Angelica's picture flashed before his mind's eye. A thrill of anticipation jolted through Flynt, shocking him with its force. That the thought of meeting the unknown Angelica seemed to be engaging his interest as much as the extraordinary corporate opportunity was more than a little disconcerting. It was so unlike him. Work was—and had always been—his consuming interest.

"Not quite, dear." Kate smiled shrewdly. "It'll take time for Brandon and his daughter to connect. One meeting simply isn't enough. Flynt, I'd like you to stay in Birmingham while Brandon and Angelica get to know each other. Then we'll sign the contract."

"And is the contract contingent upon a happy ending to this tale?" Flynt drawled. He should've known there was a catch. There always was. "Because if there is, I'm not interested. My time is too valuable to waste chasing rainbows."

"You're too young to be so cynical, my dear," Kate reproved.

Flynt grinned in spite of himself. He was thirty-six, and it had been a long time since someone had told him he was "too young" for anything. He liked Kate's take-action style. But not enough to accept the job unless the terms were sweetened in his favor.

Apparently, Kate realized that. "As much as I want Brandon's relationship with Angelica to develop into a lasting one, I realize it might not happen." She sighed.

"The contract isn't contingent on a happy ending, but there must be time and effort on your part to help their relationship along, Flynt. However, if Brandon and Angelica are simply incompatible, it won't be your fault. We'll sign that contract, regardless of the outcome."

"It's an extremely generous offer," said Sterling. "If I were legally representing you, I'd urge you to accept it, Corrigan."

It took Flynt all of one minute to follow Sterling's advice. "With computers and faxes and phone conferences, I can temporarily run the business from Alabama as well as from anywhere. I'll schedule a trip to Birmingham with Brandon," Flynt said decisively. "Is tomorrow too soon to go, Brandon?"

Brandon wore the expression of a man poised on the ledge of a building, trying to decide whether or not to jump.

"Tomorrow would be wonderful," Kate answered for her son. "Isn't that right, Brandon?"

Brandon's panicked eyes met Flynt's, who took pity on him. He gave him a bolstering, fraternal pat on the back. "Brandon, pack your bags. We're heading for Birmingham."

Chapter 1

Flynt knocked on the door of the small, white frame house and wondered if he'd erred on the side of caution by not bringing Brandon along with him for this first visit to the Carrolls. Did he really need to play "advance man"?

Word around this well-tended, working-class neighborhood was that Romina Carroll tended to keep to herself but was hardworking and well thought of. She supported herself and her two youngest children by running a pet-sitting service, caring for the pets of people on vacation and others who worked during the day. She also baked and sold cookies to college students at Samford University and the University of Alabama's Birmingham branch campus.

He knocked again, and the door opened a crack. Flynt tried to make himself look innocuous; he even managed what he hoped was a cheery smile. The mouthwatering smell of freshly baked cookies drifted from the house, and he inhaled deeply. And decided to act on a hunch. "I'm not from the State or the City Health Department, I swear."

"The neighbors called to warn us that somebody was snooping around, asking questions about us," a husky feminine voice replied from within.

"I bet it was old Mr. Willard next door who sounded the alarm about the Health Department," Flynt said dryly, trying to see inside. It was almost impossible, with the door barely cracked. "He asked me more questions than I asked him, and they were all about permits and inspections and cookies like his mother used to make without government harassment."

"Mr. Willard claims government jackals want a piece of everybody's pie." The female voice sounded amused. Yet wary and still on guard.

Flynt was tired of being stalled; it was past time to come to the point. "I'm Flynt Corrigan." He slipped his business card through the crack. "I need to speak to Angelica Carroll."

"What about?"

"I need to speak to Angelica Carroll," he repeated.

"This card says you're president of something called Security Management Services." The insider's voice was not only skeptical, it blatantly mocked him. "Am I supposed to believe that a president of a company is going door-to-door selling— What exactly are you hawking, anyway? Home security alarm systems? Well, we don't need one, we're already protected. Maybe you didn't notice the sign posted in the yard? Or the decal on the front window?"

"You think I'm an incompetent salesman with a bogus business card?" Flynt shook his head, his voice laced with irony. "Ouch. My ego is decimated."

"Goodbye, Mr. Corrigan."

He knew the door was about to be closed and wouldn't be reopened to him. All his law-enforcement reflexes were instantly activated. Flynt went straight for the door, wedged himself in the opening crack and pushed hard.

He heard an indignant gasp but he kept pushing, until the door was wide open and he was standing inside the house in a small, dimly lit vestibule.

"If you come one step closer, you're toast, mister." The threat was delivered by his husky-voiced sparring partner, but her words didn't fully register with him.

Instead, Flynt found himself gulping for air. The sight of the young woman standing in the shadows a few feet away from him had literally taken his breath away.

It was Angelica Carroll. After all the time he'd spent studying her picture, Flynt knew he would've recognized her anywhere. What he hadn't expected was her powerful physical impact on him. She had been intriguing in that grainy photo, but in person she absolutely captivated him. He reminded himself to inhale while his observational skills catalogued her.

Since he'd investigated her background, he knew of her mother's mixed Romanian-Spanish descent. Those elements, combined with the distinctive Fortune good looks, created an ethnic hodgepodge mixing exotic, adorable and classic features into one unforgettable face, Flynt thought dizzily. He was at once amazed and dazed in a way he'd never been before. He couldn't take his eyes off her.

She was small-boned, and he gauged her height at somewhere around five foot three or four. Her big dark eyes were framed by dark lashes and brows, her mouth beautifully shaped, the lips sensuously full. She had an ivory complexion, a striking contrast with the inky black color of her hair. It fell around her shoulders in a thick, silken curtain.

He blinked. And then visibly started. For not only was she incredibly attractive, she was also holding a gun, a snub-nosed .38, pointed straight at his chest.

"I'm not kidding," Angelica said sternly. "One false move and you're—"

"Toast," Flynt completed the threat. "Yes, you mentioned that already."

"You don't really believe I'll do it, do you?" Angelica sounded disgruntled. "Well, don't challenge me or else—"

"I'll be *burned* toast?" Flynt suggested.

Perhaps he was being reckless, but he wasn't afraid of being shot by Angelica Carroll. The uncanny spell she seemed to have cast upon him struck him as far more dangerous than that gun, Flynt mused. Why else would he be gazing at her like a dumbstruck yokel in the presence of a royal princess?

"Angel, I heard voices, what's going on? Who is this?"

The woman who joined them in the vestibule just had to be Romina, Flynt decided. Angelica's response confirmed his hunch.

"Everything is under control, Mama. Don't worry."

"He's with the FBI!" Romina exclaimed, her dark eyes pinning Flynt with a laser stare.

Flynt felt a peculiar frisson ripple through him. He was dressed in jeans, a white T-shirt and a jacket and knew his hair was a tad too long for regulation Bureau standards.

"What makes you think that?" He tried to sound casual but Romina's response disconcerted him. He'd rarely been so quickly identified on sight as an agent, even when he actually had been working for the FBI.

"Instincts, honey. I operate on them," Romina said flatly.

Flynt attempted to study Romina a bit more covertly than the frank way she was studying him. She looked like a version of Cher, he decided. Long, dark, straight hair and bangs, piercing dark eyes. Average height, average weight. Dressed in black leggings and an extra-long, crimson University of Alabama T-shirt.

Since his presence so far had only inspired Angelica to threaten to shoot him, he decided to address Romina instead. "I'm Flynt Corrigan, of Security Management Services, and I'd like to talk to you about your daughter, Angelica."

"What about my Angel?" Romina bristled, her body language as defensive as her tone.

"I've been retained by the Fortu—" Flynt began, before Romina let out an ear-piercing scream.

"Mama, it's all right," Angelica said to calm her.

"Ms. Carroll, Romina, please get control of yourself," Flynt ordered, but Romina kept screaming.

Within seconds, a teenage girl and a younger boy came racing into the vestibule.

"Mama, what's wrong?" cried the boy.

The girl took action. She seized an umbrella from the tall ceramic stand in the corner and began to smack Flynt with it. "What did you do to our mama? Get out of here! Get out now!"

The attack was so unexpected that the girl got in two good whacks across his back and shoulders before Flynt's trained reflexes kicked in. He grabbed the end of the umbrella and yanked it out of the teenager's hands.

The boy emitted what may have been an attempt at a warrior's whoop and charged Flynt, who easily side-stepped him. The young charger crashed into the wall instead.

"Oh, Casper!" Romina heaved a deep sigh.

"Stop right there, son!" Flynt's voice, which had once caused criminals to halt in their tracks, proved just as effective on the boy, who was about to rush at him again. Casper froze in place. The girl shrank against Romina.

"There is no cause for alarm." Flynt changed his tone into one of soothing reassurance.

He directed his attention to the boy and girl. They had to be Romina's younger children, fourteen-year-old Sarah and twelve-year-old Casper, who'd been mere footnotes in his fact-finding probe. Now here they were in the flesh. Flynt knew there was another sibling too, Daniel, a twenty-one-year-old Marine currently serving in Bosnia.

Sarah looked wholesome and perky in her cheerleading outfit, her hair caught up in a dark ponytail. Young Casper, short and skinny with his thick-lensed eyeglasses sliding down his nose, was small and scared and literally trembling. Flynt felt sorry for him.

"I'm Flynt Corrigan, and I came here to talk to your mother and older sister." He knew he'd better talk fast because Romina looked like she was gearing up to shriek again. "I think your mom must have misinterpreted what I said, because I certainly have no intention of causing trouble or harm to any of you."

"Very impressive," Angelica said coolly. "You play both bad cop and good cop, and you segue from one to the other without missing a beat. Now, drop the umbrella or I'll shoot it out of your hand."

Flynt realized that he was indeed still holding the umbrella. He let go, and it clattered to the scuffed wood floor.

"Put your hands up in the air," ordered Angelica. "The way they do on TV."

He reluctantly raised his hands in TV-style surrender. He had a feeling this scene was being enacted straight from a television cop show Angelica had watched. Unfortunately he'd landed the hapless role of criminal intruder.

"He did it!" Casper exclaimed, his voice squeaky with relief. "He listened to you, Angel."

"When someone has a gun pointed at you, it's wise to go along with the suggestion, son," said Flynt.

"It wasn't a suggestion, it was an order," snapped Angelica.

"And I'm not your son," said the boy. He adjusted the frames of his thick glasses, his face scrunched in sudden confusion. "Am I, Mama?"

"No, I've never seen the man before in my life."

Romina took a few steps closer. Automatically, Sarah and Casper moved closer, too. They studied Flynt, their faces reflecting suspicion mingled with curiosity and fear.

"What I really think," Romina said confidentially, "is that he's some kind of undercover cop."

Angelica appeared to consider the likelihood of this. "If so, he's refined the usual police procedure. He seems to be *trying* to be personable."

"Am I succeeding?" Flynt asked lightly.

"I'd swear he's FBI, but the haircut doesn't jibe." Romina frowned thoughtfully.

Flynt watched them, listening, his investigatory instincts on full alert. Something was going on here. Had they actually been interrogated by an FBI agent at some point? If so, why? And if not, why the paranoia?

Unless they had sent that blackmail note to Brandon and now feared they'd been caught?

His eyes swept over Angelica Carroll. God, she was a knockout! She had the face of an angel—it seemed altogether fitting that her nickname was Angel. But her faded, snug jeans and ribbed sky blue shirt displayed a curvy, enticing figure that did not conjure up celestial thoughts. Far from it.

Flynt swallowed hard. She somehow combined a sweet wholesomeness with sexual intensity, an intriguing combination that fascinated him despite his efforts to ignore her allure.

It occurred to him how very much he did not want Angelica to be the blackmailer, and he tried to admonish himself for his uncharacteristic loss of objectivity.

"Why don't you just drop your act and tell us the

truth, Mr. Corrigan?'' Angelica's eyes met his, and he felt another jolt of awareness.

He quickly looked away from her, uncomfortable with the disturbing sensual power this woman he did not know—and most certainly couldn't trust—seemed to hold over him.

''All right, I'll tell you the truth. There is no reason not to, I have nothing to hide.'' He knew he sounded slightly defensive. ''I used to be a field agent with the FBI, but I retired from the Bureau five years ago to form my own company. We handle investigations and security for companies, universities and certain private individuals.''

''You *used* to be an FBI agent?'' Sarah repeated doubtfully. ''Why'd you quit?''

''Because the hours and the pay in the private sector are a lot better than working for the government.'' Flynt injected a note of friendly humor in his voice, remembering their neighbor's antipathy for ''government jackals.''

He watched the Carrolls exchange glances, but could discern nothing from their blank expressions. Which were suddenly so thoroughly blank, the effect had to be calculated. Contrived. Flynt recognized a mask when he saw it, and right now he was seeing four.

Such total uniformity wasn't accidental, Flynt decided, it had to have been previously rehearsed. *He* might have nothing to hide, but these people definitely did.

The question was what? Their plan to milk their connection to the wealthy Fortunes for all it was worth? They didn't look like a clan of conniving blackmailers, but he knew from experience that judging on appearance could prove to be extremely unreliable.

"Could you put the gun down now, Angelica?" he asked.

"You didn't say please." Her tone matched the pseudo courtesy of his, word for word.

"By all means, let's keep this party polite." Flynt managed a forced chuckle. "Please, Angelica. You possess a remarkably steady hand, but being held at gunpoint is making me a little uneasy." He was aware that he was trying—too hard?—to sound personable.

"I understand. And you're not only uneasy, you're insulted," Angelica said sweetly. "Having a *girl* point a gun at you is insulting, isn't it? After all, you have your big macho male image to maintain." She kept the gun trained on him.

"I think you're actually enjoying this." Flynt was more than a little embarrassed. She'd hit the proverbial nail right on its clichéd head. What redblooded male, particularly a former lawman, wanted a pretty girl to pull a gun on him? And worse, keep it on him! A hopeful thought struck. "Maybe your gun isn't actually loaded?"

"Oh, it is," Angelica assured him. "Never doubt that. And keep your hands up, Ex-Agent Corrigan."

"We have a weapons permit, so you can't haul us in on that one," added Casper rather gleefully.

Flynt heaved a sigh. "Look, I'm getting tired of this." He slowly lowered his hands, taking heart that Angelica did not shoot him. But she did keep the gun pointed directly at him.

They were clearly at a standoff. Which might all too

easily escalate to a face-off, unless he managed to defuse the tension. Flynt ran his hand through his thick, dark hair, spiking it in a dozen different directions. Angelica, her mother, sister and brother resumed staring at him with their exasperatingly impassive expressions.

"Do you know who the Fortune family is?" he asked sternly, aware that he'd unintentionally lapsed into bad cop mode.

"Who doesn't?" Angelica replied, lifting one perfectly arched dark brow in a gesture of derision. She recognized his bad cop was back and wasn't at all intimidated.

"I don't," said Casper.

"Neither do I," said Sarah. "Who are they?"

"Keep still," barked Romina.

Both children looked downcast, their coolly impervious air gone. Flynt had no trouble reading their young faces now. They regretted displeasing their mother. His eyes shifted to Angelica, who was watching him closely.

He frowned. How should he play this? Angelica would probably laugh in his face if he segued into the role of Good Cop. Did she already know who her father was? And if she didn't, shouldn't she have some sort of preparation for such a momentous disclosure?

He scorned himself for even considering her reaction, let alone caring about it. He should be hoping she'd be so stunned, she would drop the damn gun!

He glanced at Romina. Why didn't she say something? What was going on with these people?

Flynt felt his body churn with unaccustomed frustration. Never had he felt so clueless. He'd long prided himself as an expert in interpreting facial nuances and body language, in gauging motive and reaction. Not now. In the Carrolls, he'd hit a human brick wall.

"Feel free to jump in at any time, Romina. Otherwise, I'll just go ahead and say it." He looked at Romina. Who still didn't say a thing.

"So go on and say whatever it is, why don't you?" Casper taunted.

"Don't bother," said Angelica. "We're not afraid of any threats you came here to make, so stop wasting our time—and your own—and leave. Now."

Her finger lightly caressed the trigger in a gesture so obvious, Flynt knew she'd deliberately done it to goad him.

"This is ridiculous." He sucked in his cheeks. "I don't know what game you're all playing—Family Stonewall, maybe?—but I've had enough."

He took a deep breath and forged ahead. "I am not here to make threats. And I am not leaving until I tell you why I really am here."

"Okay, let's hear it. And then get out," Angelica commanded.

"I arrived in Birmingham today, accompanied by Brandon Malone Fortune. He is your father, Angelica, and he wants to meet you as soon as possible. I came here first as a kind of advance man, a facilitator, to, uh, help ease whatever initial awkwardness there might be."

He thought it best not to mention the blackmail threat just yet.

Anticipating some initial awkwardness had been optimistic, Flynt thought grimly. The silent tension that blanketed the room reminded him of the eerie, thick stillness that preceded weather phenomena, like killer tornados.

The silence stretched on for so long that Flynt himself felt the need to break it. "Somebody say *something*." He made it a demand, not a request.

"Brandon in Birmingham." Romina finally spoke. Her voice was cold and devoid of emotion. "Well, that's good for a laugh, I guess. And since there aren't any world-famous, luxury hotels in town, I'm sure neither of you will be staying. Brandon isn't one to compromise his standards and settle for anything less."

"We're staying at the Premier Living Suites," replied Flynt, naming a complex for business travelers. Romina's insight surprised him. Even after all the years spent apart from him, she had accurately pegged Brandon's reaction to accommodations lacking the prestigious five-star or diamond ranking. Brandon would have been satisfied to arrive and leave the city the same day that he squeezed in a meeting with his daughter, but Kate's determination that he stay and try to develop a relationship with Angelica nixed a quick exit. Besides he'd grown fond of Kate and didn't want to disappoint her. When their meeting had ended, the Fortune matriarch had drawn him aside and told him she had high hopes that having a daughter would give purpose and direction to Brandon's life.

"Brandon is willing to meet you at his suite or here in this house or wherever you say, Angelica. It's entirely your call," said Flynt, hoping he sounded reassuring.

Unfortunately his irritation at Romina for placing him in the position of news breaker, gave his voice a harsher edge. Worse, he could tell that the news he'd broken really was news to Angelica and the kids.

For Flynt had seen the flash of shock and something that might have been pain cross Angelica's face in the seconds before she composed her lovely features back into a mask of stoic cool.

"I'm well aware that Brandon Malone Fortune is my father, Mr. Corrigan." Angelica sounded bored. "And I don't want to meet him—anytime or anywhere."

But Flynt was alert to the almost imperceptible pauses before she'd spoken her father's name. Before she'd said the word *father*. She was covering well, but he perceived that the news had made an emotional impact upon her.

Angelica had not known Brandon Fortune was her father; every instinct Flynt possessed told him so.

Her next action confirmed it. Angelica silently walked to the bookcase in the living room, just off to the right, and placed the gun on the top shelf. Flynt watched her, his eyes fixed on the gentle sway of her hips as she walked. On the smooth white skin of her midriff, exposed when her shirt rode up as she stretched to stand on her toes to reach the highest shelf.

Tension hummed in his body. He continued to stare as she rejoined them in the small vestibule.

Angelica looked up at him, as if surprised to still find him there. "I told you I didn't want to meet Mr. Fortune. Now why don't you go back and tell him so, like a good, loyal lackey?"

That stung. Flynt scowled. "I'm nobody's lackey, little girl. Remember that."

"Only if you'll remember not to *ever* refer to me as 'little girl' again." Angelica's eyes were flashing.

"You can reveal a lot in anger, Angel," Romina warned. "Far too much."

"I don't mind revealing that I do not appreciate sexist comments about my height or my gender, Mama." Angelica was ostensibly speaking to her mother, but her dark gaze was fastened on Flynt.

"Your uncle Gabe calls his wife, that's your aunt Rebecca, 'Shorty,' and she doesn't seem to mind," Flynt said conversationally. "Of course, she's not actually short so maybe it doesn't seem to be that big a deal to her."

"Angelica, just think, you have aunts and uncles!" exclaimed Sarah. "Tell us about Angelica's father, Mr. Corrigan!" The girl was clearly astounded by the revelation and didn't bother to conceal it. "Is he my dad, too?"

"And mine?" echoed Casper, who looked so hopeful that Flynt felt an overwhelming urge to throttle Romina.

Why had she let it happen this way? Why had she permitted her children to hear such personal, sensitive news from a stranger? *From him!* He felt like a purveyor of sleaze for the lowliest tabloid.

"Brandon Fortune is Angelica's father, kids, but not yours," Flynt said, when it became clear that Romina wasn't going to answer them.

Was that the shine of tears in Angelica's dark eyes? Flynt stared at her, watched her struggle to maintain her facade of control. He wanted to break through it, to get an emotional reaction from her. And wondered why.

After all, his own wall of reserve was as strong as a

fortress. If he'd been in Angelica's position, he would have responded exactly the same way she had. By concealing any pain. Controlling it by denying it. So why did he care?

Chapter 2

"Why did her father come here to Birmingham?" quizzed Casper. And then his eyes widened and his mouth formed a round, shocked *O*. "Does he want to get back together with Mama?"

"Of course not, Casper," Romina finally said. "I haven't seen Brandon since I was sixteen years old. I'm amazed he knows about Angelica. *If* he really does know, that is," she added darkly.

"You think I'm making this up?" Flynt was exasperated. "Why on earth would I do that?"

"Casper has asked a very good question." Romina's dark eyes were intense as lasers as they bored into Flynt. "Why did Brandon come to Birmingham to meet Angelica? After all these years, why bother now?"

"Maybe he wanted to give her some money," Casper suggested ingenuously. "Wouldn't that be cool, Angel?"

"We don't need money from Brandon Fortune, Casper." Angelica's voice was shaky. She'd either abandoned her attempt at feigning indifference or else she was unable to keep up the pretense. "Or from anyone else."

"We do, too, need money," protested Casper. "We never have enough. There's lots of stuff I don't have and the other kids do. Like a computer. I learned everything about them in school. I know more than anybody in my class, but I don't have my own computer. And I don't have any video games, either. Everybody has them but me."

"You have plenty of games," countered Romina crossly, looking defensive.

"Games that nobody wants to play!" Casper's thin face was flushed. "A deck of cards and a chess set. Chinese checkers. Clue and Monopoly—and not even the deluxe editions."

"You should be thankful for what you have, not greedy for what you don't have, young man!" Romina glared at her son.

"Mama, I think Casper is—" Angelica began, attempting to make peace between the pair.

"You know how hard I've worked to make things better than they were for you at his age, Angelica. But you never complained. I never heard one word of self-pity out of you. From the age of nine, you went out and earned money baby-sitting, and you always watched the little kids for me while I worked nights. You were a perfect child."

"Not this again!" Casper howled, his temper flaring anew. "I'm sick of hearing about how perfect Angel and

Danny were when they were kids. You don't even try to understand.'' He burst into tears and ran out of the room.

''Mama, don't.'' Angelica laid her hand on her mother's shoulder as she saw her mother brush aside a tear. ''This is a hard age for him. He's going through a rough time at school and he—''

''Oh, Angelica, don't give me that psychology junk you learned in nursing school,'' Romina said impatiently, before turning on her heels. Sarah followed, leaving Angelica and Flynt facing each other in the vestibule.

''Mama tries her best.'' Angelica looked forlorn. ''She always has. But she and Casper—well, they just—just—''

''Rub each other the wrong way?'' suggested Flynt. ''Believe me, I've been there.''

''You don't get along with one of your children?'' Angelica asked, her dark eyes wide as saucers.

A smile twitched at the corners of his lips. ''I don't have any kids. Or a wife, either, for that matter. I meant that, growing up, I played Casper's role. I always managed to do or say exactly what would get on poor Mom's last nerve. She always claimed she was doing her best, too.''

He felt Angelica studying him, and a peculiar warmth began to spread through him. ''I'm waiting for you to express your deepest sympathy for my mom. To say that an obnoxious adult like me could've only been a hellacious kid, one that would drive any well-meaning mother into a frenzy.''

''Do you get along with her now?'' Angelica said

instead. "Did things between you and your mother get better when you grew up?"

"After I left home, things between us definitely improved. Because I wasn't there." Flynt was glib. He wanted to drop the subject; Corrigan family history was not something he ever cared to dwell upon.

"Do you keep in touch with your mother?" Angelica pressed. "Do you phone or visit her often?"

She was watching him, both curious and determined. As a dogged interrogator himself, Flynt realized that she wouldn't let up till she got some answers. Well, he was willing to provide some, but if she was hoping to hear about a fractious mother-son relationship turned harmonious, she was out of luck.

"There is the occasional phone call," he admitted. "But I limit my visits to one afternoon a year, on Christmas Day. My aunts, uncles and cousins are around to keep the conversation, and the eggnog, flowing. The TV set is on all day and that helps, too."

He shrugged his shoulders. "Sorry I can't paint a more glowing picture for Casper's future relationship with your mother, but who can tell? Maybe it will be better for them, maybe they'll end up the best of friends. Now, about Brandon—"

"What about your sisters and brothers?" Angelica dismissed his attempt to switch topics. "Are you close to them? Are they—"

"There aren't any," Flynt said tersely.

He felt the familiar ache that struck whenever anyone posed casual, innocuous questions about siblings. If he replied that he had none, he felt he was denying that Mark had ever existed at all.

But mentioning his younger brother often led to more questions, ones that inevitably culminated in the pain and dread that had shadowed his childhood. And his adult life, too. How could it not?

"You look strange," Angelica observed. She'd moved to stand closer to him and was eyeing him intently.

She was close enough for him to inhale the subtle scent of her perfume, a fresh citrusy aroma that reminded him of sunshine and... Flynt gulped. And sex.

The sexual arousal was based strictly on his strong attraction to her, not the perfume, Flynt conceded. Because never before had the delicate scent of orange blossoms turned him on.

He was definitely turned on now. Heat streaked through him, from the top of his head to his feet, pooling sensually, deliciously, *inconveniently,* deep in his groin. If she were to lower her eyes, she would notice that the fit of his jeans had been altered quite visibly by his arousal.

Flynt fervently hoped that she wouldn't see.

"Of course I look strange." He retreated a few steps, desperately needing to marshal his defenses against her all-too-potent allure. "I've just been held at gunpoint, and then got stuck witnessing a nasty family quarrel," he said flippantly. "It would be strange if I didn't look strange."

"You didn't look strange till I asked you about sisters and brothers," Angelica persisted. "I can tell that's obviously a sensitive subject with you."

She took a step closer, and Flynt shifted under the

intensity of her gaze. That laser stare of Romina's seemed to be a genetic trait.

"Don't give me that psychology junk you learned in nursing school, Angelica." Flynt did a rather credible imitation of Romina's rebuke.

Instead of taking offense, Angelica smiled. And Flynt felt as if he'd been struck by a bolt of sensual lightning. He'd thought she was enticing from the moment he'd laid eyes on her, but when she smiled like that, her eyes bright, her face alight, she was well-nigh irresistible.

"Nice dodge, but it won't work, Mr. Corrigan," Angelica said, tilting her head.

She was still smiling, and he gazed at her, transfixed.

"You've had a firsthand look at the Carroll family, now it's your turn to cough up some personal information about the Corrigans."

Was she flirting with him? Flynt clamped his teeth together to keep his jaw from hanging agape like a star-struck idiot.

And then her words filtered through the sensual clouds and abruptly quashed every amatory feeling. An abrupt transition, akin to being thrown into an icy lake. Which was a good thing, he concluded. He had been too distracted by her appeal, he'd lost his focus on the job at hand. That was unacceptable.

"I'm here to talk about your father, not me." His lips thinned to a hard, straight line. "To set up the initial meeting between the two of you, and the sooner, the better."

Angelica stared at him. His transformation was startling. For a few moments there, his mood had been light, almost playful, now he was strictly business.

Fortune business. She flinched. "I have no desire to meet—"

"You didn't know Brandon was your father, did you?" Flynt lowered his voice and she leaned in closer to hear. "You don't have to don the family mask, no one is here but me. Be honest, Angelica."

"No, I didn't," she confessed. "I guess there's really no harm in admitting that."

"Any particular reason why you pretended that you knew?" He sounded almost amused.

"I just did, that's all."

"Because you were raised to automatically lie when faced with the unknown, according to your mother's 'trust no one' philosophy?"

Bingo! He'd hit it. Not that Angelica was about to tell him so. "*Now* who's overindulging in psychology, Agent Corrigan?"

"Ex-agent, remember?" he corrected. "And call me Flynt."

Their eyes met again, and Angelica felt her pulses jump queerly. He had an unnerving effect on her. A most unusual one. Because when she'd been holding him at gunpoint, when she suspected him of being sent here to investigate them, of being one of the enemy, she'd felt an unexpected, unwelcome sexual awareness of him.

That had never happened to her before. Being attracted to a man who could bring their lives crashing down on them? Good Lord, it was something her mother might do! But not perceptive, practical Angelica, who had been blessed with an abundance of common sense. And a steely self-control dating back to her nursery school days.

It occurred to her that somewhere along the line she'd begun to trust Flynt Corrigan, at least a little. Enough to believe he was telling the truth about why he'd come, that he actually was here representing her newfound father.

If he were one of *them,* he wouldn't have lingered so long talking in the vestibule; *they* liked to burst onto the scene like a SWAT team. Time was always of the essence in *their* hateful surprise searches.

Most convincing of all, her mother didn't view him as a threat, and her mother's instincts in such cases were impeccable.

"You're a million miles away." Flynt's voice, deep and male, broke into her thoughts. "I know you must have plenty of questions about Brandon and how he found you, so just ask, Angelica. I'm here to give you the answers."

She was standing way too close to him, Angelica realized with a start. They were in each other's personal space, within easy touching distance, and the longer she looked into his light blue eyes, the less clearly she was able to think.

He had beautiful eyes, the palest of blue, a distinctive contrast to his dark brown hair and brows. Taken separately, his features were too irregular for him to be categorized as handsome, yet his face was one of the most interesting, arresting ones she'd ever seen. Masculine and unyielding, with the kind of virile sex appeal that probably caused a lot of women to throw themselves at him.

He had said he wasn't married. Angelica's guard, so briefly dropped, was back in full force. He was probably one of those jerks who bounced from woman to woman, unwilling or unable to make a commitment. The type of man her mother was drawn to, with hapless moth-to-a-flame predictability.

And from what she'd heard via media gossip, exactly the type of man her father Brandon Fortune was.

Angelica's stomach clenched and she took a sudden deep gulp of air. She felt like she'd been sucker punched. *Her father!* As if life weren't complicated enough, now she had a father to deal with!

"Are you okay?" Flynt was practically hovering over her now. Too close. Way, way too close.

Angelica was excruciatingly aware of his vastly superior height—he was a couple of inches over six feet, effectively dwarfing her—and of his broad shoulders, his muscular frame not at all disguised by his jacket.

He was tough and strong and looked it. She didn't like tough, strong men. She remembered too well how one swat from a big man's fist had sent her flying across the room. More than once.

"Now you're the one who looks strange." Flynt cupped his hands over her shoulders to support her. "You've gone so pale, you look ready to faint."

Angelica jumped. His touch seemed to tripwire every nerve in her body. She felt her hair stand on end. "Don't touch me!"

She roughly jerked away from him and made a wild dash to the living room.

Flynt's reflexes were on red alert status this time. He easily beat her to the bookcase and retrieved the gun from the top shelf, tucking it in the inside pocket of his jacket.

"Give that to me!" Angelica demanded thickly.

"So you can shoot me with it? Not a chance, Miss Fortune."

"Don't call me that!"

Flynt folded his arms in front of his chest. "You're going to have to deal with it, Angelica. You've been found, and your father's family wants to claim you as one of their own."

"Oh, sure! I just bet they do," she said sarcastically. Standing across the living room from him, with distance safely between them, her fighting spirits were revived…even if he did have her gun.

She had no fear that he would use it, but it was annoying to be bested so easily by him after she'd done such a splendid job of holding her own earlier.

"That's why I'm here, Angelica," Flynt said with commendable patience. "If you'll allow me to explain the circumstances surrounding your father's—"

"Spare me. I remember when Monica Malone was murdered and the news broke that her son Brandon was really the missing Fortune child who'd been kidnapped as an infant," Angelica interjected. "It was one of those sensational stories the media hyped to excess, especially since they wrongly believed Jake Fortune had killed Monica. A person would've had to be living in a cave in the remote Himalayas not to have heard about it."

"The Fortunes were all over TV and in all the papers back then," agreed Flynt. "They told me how much they hated being trapped in that media circus. Even eight years later they're still appalled by the memory of it."

"Are they still appalled by Brandon? You see, I also remember some of the more candid pictures and video clips back then. They were a real study in body language. That family looked anything but thrilled to have Monica Malone's son dumped on them, blood relative or not.''

''You picked that up from a few photos and video footage, did you?'' mocked Flynt.

She didn't back down. ''I'm right, aren't I? Well, they'll be even less happy to meet me. Not that I blame them, I don't want to meet them, either. We might be related, but we're strangers with nothing at all in common.''

''Brandon's mother, Kate—your grandmother—was happy to have Brandon back,'' countered Flynt, ''and she is looking forward to meeting and knowing you, too, Angelica. Kate's determined to see you reunited with your father, and she's made it very clear that you are to be a part of the Fortune family.''

''Well, I'm sorry but the feeling isn't mutual.''

''The last thing you need is any more family, huh?'' His lips quirked into that wry smile of his.

The one that had an odd effect on her senses. Her cheeks suddenly felt hot. ''You make it sound as if—'' She broke off, irked.

He was deliberately trying to goad her, but she didn't have to let him. ''I have nothing more to say to you, and you can tell Brandon Fortune that there is no sense in dredging up a past that is best forgotten. Now, would you please leave?''

Flynt stayed right where he was. Angelica frowned her displeasure. Well, what had she expected? If he wouldn't go when ordered at gunpoint, he'd hardly respond to a polite request.

"I can understand why you harbor certain—reservations—about having your father in your life. Having met your mother," Flynt paused, striving for tact. Which meant starting over. "Now that I've met *both* your parents, it's obvious that dealing with the two of them is going to require a deft touch. But I believe you're up to the task, Angelica."

She was wondering how to reply to that when there was a loud, almost thunderous pounding on the front door.

"Open up!" ordered the voice outside. "Police! And FBI. We have a search warrant!"

"Great, just great." Angelica groaned. "What else can go wrong today?"

At once Romina, Sarah and Casper all came running. Romina was shouting, Sarah and Casper both appeared anxious.

Angelica's eyes flew to Flynt's face. He looked as if he'd just found himself transported into the Twilight Zone.

"What the hell's going on?" Flynt demanded.

"You have till the count of three to open the door or we'll break it down!" roared the voice from outside. "You know we'll do it, Romina."

"I know you will!" Romina screamed back.

"Go away!" wailed Sarah. "Leave us alone!" She turned to her mother. "I hate it when they mess up my room, Mama. Last time they broke my softball trophy and threw my collection of stuffed animals on the floor and tramped all over them!"

"I know, honey." Romina stroked her younger daughter's hair. "They're cruel and unreasonable."

"And that's why we do what we do, right, Mama," exclaimed Casper.

Romina glanced at Flynt. "Casper, hush."

"Okay, Romina, this is it," shouted the voice. "One…"

"Where's the gun, Angelica?" Casper tugged on Angelica's arm. "Let's fight back this time. Shoot them."

Flynt stared at the four Carrolls, who seemed prepared to let their door be broken down rather then opening it. "There'll be no shooting," he said sternly. "And no forced entry, either."

"Hold on, we're going to open the door," he called as he strode to it.

The shouted threats and warnings stopped. Flynt felt the pressure of Angelica's gun in the inside pocket of his jacket. If the intruders weren't who they claimed to be, at least he was armed.

He opened the door to two uniformed policemen, one who appeared to be in his late thirties, the other about ten years younger. Flynt immediately picked out which was the FBI agent from the two men not in uniform. Mid-forties, conservative suit and shoes, neat haircut, definitely with the Bureau. The other guy was a run-of-the-mill private investigator, Flynt was certain of it; he recognized the breed.

What, he wondered, did this quartet want with Romina Carroll?

"Who are you?" growled the older police officer whose name tag identified him as Officer S. Webber.

"I guess you could say I'm a friend of the family," Flynt replied, "or something along that line. And I'd like to see that search warrant, please."

"Oh, TJ, I'm so glad it's you!" Sarah rushed onto the porch and beamed at the younger policeman. "Would *you* search my room, please? I know you won't throw stuff around and break my things on purpose like *some* people." She shot the older officer a baleful glance. "That cop, Moffet, who was here last time was awful, Officer Webber. He should be fired."

"I'm sure Moffet was just doing his job, young lady. And nobody deliberately breaks your things," growled Webber. "If your mama decided to abide by the law, you wouldn't have to go through this. We don't like it any more than you do. Go on in with her, TJ, you might as well get started," he instructed the other officer.

"C'mon, TJ," invited Sarah. "Wait'll you see what I—"

"Just a minute! No one is going inside until I've seen that search warrant," Flynt commanded.

He sounded convincingly authoritative and legally knowledgeable and was aware that his casual attire could be attributed either to an undercover law enforcement officer or a lawyer.

The four men on the porch stayed where they were.

"Who's he, Romina?" Officer Webber demanded. "Got yourself some legal aid? Or did another agency beat us over here?"

Flynt gave his card to Webber, who passed it around to the other three men. "I'm here on behalf of Angelica's father's family," he added, not bothering to reveal his exact role.

"And they're really rich and they'll make you sorry you messed with us," boasted Casper.

"What's this about your father, Angelica?" TJ, the younger officer, looked astonished.

"Seems I have a father." Angelica rolled her eyes. "I'll tell you more later."

The FBI agent showed Flynt his credentials, identifying him as Glenn Weatherall from the local FBI field office. "Officers Webber and Gibson are with the Birmingham Police Department." Weatherall indicated the uniformed officers with a nod toward them. "And this is Ike Searcy, a private investigator."

Searcy produced his own card as Weatherall handed Flynt the warrant and a few other papers.

"Flynt can kick your butts, 'cause he's not afraid of you. He used to be an FBI agent and he had a license to kill, just like James Bond. But then he decided to quit and get rich." Casper ran around the porch like a manic puppy, darting among the four men. "And when *we're* rich, we're gonna—"

"Casper, hush!" hissed Romina. "And stay still! Sit down in that chair and don't move!" She pointed to a wicker chair at the far end of the porch.

Casper flopped down on it, heaving a martyred sigh.

Flynt read through the papers he'd been given, then looked at Romina. "This is a valid search-and-seizure warrant, Romina."

Romina glared at him, then at Webber. "So go on in and tear up my house again. I already put the usual stuff-to-be-seized in a box right by the phone. My address book, phone statements and bills, and bank statements— all together for your convenience. Did I leave anything out?"

"Credit card statements," barked Searcy.

"We don't use credit cards," Angelica replied. "Mama believes in paying cash. It keeps you from living beyond your means and getting into debt."

She was saying all the right words, but her tone was—well, too angelic, mused Flynt. As if she didn't expect to be taken seriously.

"Oh, come on. We all know the *true* reason why you don't use credit," groused Webber. "Cash eliminates a paper trail."

"This is such a big waste of time," Romina huffed impatiently. "You won't find anything here. You never do."

"You mean *anybody*," Searcy corrected. "Damn, we're too late again! I know Darlene Carson and her kids were here. You've already helped them move on, Romina," he added accusingly.

Romina shrugged. "You have a good imagination. Ever think of writing for TV?"

"You may as well get started," Angelica spoke up. "I was going to go back to my apartment, but I'll stay until they leave, Mama."

"Thank you, Angel." Romina gave her a little hug, then turned to the young policeman. "TJ, are you seeing Mara tonight?"

TJ's face reddened and he nodded his head. "Yes, ma'am, I am."

"Be sure and tell her you helped tear up my house and upset my kids. Remember what Mara says about these raids, Angelica? How all the angry men stomping and yelling reminds her of that bully stepfather of hers, the one she ran away from. Remember, Angel?"

Angelica nodded. "I remember, Mama."

"You should remember some things too, TJ," Romina said to the young policeman who didn't meet her steady gaze. "Remember that Mara Quinlan was my foster child from the time she was thirteen. That we were the only ones willing to help her get away from that monster her mother married—the one your department finally got around to putting in jail after he nearly killed a man in a fight. You think about all that while you're ransacking my house."

"Give TJ a break, Mama." Angelica heaved a sigh. "He's just doing his job."

"Yeah, like the Gestapo did theirs." Romina scowled. "Did Mara ever tell you that she was here baby-sitting during that first raid, TJ? She wouldn't open the door and the cops kicked it in. Poor Mara was scared to death, she was even more upset than Sarah and Casper who were only eleven and nine at the time. You could've knocked me over with a feather when Mara told me she'd started dating a cop. After that raid, she was so hostile toward the police."

TJ made a strangled sound and followed Sarah into the house.

"Mama, don't try to make trouble for TJ with Mara," Angelica warned her mother. "He's a nice guy."

"Don't forget to add, 'for a cop,'" drawled Flynt, unable to refrain from commenting.

"I've known TJ Gibson for years, long before he became a cop." Angelica eyed him coolly. "He's a nice guy, period."

"Angel went to the Junior Prom with TJ. He was crazy about her. Of course, I can't remember when Angelica hasn't had guys crazy about her." Romina's smile could have been one of maternal pride—or of malice.

Flynt suspected the latter because she aimed it directly at him. As if he cared who Angelica had gone to the Junior Prom with…as if he cared if there were battalions of men lusting after her!

Of course he didn't care. But he found himself wondering if there was currently a particular man in her life. He hadn't investigated her private life for the Fortunes, other than her marital status and lack of offspring.

"Might as well go inside and have some iced tea." Romina was suddenly, inexplicably cheerful. "The goon squad won't be in the kitchen long, it's too small for anybody to be hidden in there. Of course, our refrigerator does have a fairly big vegetable drawer. Think you'll find somebody hiding out in it, Webber?"

"You're a zillion laughs, Romina." Webber pushed past her and marched inside.

"Can I have some iced tea, too, Mama?" Casper had jumped up from the chair and was circling the group.

"You can have a glass of milk," said Romina. "It's better for you."

"Can I have some cookies?" the boy asked.

"They're the special orders for campus delivery and—oh, all right, you can have one oatmeal cookie." Romina entered the house. "But just one."

"I want two, an oatmeal and a chocolate chip. I'm too skinny, I need to bulk up." Casper continued to badger his mother as he trailed her inside.

"Okay, okay. You can have two. Now stop nagging!"

Angelica started after them. Flynt caught her arm, pulling her back to him.

"The warrant, the search, the items listed to be seized as evidence—" he took a sharp breath "—this is serious business, Angelica. The affidavit cites possible federal charges against your mother for aiding and abetting a fugitive and for violating custody laws. Conspiracy and obstruction of justice charges are mentioned. And then there are additional state charges filed in New Jersey for interfering with custody arrangements. I don't get it. What on earth is your mother—"

"My mother doesn't deserve to be treated like a common criminal," Angelica said stiffly. "Unfortunately, that doesn't stop it from happening."

Flynt noticed that she was staring at Weatherall and Searcy as she spoke, her words directed to them as much as to him. The two men had remained on the porch while the uniformed officers were inside the house, presumably searching and seizing.

What were they looking for? Flynt wondered. Or who? He was truly flummoxed.

"Did you use to work for the Bureau, like the kid said, Corrigan?" Weatherall asked him curiously.

"For seven years." Flynt nodded. "Minus the license to kill of course." Maybe supplying a few details of his former career would win him some information in exchange. "I was based in California. Mostly Silicon Valley, investigating economic espionage."

"No kidding?" Weatherall looked interested. "I've heard there's a lot of industrial espionage and commercial spying out there in those high-tech companies."

"Research and development, manufacturing and marketing plans, and customer lists are all at risk," affirmed Flynt.

"Also heard you electronic whiz kids are always being lured away from the Bureau by private industry. You can name your own price when you decide to leave," Weatherall added, a little wistfully.

Flynt shrugged. "I decided I'd rather be my own boss, so I started Security Management Systems five years ago. Agent Weatherall, would you mind telling me what's going on around here?"

"Seems pretty obvious." Searcy was sarcastic. "The cops are searching the place. Whiz kid like you couldn't figure that out?"

Flynt ignored him. "I tracked down Romina Carroll for the Fortune Corporation and found no record of any criminal activity," he persisted.

"Don't beat yourself up over it. Romina's never been charged with anything. Probably never will be, at this rate," Weatherall said, his tone consoling. "She's downright gifted at making investigators feel stupid."

"Did you ever consider that you feel stupid because Mama is not a criminal and that's why she's never been charged with anything?" Angelica argued crossly. She looked up at Flynt, her dark eyes glittering. "The reason you didn't find records of criminal activity is because there aren't any."

"Yeah, Romina is a regular heroine," Searcy said snidely. "So I guess that makes Ted Carson and me the villains, huh, babe?"

"You said it, not me," snapped Angelica.

She looked like she wanted to rip out Searcy's lungs with her bare hands. Flynt made a mental note not to ever call her "babe." And then he realized that he was still holding her arm, just above the elbow. Unable to stop himself, he lightly stroked the inner skin with his thumb. It was exquisitely soft, smooth as satin, and he felt the effects deep down inside him.

Angelica's heart jumped at the subtle caress. She swiftly glanced down to see Flynt's fingers wrapped around her arm and realized how strange it was that she had actually forgotten he was holding on to her. But she'd remained unaware of it until...

His thumb continued its gentle, sensuous movements. She lifted her eyes to his. Her heartbeat seemed to be roaring in her head. It felt good, having Flynt touch her. So good she wanted more. Angelica shivered and moved even closer to him, seized by an impulsive urge to press herself against him. The urge swiftly was transformed into yearning, deep and unfamiliar, yet thoroughly enticing.

She jerked up her head and locked eyes with Flynt. Oh, his eyes! If eyes were the window to the soul, as poets claimed, then Flynt's was an alert, intelligent and breathtakingly sexy one. The turn her thoughts had taken astonished her. But then, never before had she looked into a man's eyes and felt such—such—

Desire. The admission hit her hard. Angelica panicked. Her inexplicable affinity for Flynt Corrigan was leading her down a road she was too apprehensive, too controlled to dare to go.

It was dangerous for her to have these feelings. Not to mention stupid. Angelica attempted to whip herself back into her safe, smart preFlynt self.

"Let go of my arm right now or I'll—" She paused to think of a suitable threat. None came to mind. Truth be told, she didn't want him to let go of her arm. What a scary admission!

"Here's an idea for you, babe. Assault him." Searcy sniggered. "Maybe putting you in the slammer would give us the leverage we need to bargain with that psycho mother of yours."

"There is no need for insults," Flynt said, dropping his hand from Angelica's arm. "Angelica's mother isn't psycho."

Angelica reluctantly moved away from him. He'd released her and now she had no choice but to put distance between them. And she didn't want to. If her reaction to Flynt's touch had unnerved her, his defense of her mother made her want to throw her arms around him. She wasn't used to having someone stand up for her, and she liked it.

She liked it too much. Angelica was nervous again.

"Anyway, I truly don't think an assault on Corrigan by little Angelica would result in charges being drawn up against her," Weatherall pointed out amiably. "Corrigan might've left the bureau, but he hasn't turned into a flaccid desk jockey who gets himself clobbered by a woman."

"Obviously not." Searcy directed a leer toward the vicinity of Flynt's groin, where his hardening arousal was becoming apparent against the metal-buttoned fly of his jeans.

Weatherall coughed and gazed discreetly in the other direction. Angelica abruptly turned and rushed into the house, slamming the door behind her.

Flynt felt his face flush a dark crimson. She must've

looked—and what she'd seen hadn't pleased her. He stifled a groan.

"A little friendly advice, from me to you," Searcy offered Flynt. "Sure, she's a hot babe, but you'd be crazy to get mixed up with her. Her mother is trouble spelled in capitals, and the girl's gotta be, too."

"I'm not mixed up with her," Flynt said weakly. His denial sounded lame even to himself. "Angelica Carroll's father—and his family—are clients of mine."

"I'm going inside," Weatherall announced.

Flynt was grateful for the chance to change the subject. "Do you expect to find what you're looking for?"

"No. I agree with Searcy. If Darlene Carson was here before, she isn't now. And Romina is a real pro when it comes to getting rid of every trace of evidence. We can go over this house with a fine-tooth comb and never confirm that Darlene and those kids were ever here. Wonder what—or who—tipped them off this time?"

Searcy uttered an expletive and tossed down the butt of his cigarette before trooping into the house after Weatherall. Flynt went in, too, though he felt certain Angelica wasn't going to be pleased to see him. So why was *he* so eager to see *her?* Flynt's lips curved into a hard, self-mocking smile. And if he were honest with himself, he wanted to do more than just look at Angelica again. Much more...

Chapter 3

Angelica and Romina were in the kitchen seated at the table with tall glasses of iced tea in front of them. Weatherall and Searcy stood a few feet away. Footsteps sounded in the room above them—Birmingham PD carrying out the search, Flynt assumed. Sarah and Casper were nowhere in sight.

"Agent Weatherall, Agent Corrigan, sit down," Romina invited, gesturing to the two empty chairs at the table. "Would you like some iced tea? And how about a cookie? I have oatmeal and chocolate chip, freshly baked."

Weatherall sat down, and Searcy moved to take the last empty chair.

"Not you!" Romina said fiercely, dropping any pretense of hospitality. The animosity between her and the P.I. was clearly personal. "That seat is for Flynt. Angel, honey, pour the agents some tea."

Flynt gingerly sat down in the chair next to Angelica. The table wasn't very large and his knee bumped hers under it. She drew back as if she'd been burned. He noticed that her hand wasn't very steady as she poured the two glasses of iced tea from the pitcher.

Because his sensual effect on her was as unsettling as hers upon him? Or because the pitcher was heavy? His knowledge of the subtle nuances between the sexes was definitely lacking, Flynt conceded. Until now, he hadn't minded.

Romina passed a plate of cookies, pointedly excluding Searcy who sullenly watched them as he leaned against the wall.

A heavy silence fell. The footsteps continued to thud above them. Flynt was excruciatingly aware of Angelica sitting beside him—and also aware that she was avoiding even glancing in his direction.

He needed a diversion—and fast. "Would it be out of line if I asked to be filled in on the situation here, Glenn?" Flynt easily lapsed into his between-us-agents tone.

"Go ahead, Glenn, fill him in," Angelica imitated him, her expression derisive.

Or was it baiting? Maybe she wanted his attention, after all. Deliberately, Flynt let his knee touch hers again. Angelica's eyes met his, and he saw something flare in the velvety dark depths. Instead of jumping away, she let her leg rest against his while their gazes held.

And then Weatherall finished his cookie and began to speak.

Angelica shifted away from Flynt, breaking contact between them on both the physical and unspoken levels.

"We think—hell, we *know*, although we can't prove it," drawled Weatherall, "that Romina Carroll is part of an underground network, hiding women on the run with their kids. Almost all of them are fleeing court-ordered custody decrees, although there are some who'll take off to prevent any contact at all between the father and child. The bureau is involved because parental kidnapping that violates legal custody or visitation rights is still viewed as a kidnapping under the law."

"Although the cops and FBI don't treat parental abduction as seriously as stranger abduction," Searcy interjected testily. "Which is why guys like me get hired by the fathers who've been shafted twice. First, the ex-wife disappears with the kids, then the law ignores it. Sometimes the cops and agents actually help the underground by deliberately turning a blind eye to the people running the safe houses. Sometimes they'll even tip 'em off about a raid."

"Do you actually believe that Officer Webber would call Mama and tip her off?" Angelica was incredulous.

"That does seem unlikely," agreed Flynt, hoping to forestall additional sniping between the Carrolls and the P.I. "I'd like to hear more about this underground."

"How about if I tell you why the need for it exists?" Romina's voice rose with urgency. "Ever heard of domestic violence? Or sexual abuse? What about ineffective law enforcement or judges who won't believe the very real claims of abuse that mothers make against the monsters who are beating them up or molesting their own kids?"

"Until the courts consider the evidence presented about the children's safety, mothers are going to be forced into taking action on their own," Angelica chimed in. "They have to protect their kids, no matter what."

Flynt saw where they were going with this—and disapproved. "Even if 'no matter what' means breaking the law?" he challenged.

"That's right." Angelica met his gaze defiantly. "Because the law can be wrong."

"Now *there's* a familiar refrain." Flynt grimaced. "Every perp I ever arrested was quick to point out that they'd done nothing wrong, that they were clearly the victims of a bad law."

"There are some cases involving violence and abuse that have been bungled by the courts," Weatherall pointed out. "For their children's sakes, the mothers feel they have no choice but to take off and stay hidden. They view the underground as the only way to keep their kids safely away from the abuser."

"You're spouting *their* propaganda, Weatherall! It's like listening to Romina or Nancy Portland, the head honcho herself!" ranted Searcy.

"I'm simply presenting all sides of the issue to Corrigan," Weatherall said calmly, refusing to rise to the bait.

"That's very fair of you, Glenn." Romina placed another cookie in front of him.

"What's this underground network?" asked Flynt. "And who is Nancy Portland?"

"A living saint. Tell him about Nancy, Angelica," Romina prompted.

"Nancy Portland is from a wealthy, well-respected family and has been happily married for years," Angelica said, turning to gaze into Flynt's eyes.

She leaned forward. The table was so small that her action brought them back into close proximity. Her shoulder brushed his arm; her thigh touched his. This time Angelica didn't jerk away. Flynt could tell by the fervid glow in her eyes that her subject was so important to her that nothing could divert her.

He wished he were similarly preoccupied. But the controversial Nancy Portland did not engage his interest the way Angelica did.

Prickles of heat shot through him. The sizzling sexual awareness he felt in her presence caused Searcy and the others to fade into irrelevance. Flynt could see and hear only Angelica.

"Nancy is smart and brave and a brilliant organizer," Angelica said, her face rapt with admiration. "She lives in Tampa and heads an underground of secret safe houses all over the country where women running from their former abusive spouses can hide with their children. The mothers and kids are supplied with false identity papers and are often helped financially when it becomes necessary to leave one safe house for another."

"Portland's blatantly anti-male! She's never helped a father and kids running away from a physically abusive mother," shouted Searcy. "As for the sexual abuse allegations, Nancy Portland doesn't even try to learn the true facts. She believes whatever trumped-up tales these women concoct to get her to help them."

"It's true Nancy doesn't help men," Romina confirmed. "Because men are the ones with the power and the money and the connections. Nancy helps women be-cause they're powerless with nowhere else to turn.''

"But before she gets involved in any case, Nancy Portland interviews the women and their children,'' Angelica put in. "She can tell who is lying, she knows if the children are genuinely scared of their fathers and want to get away. Nancy won't assist a woman making false accusations. She'll turn them away and advise them to work things out with the children's fathers.''

"That's not what she told Darlene Carson who's made plenty of false accusations about my client and brain-washed their kids against him,'' Searcy raged. "Ted Carson won legal custody of their two daughters, now aged six and seven, after a bitter divorce. The kids went missing with that lunatic Darlene a year-and-a-half ago, and Ted hired me to find them after the initial police investigation went nowhere. I traced them to Birmingham two days ago. And Birmingham, of course, means Romina Carroll. But now—'' He threw his hands up in the air and cursed some more.

"You traced them to Birmingham, then assumed they were with Romina?'' Flynt repeated slowly. "Why?''

It seemed an unlikely assumption to make. The neighborhood was crowded, and he'd learned from his own inquiries that a number of residents spent a lot of time at their windows, watching the comings and goings on the street.

How could women and children be smuggled in and out without others knowing about it? And when a number of people viewed strange happenings, they liked to talk about them. Flynt had learned that basic investigatory truth early on. Conspiracy buffs to the contrary, the idea of a vast collusion of silence about anything was extremely improbable.

And this house was so small! Though he hadn't seen the upstairs, the area couldn't exceed the size of the rooms downstairs—the cramped living room, the eat-in kitchen, and tiny vestibule. Keeping extra people hidden without a trace required a mansion, and this tidy little box simply didn't fit the bill.

Flynt stared at Romina. What in her background had contributed to her seeming beyond-the-ordinary with sympathy for runaway women? Romina was an activist; he certainly hadn't expected *that* when he was doing his cursory case legwork. His musing carried him one step further. How had Romina's children—including Brandon's daughter!—been affected by what they'd seen and experienced from their mother's cause?

"Good question, Flynt!" Romina exclaimed, her voice piercing his reverie. "For the past three years, we've had to endure these raids because Searcy and other paid snoops show up in Birmingham and work the cops and local field agents into an uproar. Do you know there's been a tap on my phone for the past three years?"

"Our family's privacy is invaded and our rights are trampled on." Angelica was indignant. "Hard to believe it could happen in America, but we're living proof that it can—and does."

"It's not a tap," Weatherall said quickly. "The phone is attached to a number-tracer registry, which is perfectly legal. Conversations can't be overheard, a number is simply logged into a computer and the origin of the calls can be traced."

"And guess what? Records show that Romina gets calls from phone booths all over the country. Explain that!" demanded Searcy.

Angelica shrugged. "Mama has lots of friends who live all over the country and like to stay in touch."

"And none of them have their own phones?" howled Searcy.

Flynt cleared his throat. "Any record of outgoing calls?"

"The outgoing calls are all to local numbers, and they all check out." Weatherall smiled slightly. "If Romina calls friends all over the country to stay in touch, she uses phone booths too. Using coins. There are no telephone credit card numbers on record."

Neither Romina nor Angelica offered any explanation. And Flynt faced the fact that these raids weren't instigated on the whims of "Searcy and other paid snoops." He knew that whatever the evidence in this case and others, it was strong enough to authorize police and FBI involvement, compelling enough for a judge to issue a warrant.

And all this had been going on for the past three years!

What he'd deemed odd about the Carrolls, their suspicion-bordering-on-paranoia, their rehearsed blank expressions, designed to give away nothing, made sense in light of the facts he'd just learned. He had thought their initial behavior was that of people with something to hide. Well, it appeared what they were hiding were people!

No wonder Angelica had held him at gunpoint until his identity had been established to her satisfaction. Until she'd believed that he wasn't a doggedly determined P.I. like Searcy or an infuriated ex-spouse who might use force against them to demand information about missing children. Once again, he found himself contemplating the kind of men in Romina Carroll's life since her early affair with Brandon. Had a string of abusive men in her personal life turned her pro-active? He could only imagine the effects of it all on Romina's family. On Angelica.

As if the Carrolls' secret world wasn't bizarre enough, he was about to introduce Brandon and the Fortunes into it. And now there was another angle to be considered.

Flynt thought back to that meeting in the Fortune mansion, when he'd broken the news of the existence of Brandon's daughter. They had all contemplated the likely possibility that either Romina or Angelica or both were behind the extortion attempt.

But with the revelation of Romina's involvement in this underground network, the list of suspects widened considerably. Suppose Romina had mentioned her past relationship with Brandon to one of the fugitives she'd sheltered?

A woman on the run, desperate for money, might easily view Angelica as a direct conduit to the Fortunes—and their fortune. Such a person might decide that exploiting the secret connection promised a cash bonanza.

For the first time since reading that amateurish blackmail note, Flynt found himself seriously considering the death threat it contained—*if you don't pay big bucks your daughter will be killed and you'll be framed for her murder.*

It was time for a swift re-evaluation of the situation. Exactly who were they dealing with?

Angelica hadn't known Brandon was her father, which immediately eliminated her as the blackmailer. And now, upon meeting and observing her, all Flynt's instincts told him that Romina hadn't sent that note either. Romina would've known of Brandon's connection to the Fortunes for the past nine years, since the media broke the scandalous story of the child Monica Malone had obtained through blackmail. Yet she had made no attempts to contact any of them in all that time. When Romina Carroll cut her ties, they stayed severed.

Flynt recalled some basic facts from his investigation. After Romina's parents had accepted a bribe from Monica Malone, on the condition that they keep Romina's pregnancy a secret from Brandon—and preferably end it—Romina had run away, never to return. She hadn't contacted her own parents for twenty-six years!

For a moment, he allowed his imagination free reign and considered the possibility of the other Carrolls as culprits. Could Sarah or Casper be the blackmailer? Almost instantly, he dismissed the notion; Sarah and Casper Carroll were mere children, and though he'd only met them briefly, neither seemed criminally inclined.

No, it was Nancy Portland and the underground she headed, which raised all manner of questions. How was this clandestine organization financed? Blackmail could be one convenient source of cash, if a profitable secret was unearthed. If Romina had mentioned Angelica's paternity to Nancy, the massive Fortune Corporation and its assets would certainly offer a lucrative target. Was the Portland woman capable of blackmail—and of carrying out the threats made in that note?

He didn't know. He'd never heard of Nancy Portland

until today, but from what he discerned, the woman continually, defiantly flouted the law. Running an underground operation undoubtedly required association with other individuals who weren't law-abiding either. Computer hackers, forgers…hit men?

Your daughter will be killed. The threat echoed in Flynt's head. The additional threat to frame Brandon for murder didn't worry him. In fact, it was an incredibly stupid ploy, providing Brandon with a foolproof defense. But then, a hit man didn't have to be intelligent, only bold and greedy and lacking a conscience.

Your daughter will be killed. Flynt's insides began to churn. Brandon Fortune's daughter was no longer a faceless unknown to him. She was beautiful, feisty Angelica. Who might be in grave danger.

He turned his head to see her drinking the last of her iced tea. She set the glass down and daintily dabbed her lips with a paper napkin.

Flynt swallowed hard. Her mouth looked luscious and tempting as a ripe strawberry. Instantly he looked away from her, not daring to allow himself to follow that train of thought.

He made himself focus strictly on the problem at hand. Angelica at risk was a possibility none of them had ever seriously contemplated. Flynt considered it now.

His reason for being here had taken a crucial turn. Concern for Angelica's safety superseded everything else.

"Angelica, could I speak to you privately?" Flynt searched her face. Which was once again set in that same unreadable, impenetrable mask he'd seen earlier. "I want to show you something."

"I bet I can guess exactly what you want to show her." Searcy smirked. "Yeah, you'll need privacy for that. I suggest you two get a room."

Romina jumped to her feet, pitcher in hand. She looked ready to throw it at him. "Get out of my house, Searcy! The others might have a legal right to be here, but you don't! So leave, right now, or else I'll have you arrested for breaking and entering. Or stalking. Or *something!*"

"Try it!" taunted Searcy. "And I'll—"

"Time out, you two." Weatherall stood up. "Searcy, Romina asked you to leave. This is her home and you'll have to abide by her wishes."

"Fine! But I'm not giving up," Searcy said as he stomped out.

"Searcy is frustrated," said Weatherall. "He gets so close and then—nothing. His contract specifies a big bonus if he locates his clients' missing kids and they're brought back. So far, he's never collected that bonus."

"And he never will, either. Glenn, would you mind coming upstairs with me to check on those cops?" Romina asked politely. "That'll give Flynt and Angel a chance to talk privately about her father."

Weatherall and Romina left the kitchen. For a few moments Angelica and Flynt sat in silence. The reasonable side of Romina had caught him by surprise, Flynt mused.

"What did you want to talk to me about?" Angelica asked at last. "If it's about Brandon Fortune, I'll tell you for the last time—I'm not interested in hearing it. I am not going to meet him.''

"Angelica, you are.''

"Flynt, I'm not.''

He was momentarily riveted. It was the first time she'd called him Flynt, despite his earlier request that she do so. He liked her husky voice and the sound of his name on her lips. He wanted to hear her say it again.

"Go back to—Brandon Fortune,'' Angelica gulped the name, "and tell him I hope he has a nice life but not to expect me to be in it.''

"This has turned into something more than Brandon being your father, Angelica.'' Flynt reached into his jacket pocket for the letter. His knuckles brushed her gun nestled in his pocket.

"And not so incidentally, you shouldn't keep a loaded gun in a house with kids. It's a tragedy waiting to happen,'' he admonished.

"I know.'' She surprised him by agreeing. "It's Mama's, and she wants it here. She says she keeps it hidden, that only I know where it is—''

"We all saw you put the gun on the bookshelf, Angelica.''

"That isn't Mama's hiding place. I just set it there when I knew that I wouldn't have to use it.''

"When you decided not to shoot me, after all.'' Flynt almost smiled, then quickly sobered. "You don't know how many times the old 'gun is kept hidden' statement has been made at the scene of an accidental shooting, Angelica.''

"I—I know. And I worry that Casper might get hold of it.''

"You should. And I'm sorry to be the one to have to tell you that you have something else to worry about." He removed the letter from its envelope and smoothed it out on the table in front of her. "Read this, Angelica."

She stared at the paper with its multicolored letters individually cut out from magazines and pasted together to form words. "It looks like a soap opera prop," she said glibly. "Reads like one, too."

Flynt's expression was grim. "Unfortunately it's very real, Angelica."

She looked up from the crumpled note. "And what does it have to do with me?" Surely he didn't expect her to be concerned about this kindergarten project gone awry?

"That note was sent to Brandon Fortune, Angelica. You are the daughter mentioned in it."

"The daughter who'll be killed if *big bucks* aren't paid to the anonymous sender?" hooted Angelica. "And then poor Brandon Fortune will be framed for my murder?"

"May I point out that this is a threat on your life? You're certainly treating it cavalierly."

"You expect me to be scared? Brandon Fortune is the one who wrote—or should I say, cut and pasted—this note himself. It's an idiotic attempt to extort money from his own family."

"Brandon had nothing to do with this note. Why would you think he did?" Flynt demanded, irked.

Never mind that had been his first thought, too. Not to mention Sterling Foster's, Gabe Devereax's and various Fortunes' initial impressions, as well. Except for

Kate, of course. She had never doubted Brandon's fervid claims of innocence.

But now after profoundly doubting Brandon's integrity, Flynt felt obliged to defend him.

"Why wouldn't I think it?" retorted Angelica. "From what I've heard from Mama, who zealously follows even quasi-celebrity news, Brandon Fortune always needs money. Some of his spending sprees have been well publicized. I remember Mama saying that he—" She broke off and stared blindly into space, her hands balled into fists.

"So your mother has followed the travails of Brandon Fortune pretty closely?" Flynt picked up her train of thought. He shifted in his chair. It was hard and uncomfortable and he was tired of sitting in it.

He stood up. Big mistake. From his standing position, he could look down the modest V-neck of her blue shirt. Flynt spied the shadowy hint of cleavage, and his mouth grew dry. Her small breasts were softly rounded beneath the ribbed knit material.

Now *he* was hard and uncomfortable. His mind went completely blank.

Unaware of his scrutiny, Angelica leaned back in her chair. "Mama tunes in to all those TV talk shows and reads the celebrity tabloids. She avidly followed the Monica Malone murder...I guess now I know why. Mama talked a lot about it at the time, but no more than any other sensational Hollywood story. And she's followed them all."

"But you never had any hints, any suspicions at all that Brandon Fortune was your father?"

"Not until you blurted it out this afternoon." Angelica stood up and carried the empty iced tea glasses to the sink. "And right in front of Sarah and Casper, too. That was princely of you, Corrigan."

"I didn't want it to be that way. You have to admit, I tried to give your mother a chance to tell—" Flynt shoved his hands into the pockets of his jeans. "I'm sorry, Angelica. I didn't want to hurt you by springing the news on you like that. So, uh, what do you think about Brandon being your dad?"

"I never particularly wanted any *dad* at all—and now I have Brandon Fortune." Angelica groaned. "Mama occasionally would drop hints about who my father was. She said he was related to somebody famous. That would've been Monica Malone, of course. A few years ago she started adding that he had a rich famous family."

"And you started wondering if maybe you were a Kennedy?"

"I never wondered because I didn't care. It didn't matter," Angelica said firmly. "It still doesn't."

"I don't believe that for a minute, Angelica."

Her response was stony silence.

"Do you know who Sarah's and Casper's fathers are?" Flynt was unable to resist asking. He thought of the expression on the kids' faces during the brief fatherhood discussion. Confused. Hopeful. It had been painful to see. "Because they obviously don't."

"And you're wondering who else is going to arrive at the door wanting to establish a relationship with their newly found offspring?" Angelica finished washing the glasses and reached for a dish towel to dry them.

"The thought's crossed my mind. From what I've

seen around here today, you never know what or who will show up at this door.''

"Don't worry, I know who Danny's, Sarah's, and Casper's fathers are, and it's nobody rich or famous. None of them will ever come here. Each of those men are aware that mama had his child, but it doesn't matter to them.''

"All three guys know they have kids by Romina and don't care?'' Flynt frowned. "What sort of lowlife goes around fathering and abandoning children?''

"A selfish, irresponsible lowlife, that's who,'' Angelica said bitterly.

"And your mother managed to find *three* of them?'' Flynt watched Angelica put the glasses away. Her movements were graceful, precise. "Romina has a real talent for picking men.''

Angelica whirled to confront him. Though censure was missing from his tone, she expected to see it reflected on his face. She found him looking at her, his expression curious but not judgmental.

"Mama has a talent for trusting the wrong men,'' Angelica acknowledged with a wistful sigh. "I know this will probably sound like an over-used cliché, but my mother has a heart of gold and the men she's chosen have pretty much smashed it. Finally, she was galvanized to help other women. It was a gradual process and she—''

Angelica abruptly lapsed into silence. Flynt Corrigan had been an FBI agent, she reminded herself, a professional investigator who'd made his living interrogating people. She had to proceed with caution around him. But it was hard to remember that because he was so easy to talk to. So easy to confide in.

It was mystifying. Angelica was thoroughly bemused. She'd never been the open, trusting type who shared secrets and sought advice; from an early age, she had found it best to keep her thoughts and feelings to herself. Yet here she was, chatting away about mama's men with Flynt as if they were long-time confidantes, just like she'd done with Mara, who was her best friend, fellow nurse, former foster sister and current roommate.

Of course, the feelings Flynt evoked in her were definitely not the comradely ones Mara inspired. Angelica noticed that Flynt was watching her, and her heart began to beat erratically. Needles of sexual excitement pricked her, and she was suddenly, sharply aware of how quickly she'd shifted from being mentally attuned to him to this aching sensual awareness of him.

"Why hasn't your mother told the kids who their dads are?" Flynt asked.

Angelica dragged her eyes away from him, wishing that they were talking about something else, not this subject that had caused so much pain.

She swallowed hard. "There's no deep dark secret why mama hasn't told the kids who their dads are. My brother Danny knows, but he's old enough to deal with it. Sarah and Casper aren't. Mama doesn't want them to know their fathers' names because she's afraid the kids might try to contact their fathers and be hurt when they're rejected by them, which they definitely would be."

"Help!" Casper came running into the kitchen with an armful of dishes. "I ate ice cream and spaghetti and pie and chocolate pudding in my room, and this gunk got crusted on, and now there's roaches in my room and mama's gonna kill me.'' He dumped the dirty dishes onto the counter and ran out the back door without pausing to take a breath.

Flynt joined Angelica at the counter and picked up one of Casper's discarded bowls. ''It's encrusted with gunk, all right,'' he said lightly. ''I'm surprised that any self-respecting roach would go near this.''

Angelica began to fill the sink with detergent once again. ''Mama is something of a neat freak. Gunk and roaches aren't going to improve her relationship with Casper.'' She took two of the bowls and submerged them in the sink of soap bubbles.

She found herself resorting to her own private fantasy that something—somebody!—would come along to help improve the relationship between her mother and baby brother. More specifically, a good man who could relate to both Casper and Romina because it was achingly clear that Casper needed a strong male presence in his life, especially with Danny gone. Immediately, Angelica reproved herself. A good man to set everything right? How embarrassing! Her fantasies were becoming downright retro; she'd undoubtedly watched one too many reruns of those old heartwarming family sitcoms. Next she'd be proclaiming that ''Father Knows Best.''

She cast a stealthy glance at Flynt. He'd pushed up the sleeves of his jacket and reached for a plate coated with an ominous-looking blue substance. He tentatively dipped it into the sink.

Angelica was totally diverted by the sight of his muscular forearms, now exposed by the rolled up sleeves of his jacket. They were covered with a light dusting of wiry hair. Her stomach turned a wild somersault. She'd seen plenty of bare forearms—the doctors in the hospital scrubbed to their elbows—but none of them ever had impacted upon her like the sight of Flynt Corrigan's. And his hands...

She stared at his big hands, the long, well-shaped fingers. Not even the fact that those fingers were now holding two of the most disgustingly filthy bowls she'd ever seen detracted from the compelling masculinity of his hands. She watched him reach for the scrub brush.

"Don't bother," she said hastily. "These dishes need to soak for hours."

"Sounds like you're experienced with this sort of thing."

"Pretty much," Angelica murmured, as an entirely new wave of sensation rolled over her. She had been so riveted by the sight of his hands she hadn't noticed that when he'd moved to stand next to her at the sink, their hips had made contact. And remained touching as they stood together.

Her head seemed to be spinning. Just being near him, their bodies touching in exciting yet comfortable familiarity was a sensual experience that she wanted to prolong, to savor. She stood, dazed by these strange new feelings, watching Flynt helpfully finish putting the dishes into the sink to soak.

"Thank you," she said softly, suddenly feeling overwhelmingly shy.

Flynt nodded and pulled off three squares from the roll of paper towels. Angelica couldn't help but count;

their mother had drilled them into the one-square rule since toddlerhood.

"Would you say you owed me a favor?" He scrunched the paper towel into a ball and slamdunked it into the trash can.

Angelica knew she should be suspicious. Instead, her heart pounded with nervous anticipation. "That depends." She inhaled sharply. "What does this favor involve?"

"Your father, Brandon Fortune."

Chapter 4

Disappointment rolled through Angelica in waves. Flynt was standing close to her, their bodies touching; she was aware of his masculinity in a way that enticed her instead of intimidating her.

But Flynt didn't appear to notice, or at least, he didn't intend to talk about it. The question he'd asked about her owing him a favor contained no sexual innuendo whatsoever. Damn! exclaimed a naughty, previously unheard-from little voice in her head. Angelica firmly stifled it.

Flynt wanted to talk about her father Brandon Fortune. Mortification swiftly replaced disappointment. She could only be grateful that he didn't know how wildly she had misinterpreted his request.

"You said your mom told the other men in her life that they were fathers, but they chose to ignore that fact—and their kids." Flynt stated his premise.

Angelica could picture him using a similar technique with suspects during his FBI days. She purposefully moved away from the sink. Away from Flynt. She stood in the doorway of the kitchen, her arms folded in front of her chest in classic defensive body language.

"That's true," she said shortly.

"Well, Brandon never knew about your existence. Your mother didn't tell him that she was pregnant, she broke up with him and then ran away from home." Flynt's voice rose slightly. "He knows about you now, and he's here to acknowledge you as his daughter, Angelica. Doesn't that count for something?"

"How about the Father of the Year Award?" Angelica was flippant.

Flynt didn't let her get away with it. "Angelica, be fair. This time it's not a case of a father deliberately abandoning his child. This was your mother's choice not to tell Brandon about you."

"Mama once told me that she was scared to tell him— my father—that she was pregnant." Angelica defended her mother, her voice warm with compassion. "After all, when she finally worked up the courage to tell her own parents they were terrible to her. They threatened her, and she had to run away to have me."

"I've talked to your mother's parents, Angelica. They admitted that they went to see Monica Malone when they found out that Romina was pregnant. Monica— uh—paid them some money…" He paused, searching for a tactful phrase.

"Monica Malone bribed them to make Mama get rid of me," Angelica said bluntly. "That squares with what Mama told me about her parents."

"Without condoning their actions, keep in mind that your mother was only sixteen years old at the time, Angelica. Only two years older than Sarah is now."

"Yet they never bothered to look for her," Angelica shot back. "Mama was an underaged runaway and could've been found easily enough, but they never even reported her missing. All these years and they made no attempt to find her."

"She knows that? She's looked into it?"

Angelica nodded solemnly. "She knows."

"Do you think Romina expected to be found? Maybe *hoped* to be found? She was remarkably easy to trace, she never attempted to use false identity or conceal her whereabouts." Flynt frowned thoughtfully. "Romina's parents admitted to me that they never looked for her."

"What kind of people are they? I can't imagine not knowing where your own child is." Angelica's voice grew husky with emotion. "If my sister or brothers or one of my own children were ever missing, I'd never stop looking for them. Never."

"Yet you don't mind that your mother helps fugitive women hide their kids from their fathers? That those men are consigned to the very fate that you just said you would never accept—not knowing where their kids are?"

"That's different! Those children were abused by their fathers! Men like that don't deserve to—" Her jaw dropped. "I—I mean, speaking hypothetically, of course. There is no proof that Mama is involved in—anything unlawful."

Angelica looked at the ground, unable to meet his eyes, aghast at her slip. She had almost admitted that her mother was a part of Nancy Portland's underground network, something she'd never come close to doing with anyone else. Even after warning herself to be careful what she said around Flynt, she'd been indiscreet. She flushed, angry with herself for her inexcusable lapse. And with Flynt for causing her to make it.

He knew it, too; she could tell. She was darn lucky he'd opted out of law enforcement, Angelica thought grimly. Back in his agent days, Flynt Corrigan had probably weasled confessions out of suspects before they'd ever realized what they were saying.

"Relax, Angelica, I'm not here to grill you or your mother about any disputed custody cases. I'm no longer an officer of the law, I'm here strictly as a—friend—of your father. To convince you to give him a chance to know you."

Angelica heaved an impatient sigh. "Look, if I agree to meet Brandon Fortune, will you both go away and leave me alone?"

Getting rid of Flynt was paramount at this point. He penetrated her defenses too easily. Of course, that meant agreeing to meet Brandon Fortune. Her father. Angelica felt a peculiar tightness in her chest.

"Will you be available to meet Brandon tonight? For dinner?"

"I already have dinner plans." Angelica decided it was none of his business that those plans were to nuke a frozen dinner in the microwave and watch the evening news with the cat in the apartment she shared with Mara Quinlan. After all, plans were plans. "But I suppose I could meet you afterward," Angelica said.

She could tell he didn't buy her dinner plans excuse;

he was staring at her in patent disbelief. And she'd learned enough about him in this short time to know that he wasn't going to simply give up and go away. Not until she agreed to meet her father.

"Afterward, then," Flynt said stiffly.

"But I might not be able to stay very long. I have three patients who are due to deliver any time, so I'm on call for them."

Angelica concocted her plan as she spoke. She could ask Mara to page her beeper, whether any patients actually went into labor or not. It was a built-in excuse to end the evening quickly and diplomatically.

"I'm a nurse-midwife," she explained.

"Yes, I know."

Angelica eyed him with disapproval. "It's more than a little creepy knowing you investigated me, the way that—that reptile Searcy is always snooping around trying to find dirt on my mother."

She decided that she was definitely going to arrange to have herself paged by Mara.

"I wasn't looking for any dirt, nor did I find any, Angelica. And I only know a few basic facts about you. At this point, I've told you as much about myself as I know about you."

They stared at each other. Angelica was surprised to see how wary and alert, how very much on guard he appeared to be. In fact, he looked the way she felt.

That struck her as strange. Why should Flynt be uneasy around her? She couldn't disrupt his life, the way he'd most certainly disrupted hers. Unless...

She remembered Searcy's crude comment on the porch, and her own foolishly impulsive glance at Flynt's groin. Angelica felt her cheeks begin to grow warm. She was blushing!

This was a nurse? One whose career was based on the results of reproduction? It was disconcerting to realize that she could comfortably and competently discuss the anatomy and other clinical aspects of sex with any man, woman or child on the planet, yet the flash memory of Flynt Corrigan's bulging fly made her flush as crimson as a sheltered Victorian maiden.

It was also mortifying!

She couldn't let him know how he affected her, that he was capable of turning her into a blushing schoolgirl. But then, his own actions made it clear that he didn't want to acknowledge her erotic effect on him, either. Flynt had tried to ignore the evidence as much as she had; he'd not even hinted at making a pass at her.

The realization bolstered her self-confidence. The two of them could operate under an unspoken agreement, without admitting their mutual sexual awareness. Such an arrangement would permit them both to maintain control. Which would be as important to Flynt as it was to her. She recognized a fellow control freak when their paths crossed, Angelica mused wryly.

"I'll check with Brandon and then get back to you about tonight," Flynt said, already heading out of the kitchen. "Where can I reach you? Here or—"

"I'll be at my own apartment." Angelica scribbled down her phone number on the ransom note and handed it to him. "Oops. Did I just tamper with evidence or something?" she asked snidely.

"Brandon isn't responsible for this, Angelica. Believe it."

"Then maybe it was Searcy," mocked Angelica. "I wouldn't put anything past *him*."

"You could be right. There's a whole world of suspects out there, now that you and your mother have been eliminated."

They reached the small vestibule. The umbrella was still lying on the floor where she had forced him to drop it. Flynt stooped down and picked it up.

"You suspected *me* of extortion?" Angelica was incensed. "Or Mama?"

"You two were the first ones we suspected," drawled Flynt. "See how easy—and how foolish—it is to jump to conclusions?" He placed the umbrella in her hand. "I'll talk to Brandon and then call you, probably within the next hour."

"Can't wait," Angelica muttered, watching him stride down the walk.

She tried to ignore the unwelcome fluttering in her stomach. She was *not* nervous! That threatening note was too amateurish to be taken seriously, she decided. The pasted letters were too ridiculous, like something out of a junior detective novel. Anyway, she didn't feel like a Fortune, she didn't feel like Brandon's daughter so the threat didn't really apply to her, no matter what Flynt might say.

Nor was she nervous about meeting her father for the first time; she didn't care enough to be nervous, Angelica staunchly reminded herself.

"Fathers!" She said the word aloud and heard the scorn in her voice. "Who needs them?"

Who needed them, indeed? She remembered her brother Daniel's father, Tom Harper, though she had only been seven years old the final time she'd seen him. He was a big, rough, hard-drinking cowboy in East Texas, who'd resented even the slight domesticity forced on him during his visits to Romina's tiny apartment and was abusive to the mother of his son.

Angelica thought of that last evening when Tom Harper and her mother had been fighting as usual, with Mama screaming, Tom cursing, and both of them throwing things. Poor little Danny, not quite two, had cried and cried. In her mind's eye, Angelica could still see Tom Harper bursting into the small bedroom, bending over the crib to grab the terrified toddler.

She saw her young self charging Tom like a bull in the rodeo, knocking him off his already unsteady feet. He had risen up like an enraged giant, and then it was Angelica who'd been thrown, right into the wall.

That had done it for Romina, who'd endured Tom's abuse but wouldn't tolerate a man's hand being raised against her children. She'd immediately decided they were leaving Tom Harper and Texas the next day. For a long time afterward, Romina had boyfriends only, sparing Angelica and Danny any further interactions with fathers until she met Sarah's, in Baton Rouge, Louisiana, seven years later.

Barry North, a charming, smiling man, Angelica recalled. Handsome and well-groomed, some kind of professional because he always wore a suit when he came to visit. A married man. She and Danny had rummaged through his wallet once when he was in the other room with mama, and had seen the family photo he proudly carried. There they were, the North family. Barry, his wife and three kids.

Barry North was not interested in having a fourth child, at least not with Romina. After Romina told him she was pregnant, they never saw him again.

Shortly after Sarah's birth, they had moved to Birmingham, Alabama. Romina met Casper's father, Jurgen Heintz, an introverted physics professor at the university, on one of her cookie runs to the campus. He'd made it clear during his infrequent visits that the presence of Angelica, Danny and little Sarah unnerved him. He did not like children, and he certainly didn't want any of his own.

Angelica knew that because at fourteen she'd become her mother's confidante—or confessor. Jurgen Heintz refused to have anything to do with his child and arranged for a departmental transfer to the main campus at Huntsville. Before leaving town, he gave Romina a lump sum of cash.

"He bought his way out of Casper's life for six thousand dollars," Angelica remembered her mother saying as she clutched the professor's check.

They'd used it as a down payment on this house.

At least Jurgen had provided them with that much; Tom Harper and Barry North hadn't donated a penny toward their children's welfare. Yet even as she credited Jurgen Heintz for his contribution, Angelica thought of Casper, wanting all those expensive, exciting, challenging things they couldn't afford.

"Casper is too smart for his own good," Romina often said. "It's too bad he inherited that high IQ from his father."

Fathers. Angelica shivered. She'd always felt lucky

to be spared knowledge of her own. Now that was about to change.

The fluttering in Angelica's stomach became genuine pangs. Which could not be anxiety! She refused to be anxious about meeting some guy from her mother's past—which was all that Brandon Fortune meant to her.

"Is she coming?" Brandon asked Flynt for what seemed like the thousandth time since they'd taken a booth in the trendy Southside nightspot called Swank.

The place had been Brandon's choice. He'd polled the staff at the Premier Living Suites for the "hottest new place in town" and been told Swank was it.

The place boasted no fewer than seventy-five varieties of beer, plus a cigar bar stocked with fancy smokes, cognacs, wines and premium cocktails. There was also a billiard room, a smoke-free lounge with thick-velvet upholstered chairs and sofas and a marble dance floor. Flynt and Brandon were currently occupying one of the dark leather booths in the softly lit Martini Lounge. Strains of a yearning ballad filtered in from the dancing area.

"The setting's gotta be right. I want my kid to think her dad is the coolest dude ever," Brandon had explained to Flynt. When Flynt mentioned Swank to Angelica, she had agreed to meet them there at nine o'clock in a tone so utterly indifferent that he *knew* she was faking it.

"Do you see her? Is she here yet?" pressed Brandon.

"No, I don't see her, she's not here yet," Flynt replied, for what felt like the thousandth time.

He'd followed the traditional security seating arrangements and faced the entrance of the lounge, putting himself on guard duty. Meanwhile, waiting with Brandon for Angelica to arrive seemed to him a lot like watching for Santa on Christmas Eve with an eager kindergartner. Neither possessed much patience or any sense of time.

"I'll have another drink, Kimmy," Brandon called to the waitress. "Same as the last."

"That'll be your third martini, Brandon." Flynt took a sip of his beer. His first, from a local microbrewer. "In addition to the wine with dinner. Think you'd better slow down?"

He suspected Brandon had a few drinks earlier, too. Monitoring the other man's alcohol intake made him feel like a prep school chaperone.

Apparently Brandon agreed. "What're you, a teetotaling watchdog?" he snapped, his voice slightly slurred.

"You don't want to be drunk when you meet your daughter for the first time, do you?" Flynt grimaced. He sounded like a condescending scold, but he didn't want Angelica to find her father soused upon her arrival.

Maybe another approach would be better received. "Look, Brandon, I know you're nervous about meeting Angelica—who can blame you?—but—"

Flynt paused as Brandon jumped to his feet to snatch his latest martini from the waitress's tray. Still standing, he glanced at the entrance of the lounge.

"Oh, wow!" Brandon downed a large gulp of his drink. "Flynt, is that *her?*"

Flynt followed the direction of Brandon's pop-eyed stare. A young woman in a short blue dress was striding into the lounge. She wore high-heeled strappy sandals that gave her added height and showcased a pair of shapely legs. Her thick shiny black hair flowed around her shoulders and she held her head high as she walked.

She was not only beautiful, she had presence, she radiated sexual charisma, and Flynt knew that every male eye in the lounge was on her. On Angelica.

"Can that be my little girl?" Brandon fairly gasped the words.

Flynt figured that although Brandon had seen the photograph of Angelica, he somehow, against all logic, must have been expecting "a little girl." Perhaps a sprite in pigtails and kneesocks.

"Brandon, I think you'd better sit back down," Flynt said, trying to ease him back into the seat. Poor Brandon didn't look too well.

By the time Angelica reached their booth, her father was pale and hyperventilating.

"I think he might be having an asthma attack," guessed Kimmy, who'd returned to check out the commotion.

"Or maybe a cardiac arrest," a patron at a nearby booth suggested helpfully. "Does anybody know CPR?"

"I do, I'm a nurse," said Angelica. She leaned over Brandon, holding his wrist to take his pulse. It was quite strong, not at all indicative of cardiac distress.

"I'm pretty sure he's having an anxiety attack," Flynt said quickly, before Angelica and the interested group of spectators who'd gathered could begin CPR. "A paper bag would be helpful."

Someone shoved a bag into his hands. "Breathe into this, Brandon," Flynt ordered, holding it up to his face.

Brandon took a few deep breaths and gradually resumed breathing naturally.

Angelica met Flynt's gaze over the top of Brandon's head. So this was her father? She decided to get this over even more quickly than she'd originally planned.

She would introduce herself and then take off. "Hello, I'm—"

"Don't even think it," Flynt growled, and she knew he'd read her thoughts—all too accurately.

The other customers returned to their booths. Kimmy asked if Angelica would like to order a drink.

"That's my daughter, can you believe it?" Brandon sounded like he didn't. "Give her whatever she wants. Money is no object."

No doubt her status-conscious father expected her to order a magnum of the most expensive champagne, Angelica thought. Well, she would not bow to greed. This was her first opportunity to show him that, apart from sharing a gene pool, she and Brandon Fortune were not alike in any way.

"I'll have a chocolate martini, please," said Angelica.

Flynt assumed she was being sarcastic. "Angelica, if you don't order something, I'll order for you," he gritted through his teeth.

"No, she's already ordered, Flynt." Brandon leaped to her defense. "A chocolate martini is *the* cool, up-to-the-minute drink. Of course, *my* daughter would know such things." He gazed raptly at Angelica for a long moment.

"A chocolate martini?" Flynt grimaced. "Who dreamed that one up? And why?"

"It's cool and up-to-the-minute," Angelica assured

him, a gleam of humor in her dark eyes. She kept them focused on Flynt, stealing only a covert glance at her father.

"Sit down, both of you!" Brandon played host. "We have so much catching up to do." He slid over, making room for Angelica on his side of the booth.

Instead, she slipped into the other side, across from her father, casting him a veiled sidelong glance. Brandon's eyes were slightly bloodshot, his face tanned and somewhat dissolute, his hair too blond and too long for a man of his age.

He was her father. Her father! Shouldn't she be feeling something, anything, toward this man? Some sort of allegiance based upon biology, at the very least. Instead she felt...

She felt nothing. Angelica's eyes collided with Brandon's, and she noticed that he looked away as quickly as she did.

She twisted the napkin that she hadn't even realized she'd picked up. Well, maybe she was feeling something, Angelica conceded, a confusing inner turmoil that she wasn't sure how to identify or to handle. What were she and Brandon Fortune supposed to do now? What could they possibly say to each other? He was her father, but she didn't know him.

There was no need to know him, she reminded herself, she didn't want to know him.

"My daughter, huh? I've been in some really weird places but this kind of tops them all," Brandon said, breaking the silence again. "I mean, I thought meeting my mother and sisters and brothers for the first time was—was…'' His voice trailed off. Clearly, he was at a loss for words.

''Weird?'' Angelica supplied one.

She was suddenly intensely curious about this man. *Weird* hardly covered the unsurpassingly strange series of events that comprised Brandon Fortune's life.

''Yeah, weird,'' Brandon agreed.

Flynt sat down beside Angelica, closer than he needed to be. Close enough for her to feel the sturdy strength of him, to absorb the heat from his body. Instead of being offended at this invasion of her personal space, she found his nearness to be comfortable, familiar.

''Are you okay?'' Flynt asked in a low quiet tone, for her ears only.

Angelica nodded her head, grateful for his concern. For his presence. If he had taken her hand for an encouraging squeeze, she knew she wouldn't have objected.

But Flynt rested his arms on the table, folding both his hands around his bottle of beer. ''I have to admit, I'm not sure how to proceed from here. Should I introduce you two to each other?''

''No introductions necessary, Flynt,'' said Brandon. ''Angelica and I know who we are.''

Angelica swallowed. If this wasn't the most bizarre moment of her life, it was certainly a prime contender. ''Yes, we know.''

''So what do you think of your old dad?'' Brandon asked in faux_hale-and-hearty tones.

''I don't know you well enough to be able to answer that, Mr. Fortune,'' she replied. And instantly took herself to task. No, that sounded wrong. Too cold and formal, maybe even critical which she didn't mean to be. "Um, Brandon," she amended. But that didn't sound right either.

"You can call me Dad," Brandon said rather breezily.

Flynt winced. In his book, that suggestion earned Brandon the title King of Superficiality. But Angelica's response stunned him.

She smiled. "Okay, Dad."

"Say, this is a lot easier than I thought it would be." Brandon looked pleased.

And then Flynt began to understand the dynamics between the pair. The title, the very concept of *Dad,* meant nothing to Angelica. She probably attributed the same emotional weight to the word *Dad* as she did to *man* or *person.*

And Brandon shared her attitude completely. *Dad* held no special meaning for him, either. As Brandon Malone, he'd grown up without a dad, thanks to his adoptive mother's succession of lovers and his own father's hideous betrayal. Flynt frowned thoughtfully. The more he considered it, the more *Dad* seemed an imprecation for this pair. A subtle, convenient expression of hostility.

Which was a shame. The two of them shared a common loss, without either realizing what they'd missed. Inevitably, came memories of his own dad, whom he'd deeply loved. Flynt felt the familiar dark sadness well within him and immediately suppressed it. This wasn't the time or the place to think about the late John Corrigan.

He ignored the niggling guilt, reminding him that he'd *never* found the proper time and place to think about his father, that he'd been keeping those memories at bay for too many years.

Kimmy's arrival ended his reverie, and Flynt was glad to let it go. He watched as the waitress placed a peculiar-looking drink in front of Angelica.

"So that's a chocolate martini?" He eyed it dubiously.

"Would you like a taste?" offered Angelica, lifting the glass.

"No, thanks." Flynt politely declined. He saw no reason to add that the very idea of a chocolate martini made him feel like gagging.

"Do you have a picture of your mother with you, princess?" Brandon asked Angelica. "Romina was my first love, you know. You never really forget your first love, right?"

"To be honest, I wouldn't know. I've made it a point not to fall in love. And I do have a picture of Mama." Angelica delved into her purse and found her wallet. "This was taken last year, right before my brother Danny was sent overseas. He's stationed in Bosnia. There we are, the five of us, Mama, Danny, Sarah, Casper and me."

Brandon stared at the Carroll family picture. "Romina still looks damn fine for a woman her age."

"She's younger than you are." Angelica was immediately defensive.

"Brandon was complimenting your mother, Angelica," Flynt pointed out.

"Yeah," agreed Brandon. His eyes remained riveted to the photo. "Romina looks good."

"Mama looks *very* good," Angelica proclaimed loyally. She was surprised to notice her martini was gone. She must have gulped it down, though she barely remembered tasting it.

Brandon noticed her empty glass, too. "Kimmy, another drink for my daughter," he called, then flashed a smile at Angelica and Flynt. "Would you two excuse me? Try to keep the conversation going without me, okay? Bet you won't have a bit of trouble." He gave an exaggerated wink and loped off.

"He beat me to the punch," Angelica grumbled. "*I* planned to be the one to excuse myself and hide out in the rest room."

Kimmy set another chocolate martini in front of her. Angelica automatically reached for it.

"Careful." Flynt laid his hand over hers. "Getting yourself juiced will only make things worse, Angelica."

"I'm not," she protested, then reconsidered. "You're right." She pushed the glass away.

"Pretty tough going, huh?" Flynt said softly.

Angelica turned to him. Right now, when she needed a friend, Flynt had somehow transformed himself into just that. He was her ally in this surreal episode.

"Brandon said it's easier," she cried. "*Easier?* Compared to what?"

"Brandon's worst-case scenario probably was that you'd turn out to be a histrionic drama queen like Monica Malone. Ever seen any of her movies?"

"Some of the old ones on the movie channel on TV."

"Then imagine how Miss Malone would play the scene if she were cast as the long-lost daughter of a, well, rather notorious father."

"As an actress, Monica Malone was usually way over

the top." Angelica smiled slightly. "If she were playing me, Brandon would be wearing this chocolate martini."

"And then you'd probably make him eat the glass." Flynt leaned back and draped his arm lightly around her shoulders. A supportive gesture. One of comforting warmth and friendship. He was not coming on to her, he assured himself.

"What's it like, meeting the man who is your father for the first time?" he asked huskily.

"Do you need to know for the report you're writing for Brandon's family?" Angelica resisted the surprisingly strong temptation to lean back against his arm.

"I'm not writing a report, but I admit to being personally curious. This is a fairly unique situation, you know. Most of us meet our fathers in the hospital maternity ward and have no recollection of the event."

"Mmm, that's true, I guess." Angelica felt a glowing warmth spread languorously through her veins. "I drank that first martini way too fast." She spoke her thoughts aloud, confirming what she'd just realized. That the drink was quite strong and its effects were starting to hit her.

"I thought so," Flynt agreed amiably.

"Thank you for keeping me from bolting down a second one or I'd be weaving and staggering out of here."

Her back felt stiff from her erect position, her muscles were beginning to ache from the tension of sitting forward and still. She forgot why she'd refrained from leaning back in the booth, and did it, immediately coming into contact with his arm. It felt warm and solid and she settled against him, slouching a little. Relaxing.

"I wouldn't let you weave and stagger." Flynt closed

his hand around her shoulder, and his fingers began to knead lightly. "I would've carried you out."

"A real gentleman." She shivered as his hand glided to the nape of her neck.

"Thank you." He leaned in closer, his lips almost skimming the top of her head.

Her hair smelled clean and fresh and shone like black silk. It felt sleek as silk as it brushed against his hand. The soft, feminine feel of her sent excitement skyrocketing through him.

Who was he kidding? Flynt believed in self-honesty. He was most definitely coming on to her.

Unable to resist, he lifted his other hand to her cheek, cupping the soft skin with his palm.

Angelica closed her eyes and leaned into his hand, letting the warmth envelop her. Her heart began to pound, her skin felt as if it were on fire. And while her every nerve was operating on a hypersensitivity level, her brain—at least the area in charge of her willpower and judgment—seemed to have shut down completely.

Her body took over, thinking for her. Making the decisions for her. Doing what it wanted. Otherwise, she never would've given in to the urge to lay her hand on his chest, an unmistakable sign of encouragement.

She would've pushed him away, instead of sitting here in sensual darkness, her eyes closed, enjoying the exquisite torture of waiting for his next move.

She didn't have to wait long. She felt his warm breath on her face, and a hushed whimper escaped from her throat as his mouth touched hers lightly, softly, in a tentative, almost chaste kiss.

It was so sweet, so wonderful. But it wasn't enough.

He brushed her lips with his, gently, back and forth. And it still wasn't enough for her.

Angelica spread her fingers over the smooth cotton of his shirt. Beneath it, she could feel the heat rising from his skin. Slowly she slid her fingers along his chest, pausing to stroke the hard column of his neck, his strong jawline, before curving her hand around his cheek.

"Angelica." He moaned her name.

The deep raspy sound shot through her, liquefying into urgent need. On wild bold impulse, she touched the tip of her tongue to his lips.

He needed no further invitation. Flynt opened his mouth over hers, and he kissed her hotly, hungrily, the way he had wanted to from the first moment he'd seen her. He buried one hand in her hair while his other cupped her face, anchoring her to him.

But Angelica was making no attempt to escape. The fingers of her other hand had found their way to his waist and she held on, clinging to him.

His tongue penetrated her mouth and met hers, and she welcomed it, rubbing and teasing, retreating a little, then luring him back. She felt his tongue playing with hers, exploring her mouth, and she loved it, the seductive stroking, the slow glide over her teeth.

Angelica shuddered with pleasure.

Suddenly, fiercely, aching with need, she pressed against him, seeking the pressure of his chest to soothe the throbbing of her tight, tingling nipples. She wanted to be closer to him, wanted it so badly she was almost delirious with it.

A whispery moan escaped from her lips as he angled

his mouth over hers, exerting his possession and deepening the intimacy of their kiss.

And then a shrill staccato beep shattered the sensual clouds surrounding them.

Chapter 5

The beep sounded again and again, sharp and insistent.
Flynt reluctantly lifted his mouth from Angelica's.

Her eyes flew open and stared into his. His pupils
were dilated with arousal, only a rim of light blue en-
circled the black spheres. Angelica's gaze dropped to his
mouth that was moist from kissing her, lingering on the
tantalizing sensuality of his full lower lip.

And then she realized where they were and what they
were doing. "Oh!" She frantically tried to disentangle
herself from his arms.

Flynt showed no inclination to release her, and she
gave up, turning her attention instead to fumbling with
the clasp of her purse where her beeper shrilly sounded.

"Arrange to have your mother beep you shortly after
introductions were made?" Flynt drawled, watching Angelica snatch the beeper from her purse.

''No! It's not my mother!'' Which was true; it was Mara whom she'd arranged to beep her.

The phone number of the apartment they shared was displayed on the tiny screen. Angelica pressed the button to silence the beeper.

''This is the number of my service, which means it's a patient-related emergency call,'' she lied, pulling away from him. She shrank against the wall, as far from him as she could get. Which wasn't very far, given the dimensions of the booth.

Angelica knew he was watching her, but she couldn't bring herself to look at him. She was flushed and flustered, stunned not only by her total loss of control but also by the overpowering flood of desire raging through her. The sharp, sensual ache in her belly was almost painful in its intensity, and her breasts felt swollen and ultrasensitive.

Her mind reeled. How had it happened? His mouth had hardly touched hers when she'd quite unexpectedly caught fire. And in a public place! It was unbelievable.

Angelica flinched. She wasn't the type to sensually ignite anytime or anywhere. Her high school award of Class Ice Queen had been entirely deserved; the yearbook prediction for her to achieve the status of ''oldest living virgin'' had turned out to be accurate.

In the following years, her incredulous nursing school classmates had repeatedly asked her, ''What are you saving it for?'' They'd been alternately astonished, scornful and intrigued by her chastity.

She wasn't saving anything for some nebulous future Mr. Right, Angelica had informed them; she was saving *herself* from the misery and uncertainty of all those Mr. Wrongs brought into a woman's life.

But not into hers! She had long relished her freedom from the emotional turmoils of romance.

And now this. Angelica was appalled. A virgin ice queen did *not* make out in a booth in the middle of Swank's Martini Lounge.

Angelica choked back the lump rising in her throat. She was scared. Those few ardent moments with Flynt had given her a glimpse of something she hadn't experienced before, of exciting pleasure that tempted with seductive allure.

She didn't need to remind herself how dangerous *that* was. She'd watched her mother succumb to passion all her life and decided early on that it wasn't worth the risks. Why invest time and energy in loving a man who wouldn't return her love, who would hurt and leave her? Possibly with a child!

Romina had made that choice, time after time, but Angelica swore she never would. Her plans for her own life had included getting an education and a good-paying job that she liked, having her own place to live and friends to enjoy. She was proud that she'd achieved it all.

And now this!

Angelica stared at Flynt in round-eyed horror. There was absolutely no place in her wonderfully controlled, ordered life for a man. Not even a sexy, successful, intelligent one like Flynt Corrigan.

Especially not him because he'd proven himself to be the take-charge, dominant type. The quintessential alpha male. She'd seen alphas in action; they barged into a woman's life and messed it up, fully expecting the woman not to mind.

Well, Angelica minded. She minded very much.

"Angelica," Flynt took her hand and carried it to his mouth, brushing his lips over her knuckles. "I think we—"

"Don't!" She ripped her hand away, nearly knocking over the martini glass and the beer bottle. Flynt caught them both, his quick reflexes preventing a double spill.

"Let me out." Her voice was breathless and husky, nothing like her normal, commanding tone. No wonder he didn't budge.

Angelica ran a nervous hand through her hair, tousling it even more than it already was. "Please!" She cringed at the plea in her voice. Had his alpha maleness already reduced her to a wimp?

She tried to rally, to stick with her escape scheme. "I can't wait. I have to answer this page immediately. There is a phone in the lobby I—"

"No need to go there. Here, use mine." Flynt reached into the pocket of his tan sport coat and removed a small cell phone. "Unless making a phone call wasn't part of the plan because there is no emergency? You intended to go the lobby, walk straight out the door and not return?"

Oh, yes, that had been the plan. Not that she would admit to it now. She glared at the too-conveniently available cell phone. "I'm going to answer this emergency call right now," she said frigidly.

"Go ahead. Romina will be surprised to hear from you, but I have every confidence you'll manage to fake something credible."

"It's not Mama," Angelica insisted. At least that much was true. Stubbornly, she punched in her own phone number.

Mara answered on the first ring.

"This is Angelica Carroll returning the page," she said in her best professional tones.

There was an infinitesimal pause. "Oh, I get it now! You have an audience, and we have to pretend there really is a patient about to deliver," Mara said jovially.

"Yes." Angelica cast a covert glance at Flynt.

He raised his brows, letting her know he'd seen her sneak that look at him. She turned her back to him, as much as the booth would allow.

"Okay, let's pretend something really dramatic. I've got it—a woman is having triplets!" Mara was enthused. "Of course, we'd never deliver triplets since they're in the high-risk obstetricians' domain, but Brandon Fortune won't know that."

"The mother is in labor with triplets? I'll be there right away," Angelica exclaimed with credible urgency.

Mara laughed. "Rascal and I will be here waiting for you, Angel."

Rascal was their gray-striped tabby who found new ways to live up to his name every day. And then it occurred to Angelica that Mara wasn't even supposed to be home tonight. They'd agreed on the bogus page, which could be made from anywhere, since there was no need for a return call.

"What about TJ?" Angelica heard herself blurt out.

Flynt chuckled softly. Angelica groaned. Clearly, she had lost all impulse control tonight. That chocolate martini had packed a too-potent wallop! She vowed never to order another one.

"I broke my date with TJ after I talked to your mom about the search and seizure this afternoon," said Mara. "There's no way I wanted to see him tonight after his part in that." She sounded sad.

Poor Mara. Angelica hated to hear her normal optimism quelled. After all, she'd spent hours listening to the other girl's hopeful dreams, which all included love and romance. Despite her mother's terrible marriage to an abusive alcoholic, despite her five-year stint as Romina's foster daughter, Mara still believed in True Love.

Angelica figured that TJ Gibson just might be the answer to her best friend's prayers. Although he was a cop, TJ was a gentleman, well-raised by solid, kind parents, a definite beta rather than alpha male. Mara would be safe with him. Too bad she had talked to Romina, who distrusted all police and would automatically discourage anyone from dating somebody in law enforcement.

"It's really not his fault," Angelica said, defending TJ, giving up the emergency ruse. What was the point, since Flynt had it all figured out?

"Don't make excuses for him, Angel. TJ could've refused to go to the house, citing personal reasons or something."

"Wouldn't that be like refusing to treat a patient? Think about his professional responsibility." Angelica met Flynt's eyes. "I'll see you soon, and we'll talk about it some more."

She handed Flynt his phone. "Thank you. And it wasn't my mother," she added with a touch of defiance.

"No, it was your foster sister Mara Quinlan. You arranged to have her page you to get you away on a false emergency.''

Angelica gaped at him. ''How did you know her name? And that she'd been my foster sister?''

''Your mother mentioned both when she quizzed Officer TJ about that date tonight. As soon as I heard you ask about him, I put it together. I have an eidetic memory for names and facts, Angelica. An invaluable asset in my line of work.''

''I'm sure it is,'' Angelica said coolly. ''Well, now you know how much I don't want to be here. I've met Brandon Fortune and—''

''Where is Brandon, anyway?'' A frown crossed Flynt's face. ''He's been gone a long time.''

''Maybe you'd better check the men's room.''

''Maybe I'd better.''

Before Angelica realized what he was doing, Flynt had retrieved her keys from her purse. ''Hey!'' she protested. ''Hand them over, right now!''

''Sorry.'' His tone did not indicate the slightest remorse. To the contrary, he was undeniably taunting her.

He dropped the keys into the pocket of his trousers. ''Unless I hang on to these, you'll be out of here the moment I'm out of sight. And you can't drive, Angelica. You're under the influence.''

''I only had one drink!''

''Which was strong and went straight to your head. I can cite factors like body weight and blood alcohol content, if you'd like.''

''I am in complete—'' She broke off.

Why was she arguing, when her entire defense for her wanton behavior was the effects of her too-potent drink that she'd drunk too fast? She felt her face begin to go scarlet again. Tonight she'd blushed enough to burst the capillaries in her cheeks!

"I—I probably shouldn't drive," she admitted grudgingly.

"I figured you'd see it my way, after you'd thought things through." Flynt was droll.

He knew how embarrassed she was by their little impromptu necking session! And he didn't appear the least bit embarrassed—or affected in any way at all. Angelica scowled. "May I use your phone to call myself a taxi?"

"I'll drive you home. Let me look for Brandon first. He's in no condition to drive, either, but fortunately, I drove the rental car here and I have the keys." Flynt laid down several bills beside the check before sliding out of the booth.

"Let's go." He reached for her hand, pulling her along after him.

"You are probably the most alpha, alpha male I've ever met," Angelica accused, trailing behind him as far as the length of his arm would allow.

"I'm going to assume that's not a compliment."

"You are so right. It's an insult," she added, to make sure he knew it.

"In that case, ouch." Not that Flynt appeared to be wounded in the slightest.

They reached the dimly lit lobby, which was crowded with patrons moving among the various rooms. There was a wide range of age groups, but customers in their twenties and thirties predominated.

"Wait here," ordered Flynt. He strode off, presumably in the direction of the men's rest room.

Angelica chafed at having to obey his command. She sought an alternative, glancing at the two pay phones in the corner. Both of them were currently in use. Well, it didn't matter, anyway; Flynt would be back well before any cab she called could arrive.

But Brandon had been gone long enough...

She approached the hostess and asked about a man with a blond ponytail and deep tan, wearing a black turtleneck and black jeans. With three earrings in one earlobe, two in the other, and a thick gold chain with a jeweled medallion around his neck.

The hostess remembered Brandon quite well. He had mentioned that he was visiting from California and asked her to call him a taxi. When it arrived, he'd given her a twenty-dollar tip.

Flynt joined her at that moment. "He's not in the—"

"He called a cab," Angelica cut in. "He's gone."

Flynt muttered a curse. "I'm sorry, Angelica."

"No need for you to apologize for Brandon. After all, I was ready to do the same thing and cut out on him." She folded her arms in front of her chest to prevent him from taking her hand again.

Instead, Flynt placed his hand on the small of her back, to guide her from the premises. His touch felt hot as a brand on such a sensitive area, and Angelica picked up her pace in an attempt to get ahead of him. Out of touching range.

She didn't succeed. No matter how fast she walked, his long-legged stride easily matched her own. And he kept his big hand firmly resting on her back. Finally she gave up and slowed down. Her feet were killing her; her high-heeled sandals lacked the design and comfort of track shoes, which were required if she were to even try to outrun Flynt Corrigan.

"You're upset," Flynt observed. Their current leisurely pace was more conducive to conversation. "And rightfully so. Brandon shouldn't have—"

"I've already forgotten about it." She cut him off.

It was true, her senses were too filled with Flynt to spare Brandon a thought. Which was upsetting, indeed. Imagine getting all shook up over a man, at the supposedly wise and mature age of twenty-six!

It was ridiculous; *she* was ridiculous!

"This evening has turned into a major inconvenience," Angelica said crossly, steering her troublesome thoughts in another direction. Annoyance was definitely preferable to the dangers of romantic fantasy.

"Now I'll have to ask Mara to drive me down here to pick up my car on the way to the hospital tomorrow."

"Do you keep office hours or work hospital shifts?"

The question diverted her. "I have my own practice and schedule patient appointments from nine to five on weekdays. I do hospital rounds before nine to visit any patients of mine on the maternity floor, and of course, I'm on call after hours and weekends if one of the mothers goes into labor."

"What about home deliveries? Don't midwives advocate them?"

"There is no set policy. If the mother wants a home delivery and there is no apparent risk to either her or the baby, I'll agree to it. But I always consult with both obstetricians and pediatricians before I give the go-ahead."

"Having a baby at home strikes me as nuts," Flynt

declared. "One of my crazier cousins did it. Had her husband and two older kids in the bedroom with her to see the baby being born. Hell, I think she invited the entire neighborhood in to watch."

"I assume the whole event was videotaped?"

"You assume correctly." He slid his fingers to her waist and gave a light retaliatory squeeze.

Their flash of shared humor was all too brief. Angelica stiffened, and Flynt dropped his hand at the same moment. Neither said a word.

Flynt's rental car, a gray Ford Taurus, was parked along the street nearly two blocks from Swank. A few drops of rain were just beginning to fall as she slipped into the passenger side. The raindrops were splattering harder against the windshield as Flynt settled in the driver's seat.

Angelica stared at his hands on the wheel, at his long well-shaped fingers. Compulsively, her eyes lifted to trace the strong line of his jaw, the sensual shape of his lips. She could almost feel the touch of his mouth on hers, of his strong hands holding her.

Arousal curled hot and deep within her. She shivered and squeezed her legs together. Oh, God, she wanted him. If he touched her again, she couldn't be sure she'd resist him. She certainly couldn't depend on a fortuitous page to interrupt them....

Her heart jumped in panic.

"Tonight turned out to be a big waste of time." Her tone was sharp, defensive.

She had to make him mad enough to stay away from her, and a blow to his male ego would be just the trick.

"I've spent more worthwhile evenings sitting alone watching the Weather Channel with the cat. Too bad I didn't do that tonight. At least I wouldn't be out in this thunderstorm."

As if on cue came a rumble of thunder, followed by a flash of lightning.

"It's a night for regrets, huh? Then don't forget your big date tonight. What a shame you had to cut it short to meet your own father," Flynt retorted caustically. What troubled him greatly was the streak of pure undiluted jealousy surging through him at the thought of her with another man.

Angelica suppressed a snicker, recalling the dinner date she'd invented. And the professional inquisitor with his unfailing memory had bought her story? Well, why not play along?

"Yes, what a shame. My date was very understanding, though. I told him I wasn't entertaining any illusions about Daddy Dearest. Good thing I wasn't. Brandon skipped out as if I were a bounty hunter ready to turn him in."

Flynt turned toward her. Though he'd inserted the key in the ignition, he made no attempt to start the car.

"Angelica, try not to take it personally. Brandon was nervous about meeting you. I think that seeing you affected him more than he ever dreamed it would."

"I already told you there is no need to apologize for Brandon, and there's no need to make excuses for him, either." Angelica played with the strap of her purse. "Truth be told, I expected it of him. Brandon's behavior is entirely consistent with the other men who made

Mama pregnant. All of them leave, none of them want anything to do with fatherhood.''

Her observation disturbed him because it was true. Because he knew himself what it felt like to be unwanted by a parent. ''Angelica—''

''It doesn't matter. I'm an adult and I wasn't looking for a father, anyway. Now that Brandon Fortune and I have met, he can go back to California or wherever, and I'll gladly get on with my life.''

''It's not that simple,'' growled Flynt. He wished it were. But Brandon was supposed to stay and get to know his daughter, and Flynt knew keeping Brandon in Alabama meant spending more time with Angelica himself. His body surged with hot anticipation…that was immediately followed by an impulse to pack up Brandon and catch the next plane out of the city.

When merely the thought of the sexual chemistry between him and Angelica had such an intense physical effect on him, he knew he was treading in very dangerous waters indeed.

But he couldn't run away from her. Not when there was a chance that Angelica might be in danger. The blackmail note threatening her, which they'd all dismissed as the idiotic but harmless idea of either Brandon or Romina, might be tied to the custody-thwarting underground, a sinister possibility indeed.

Furthermore, not to be discounted, was the multi-million-dollar contract for his company that Kate Fortune dangled as bait. Certainly no minor incentive.

And all threats or incentives aside, what kind of man ran away because a dark-eyed woman with the face of an angel and a curvy little body could tie him in knots with merely a glance? A coward, a man with no pride or self-control.

Certainly not Flynt Corrigan.

He stared at the rain pounding on the windshield, turning the streetlights into watery blurs. "I think both you and Brandon need to give each other another chance, Angelica."

"That must be the tone you used when you were about to read a suspect his Miranda rights," Angelica mocked him. "What's next? A choke hold till I agree to meet *Dad* again?"

"I never had to resort to choke holds." Flynt attempted a benign smile.

"And now you seamlessly morph into Good Cop, the perpetrator's pal."

Flynt's benign smile faltered. She could be seriously maddening. He resisted the urge to respond in kind to her smart-alecky retorts, made himself stay focused on the issue at hand.

How many separate attempts at father-daughter bonding would be enough for Kate to decide he'd done his part? Unfortunately Brandon's getaway and Angelica's intransigence made even a second meeting between the pair a seemingly hopeless proposition.

"If Brandon didn't feel deeply about being your father, he wouldn't have bolted, Angelica. He would've stayed and talked the glib Hollywood patter he uses when the person he's with means nothing to him."

"That would include everybody on the planet, I imagine." Angelica rolled her eyes.

"Your grandmother, Kate, is an astute judge of character, and she believes in Brandon, Angelica. She is sure that caring for his daughter will—''

"Give it up, Flynt. Brandon Fortune doesn't give a damn about me, and he never will. Luckily I don't care about him, either. Maybe if he'd come around when I was six—or even sixteen—it might've mattered, but now it's just too late.''

"Since you grew up with your mother and lived with the choices she's made, I can understand why you're hesitant to—''

"Skip the amateur psychoanalysis,'' Angelica snapped. "What does it matter to you if Brandon Fortune and I ever see each other again, anyway?''

"You've absorbed Romina's paranoid ideation well, Angelica. Be suspicious, look for ulterior motives, make accusations.''

"Leave my mother out of this. She's not the one who's trying to push me into playing daughter to a perpetual adolescent. That would be you, Flynt, and I'd be a fool not to wonder why.''

Flynt heaved a frustrated sigh. If he told her what was at stake, it would give her tremendous power over him. A chilling prospect. Putting another person in a position of power meant ceding independence and control, and that was unacceptable to him.

Flynt concentrated on studying the rivulets of rain streaming down the car windows, but Angelica commanded his mind's eye. She was desirable, feminine and pretty, but he'd met plenty of women who'd possessed those attributes. None of them had ever fascinated, confused and exhilarated him the way Angelica Carroll did.

He even liked her feisty attitude. Women who were

whiny, clingy and ineffectual had never appealed to him. She reached him on too many levels; he wanted her more than he could remember wanting any other woman.

All the more reason not to trust her. No, there would be no forthcoming explanations or confidences from him.

"I'll drive you home and then track Brandon down."

Another crash of thunder sounded simultaneously with a bolt of lightning, and the rain intensified. Flynt started the car and pulled into the line of traffic. The other cars had slowed to a crawl in deference to the reduced visibility.

Angelica felt his withdrawal viscerally. And chided herself for minding.

You don't want this attention, she reminded herself. *You can't be trusted when he turns all that masculine intensity on you, so stop pining like a lovesick schoolgirl.* Which she had never been. She'd been too savvy.

Still, she couldn't resist needling him, certainly a minor bid for attention. "Do you need directions to my apartment or did you get all that down pat when you were investigating me for the Fortunes?"

"I have no idea how to get to your apartment. And yes, I would appreciate directions."

"Take a left at the next light." She tried to match his detached tone. "And then—"

Her beeper emitted another shrill beep.

Flynt reached into his coat and tossed his cell phone onto her lap. "You can tell Mara the plan worked. You're on your way home."

Angelica retrieved her beeper and turned it off, staring

at the number it displayed. "It's not Mara. I don't recognize this number. It really must be a patient."

"Fact or fiction?" Flynt pretended to ponder the question, then shrugged. "With you, who knows?"

Angelica ignored the dig and called the number on the screen.

"Angel, thank God I got ahold of you!" Her mother's voice, high-pitched with anxiety, sounded over the line. "We have a real emergency here. Can you come right over? To 307 Blueberry Hollow Lane."

"Mama, what's going on?" Angelica's stomach began to churn with trepidation.

"I can't talk now, Angel. Please, just get here soon!" Romina hung up.

Angelica clutched the phone and tried to remember the number from the beeper's small screen so she could call her mother back.

But the only numbers she'd retained were 307. On Blueberry Hollow Lane, wherever that was.

"Do you have a map of the city?" she asked Flynt.

"Of course. I haven't navigated around Birmingham using ESP."

She didn't have the time or inclination to trade barbs. "Where's the map?"

"In the glove compartment."

"Would you mind pulling over so I can find Blueberry Hollow Lane? I have a feeling it's a street in one of the newer housing developments south of the city and that's the opposite direction of where we're headed."

Flynt steered the car onto a side street and braked to a stop alongside the curb, as she switched on the overhead light and studied the map. "I was right. We need to turn around and get onto I-65."

"I agreed to give you a ride home, not drive you all over the state," grumbled Flynt. Outside, the wind accelerated into rainy gusts. "It's a lousy night to be out on the road."

"Never mind, then. You can drop me off at my apartment, and Mara will—"

"I didn't say I wouldn't take you, I just said it's a lousy night to be out." He sighed. "At least give me some advance warning of what we're going to find at this place. Searcy and the FBI again? Birmingham PD with another search and seizure warrant?"

"I'm fairly certain this address belongs to someone that my mother pet-sits for."

"Why would Romina want you to come to a pet-sitting client's house at this hour?" Flynt was perplexed.

"Any number of reasons. I remember once when Jury, a bichon frise who belongs to Judge Newman and his wife, escaped as Mama was letting herself inside the house to take care of him. The Newmans were on vacation and Mama called us, hysterical. She'd combed the neighborhood and couldn't find Jury anywhere. So Mara, Casper, Sarah and Danny—he was home on leave that time—and I drove over to help her find the dog."

"Did you find it?"

"Two and a half hours later, we did. Jury had joined a gang of dogs in a park a mile away and was having a fabulous time, rolling in mud and chasing squirrels."

"Behaving like a common mongrel instead of a pampered, pedigreed pooch?" Flynt smiled at her.

She returned it. "And looking like one, too. It took

us another hour to get him all washed and groomed again. Poor Mama was a nervous wreck.''

''Do you think we're being summoned for another fugitive dog chase?'' Flynt glanced outside at the rain, which showed no signs of abating. ''What dog would be stupid enough to want to run around outside in this deluge?''

''There are certain breeds of dogs who don't mind water at all. They even like it.''

''Swell. The dog can revel in the rain while we play human lightning rods trying to catch it.''

''It could be a different kind of crisis, though. There was another memorable time when a pigeon flew down the chimney of Dr. Tomlin's house when the family was out of town. Mama went in to feed their cats and found the pigeon, crazed with fear, flying all over and bombarding every room while the cats stalked it. Poor Mama called us—''

''Hysterical?'' guessed Flynt.

Angelica shot him a reproving look. ''Of course she was upset. It took us hours to shoo the pigeon out and clean up the awful mess that bird had made.''

Flynt groaned. ''I can't think of two less appealing things to do tonight than having to hunt for a runaway dog in a thunderstorm or clean up after a renegade pigeon.''

''At least those stories had happy endings. Let's just pray that Mama hasn't found one of the animals dead. She lives in dread of that happening. Several of the pets she looks after are getting on in years, and she worries about them a lot.''

From what he'd observed today, Romina did not handle stress very well, and a dead animal was definitely work-related stress for a pet-sitter. Flynt grimaced. He found himself actually hoping they'd find a pigeon on the loose in the house on Blueberry Hollow Lane.

He sped along the interstate, passing every car that was cautiously inching along in the right lane. He noticed Angelica clenching her fists in white-knuckled anxiety.

"Relax, I'm an old hand at driving in the rain. I grew up in western Pennsylvania, which is the rain capital of the country."

"I thought that was Seattle," murmured Angelica, eyeing the slow, steady procession of cars they whizzed past. She knew she would've been in that long line herself, if she were behind the wheel.

"Western PA has fewer sunny days. A little-known fact because it's not exactly a selling point for the area."

The night had taken a strange turn, yet he felt oddly lighthearted. He cast a quick glance at Angelica, seated beside him. Why bother to deny it? He was glad this wild pet chase, or whatever it turned out to be, had prolonged his time with her.

Angelica directed him to the address in a posh neighborhood of newly built, luxurious houses on spacious lots.

"Lots of professional people live here," Angelica murmured, scanning the street signs and house numbers as Flynt steered the car through the rainy darkness. "Mama does a lot of pet-sitting for dual-career couples in this area."

"Does she have keys to all their houses?" Flynt asked idly.

"Of course. Mama is very trustworthy." Angelica was instantly defensive.

"I wasn't casting aspersions on Romina's character, Angelica," Flynt said. "I was just wondering how all those prominent folks reacted when their house keys and addresses were seized by the police during one of those searches."

"Oh." Angelica gnawed her lower lip. "Well, they weren't seized."

"No? It seems that a book of addresses, complete with keys, would be something to be carefully checked out, particularly considering—"

"Mama keeps that stuff at my apartment. It's not an inconvenience," Angelica explained hastily. "I only live a few blocks from her, she has a key to my place and she picks up and drops off the keys as needed."

"For exactly the reason I stated." It was a statement, not a question.

Angelica looked at him. "You must've been a pretty good FBI agent," she said with grudging admiration. "Nobody else mentioned Mama's keys and address book."

"From there, it's a quick leap to her access to empty houses when the pet owners are on vacation. If someone should need a temporary place to hide out while on the run…" His voice trailed off, inviting Angelica to finish.

She didn't say a word.

"How long has Romina kept the address book and keys at your place? For the past three years, when the search-and-seizure raids began?"

"Your memory strikes again." Angelica was glib but

rather impressed, in spite of herself. His recall of seemingly throwaway information amazed her.

"Romina knew to get that book and those keys out of her house. Obviously she was tipped off." He reached over to lightly tap her arm. "How am I doing so far?"

Angelica wet her lips with the tip of her tongue. "Mama got an anonymous phone call a few weeks before our house was searched for the first time. The caller said that if she didn't keep her pet-sitting business stuff in her house it wouldn't be subject to the search-and-seizure warrant."

"So it must've been a cop with inside information," concluded Flynt. "Your friend and Mara's admirer—TJ?"

"It was a male voice that Mama didn't recognize. Now she thinks it could've been Agent Weatherall. But she's not sure, she really isn't," Angelica added earnestly.

"Weatherall agreed that some cases involving violence and abuse have been bungled by the courts and sometimes the underground is the only way to keep children safely away from their abusers," Flynt murmured.

"There are a lot of people in law enforcement who share that view, Flynt. So they turn a blind eye to the safe houses and the people helping the mothers and children. If they didn't, the underground couldn't function."

"Custody battles are ugly, Angelica. Charges and threats are made by both sides. How do you know these women are being truthful? The truth is often sacrificed when emotions run high."

"Nancy Portland won't get involved if the woman is lying," Angelica insisted.

"So this Nancy Portland is an infallible human lie detector? Give me a break."

"She's trying to help people—unlike that disgusting sleaze Searcy, who hunts down scared little kids for money!" Angelica's voice trembled. "Are you going to tell him to harass my mother even more by making sure her address book and the house keys are seized, so she can't make a living?"

"As I said before, the truth gets lost when emotions run high, and right now yours are past flood level. I have no intention of saying anything to anyone, Angelica. I'm not involved in any case, I'm not an agent anymore, merely an objective observer."

"Stop!" she exclaimed.

For a split second, Flynt thought she was going to get out of the car because she preferred getting drenched on a dark road to sharing space with reprehensible him.

But Angelica didn't reach for the door handle. "This is Blueberry Hollow Lane," she announced.

Flynt made a sharp turn onto the narrow street.

"There's 100, 101, 103." Angelica read the house numbers. "Even numbers are on the left, off on the right—307 must be two blocks farther."

Which it was. Flynt swung the car into the wide, paved driveway of a big house with stucco walls. It had a brick facade with an arched doorway, and the brass numbers 307 were hung on the front door as well as painted on the decorative mailbox at the foot of the drive.

"Well, thanks for the ride." Angelica flung open the car door. "You may as well go. There's no need for you to be stuck here. I'll drive back with Mama."

She ran through the rain to the arched doorway.

Flynt watched her go. She was right, she could get a ride back with her mother, there was no reason for him to be stuck here. He should go back to the hotel and see if Brandon had surfaced there, he should...

Flynt swung open the car door and climbed out. He was staying whether Angelica wanted him to or not. Never mind what he ought to be doing, he couldn't leave her. A kaleidoscope of images of her tumbled through his head as he strode toward the house. He'd known her such a short time, but already she had commandeered his thoughts in a way no other woman ever had.

He remembered their passionate kiss in the booth, and heat streaked through him. It seemed that she had commandeered his body, right along with his mind.

Chapter 6

Angelica was ringing the doorbell when Flynt arrived at her side. "I wouldn't dream of deserting you," he said drolly. "If there's a dog or a pigeon on the loose, you're going to need all the extra help you can get."

Delight surged through her. He had stayed! "Just remember, I offered you an out," she replied, her tone as light as his. "That means no complaining whenever—"

The door was flung open. "Angel, thank God you—" Romina paused to gape at Flynt. "What is *he* doing here?"

"I was driving Angelica home when she got your summons," he drawled.

"Well, you can't come in." Romina's dark eyes darted from Flynt to the deserted, rainy driveway beyond him. "This isn't my house. I can't let in strangers off the street. Come on, Angel." She grabbed Angelica by the arm and pulled her inside.

At that moment an ear-splitting primal scream sounded from within. Flynt didn't hesitate. He pushed inside, and the wind blew the door shut behind him. "What's going on, Romina?"

There was another scream.

"Who is here, Romina?" Flynt started up the paneled staircase, not waiting for an explanation. "It sounds like someone being tortured." He headed in the direction of the screams, Romina and Angelica at his heels.

"She's in labor, Angel," cried Romina. "You have to help her."

"But, Mama—"

"We don't have time to talk. We can't waste a minute." Romina pushed past Flynt to race down the long second-story hall, dragging Angelica along after her. A door stood open, and the pair entered the room.

"This is my daughter, sugar." Romina's voice lowered to a soft, soothing croon as she crossed the room to stand by the bedside. Angelica remained in the doorway. "She's a licensed midwife and a registered nurse and she's delivered lots of babies. Angelica, this is—uh—well, she won't tell me her name."

"Never mind my name, you can just keep calling me sugar," whimpered the young woman sitting on the bed, the pillows propped against her back.

Flynt gauged her age to be somewhere in her twenties. She was also very pregnant—and apparently in labor. He gulped.

"Who's he?" Sugar's voice was filled with fear as she gazed at Flynt, standing directly behind Angelica.

Romina spoke up before he could. "He's Angelica's

boyfriend. You don't have to worry about him. He'll do whatever my Angel says.''

Flynt felt hot color stain his face and spiral downward. ''That—that is not true.'' He was amazed to hear himself sputtering. Romina's assertion rattled him far more than it should've. And his instant flashback to that passionate kiss only addled him further. ''I—she—we—''

''Of course, like any man he can't stand to hear the truth about himself. Which is when Angelica snaps her fingers and says 'Jump,' Flynt here says 'How high, darling?''' Romina laughed, enjoying herself.

''I do not!'' Flynt snapped. It was humbling to witness himself arguing, kindergarten style, knowing Romina had deliberately provoked him into it.

''You two can continue bickering somewhere else,'' Angelica said firmly, taking charge. She crossed the room to stand beside the bed. ''I need privacy to examine my patient.''

''Of course,'' Romina agreed at once. ''Let's go downstairs and boil some water, Flynt.'' She shoved him into the hall.

''Romina, I will not be a party to—'' Flynt began.

''Shhh! No use letting that poor girl hear us arguing, she's upset enough as it is. Come down to the kitchen with me, and I'll try to explain while we're boiling the water.''

Romina's fingers closed over Flynt's forearm, and she took off, pulling him after her, just like she'd done earlier with Angelica.

Flynt allowed himself to be dragged. There seemed to be little else he could do at this point. Bursting into the bedroom while Angelica examined the shrieking young woman in labor seemed unwise. Not to mention unnerving.

"Why are you going to boil water?" He trailed Romina into the spacious downstairs kitchen. It looked like the domain of a gourmet chef, with every possible modern convenience.

"Don't you watch TV? Somebody always boils water when a woman is in labor."

"This isn't a TV drama. For godsakes, Romina, call 911 and get an ambulance here to take that woman to a hospital."

"I can't, I promised her I wouldn't. She doesn't want to go to a hospital." Romina filled a large spaghetti pot with water and put it on the stove's electric burner. "She showed up at my door about an hour ago, crying her eyes out and said she'd heard I could help her—but she refused to tell me anything else, including her name. She's in labor, but she freaked out when I mentioned getting her to a hospital. I couldn't keep her at my place, not with Sarah and Casper there, so I brought her here to the Rydells' house. They're visiting their son in California, and I'm taking care of their dogs and their parrot."

"And then you paged Angelica."

Romina nodded her head. "I called Mara, too. She's a nurse and should be here real soon to help Angel with the delivery."

"Romina, if what you say is true, and you have no information about this young woman whatsoever, why did you bring her here?" Flynt was exasperated. "Why involve Angelica? That young woman belongs in a hospital! Her judgment is obviously impaired, no doubt due to her condition, and—''

"The poor girl is scared and needed help and said she couldn't go to the hospital. I couldn't turn my back on her," Romina said fiercely. "There were so many times when nobody helped me, times when me and my kids really could've used a helping hand but didn't get one. I promised myself that one day *I'd* be a helping hand for somebody else, for any young woman who needed me."

Either she was the world's greatest actress or she was utterly sincere. Flynt leaned against the wall and listened to another shriek reverberating through the house. This time the Rydells' dogs joined in, baying in mournful harmony from their penned area off the kitchen.

"Sounds like *The Hound of The Baskervilles*," Flynt muttered darkly. The way things were going, they probably were.

"Let's just hope the parrot doesn't start squawking again." Romina dropped onto a chair, looking tired.

Her acceptance of the bizarre situation aggravated Flynt. "We need to find out who that girl is, Romina. She must have a purse or some kind of bag to keep money and ID. And I am going to call 911. *I* didn't make any promises not to."

"Angelica is the one in charge now. Talk to her before you do anything."

"If you think I'll do whatever she says, you're wrong, Romina. I don't jump to anyone's command."

"I was only kidding when I said that. Jeez, you're touchy. Can't you even take a little joke?"

The doorbell rang, and Romina brightened considerably. "That'll be Mara. Want to let her in and take her up to Angelica and—uh—Sugar?"

Flynt strode off. Romina's passivity had only heightened his need for some kind of action. Red-haired Mara was standing at the door in a yellow slicker, already damp from the blowing rain. She clutched a large black bag.

"You have to be Flynt." Mara studied him. "You look way too young to be Angel's father, Brandon."

"Flynt Corrigan," he confirmed. "You're supposed to help Angelica with a nameless patient upstairs."

"That's what Romina said when she called." Mara trooped in, shedding her slicker as she walked.

"Does this sort of thing happen often?" Flynt demanded. They walked up the stairs together. "You're summoned out at night to deliver the baby of a young woman who suddenly appears on Romina's doorstep and refuses to give her name?"

"I guess I'll go with Romina's motto, 'Ask me no questions and I'll tell you no lies.'" Mara followed the sound of the moaning with Flynt at her side.

Angelica's eyes shone with relief at the sight of them. "Thanks for bringing my bag, Mara."

"I wouldn't leave home without it." Mara handed the medical bag to Angelica and then took the patient's hand in hers. "I'm Mara, and everything is going to be all right. Angel and I are old pros at delivering babies, if I do say so myself."

"Is he going to stay?" The young mother-to-be stared at Flynt.

"He will if you want him to," said Mara.

"Yes," the girl whispered. "He reminds me of my brother Joe."

Angelica and Flynt exchanged glances.

"Angelica, may I speak with you a moment?" Flynt placed a firm hand on her shoulder to steer her to a corner of the room, out of earshot of the patient. "I'm going to call for an ambulance. Your mother won't do it but I—"

"There isn't time, the baby will be here long before any ambulance arrives. I've examined her and there are no complications. Mara and I can handle the delivery." Angelica laid an impulsive hand on his chest. "If you want to do something for this girl, play the role of her big brother Joe for a little while."

Big Brother. The term resonated in Flynt's head. He'd been that once. And failed mightily in the role, according to his mother. His fingers curved automatically over Angelica's and for a moment, he held on tight.

Then Angelica broke away and returned to her patient.

"Come on, Flynt," urged Mara. "You can be Sugar's coach."

Flynt considered it. Him, a coach for a woman in labor, a stranger who wouldn't even tell her name. It seemed unreal. Of course from the moment he'd entered this house, it was as if he'd stepped into an alternative universe.

And in that universe, pretending to be a big brother while actually acting as a labor coach was undoubtedly the norm.

He walked slowly to the bedside, his shoulder brushing Angelica's as he passed.

"If you faint, we'll leave you on the floor, big brother," she murmured dryly.

It was just the challenge he needed. Flynt felt immediately bolstered. "I've never fainted in my life, and I'm not about to do it now." He took the anonymous Sugar's hand, and she squeezed hard and wailed as another contraction gripped her body.

"It hurts!" wailed Sugar.

"I bet it does," he agreed vigorously. "Is this your first baby, Sugar?"

"I had one ten years ago, when I was fifteen," Sugar said between pants. "I gave that one up for adoption, but this one I'm keeping."

From her position at the foot of the bed, Angelica watched Flynt interact with Sugar. He was calm and soft-spoken, holding Sugar's hand, talking to her. Angelica admired his poise. She'd seen her share of fathers-to-be, including some who had prepared for the birth with childbirth classes and videos, lose their cool when delivery was imminent. Flynt, an unprepared civilian, was doing just fine.

"This is going to happen fast, Sugar. Push!" Angelica ordered. "Push hard."

"The baby's head is crowning. I see a mop of dark hair, Sugar!" Mara exclaimed. "It won't be much longer now. Push, honey."

Sugar made a sound that was something between a gasp and a scream.

"You're doing great!" Flynt said approvingly. He held on to Sugar, helping to support her in a semiupright position.

Angelica glanced at him. His face wasn't the chalky

green color of a man who was on the verge of fainting at the sight of the emerging child. She'd had her share of those, too, the queasy fathers who crumpled to the floor at a crucial time, diverting time and attention from the patient. Flynt was conducting himself like a full-fledged member of the team. She felt an absurd glimmer of pride as she watched him.

And then the baby required her complete concentration.

"Here he is!" Angelica grasped the wriggling newborn boy who began to squall the moment he emerged.

"Listen to him roar!" Flynt hugged Sugar. "He's got a powerful set of lungs on him, Sugar."

Angelica handed the infant to Mara, who wrapped him in a blanket and carried him to his mother. Angelica felt elated, just as she always did after a successful delivery.

"He's beautiful!" Sugar wept, clutching the baby. "Oh, Joe, I love him so much."

Flynt did not correct her; if she needed him to be her brother Joe for a while longer, he was willing. "I know you love him," he said quietly. "You're going to be a good mother, Sugar."

"I promise I will," the young mother exclaimed, gazing at the baby. "And I'm going to name him Sawyer Matthew. I picked it out months ago."

"A fine name," said Flynt, his eyes moving from the infant to Angelica.

For a few blissful seconds, he allowed himself to fantasize that he was the father of Angelica's child, that he would cradle her and their baby in his arms, moments after supporting her through the birth.

"Flynt, why don't you join Romina downstairs

now?'' Mara's suggestion was an unwelcome intrusion into his enchanted fantasy. ''We want to put the baby to breast now and—''

''I'm on my way.'' Flynt knew he was being kicked out and acceded gracefully. He walked to the door.

''Flynt.'' Angelica's voice halted him in his tracks. He turned and faced her. ''You—you were a real help tonight. Thank you.''

Warmth radiated through him. He left the room with a smile as broad as a proud father's. Or big brother's.

''Renee Riley is on her way to my little getaway cabin in Wyoming.'' Back in Minneapolis, Kate Fortune hung up the phone, looking pleased.

Sterling lit his pipe. ''Kate, my dear, you have a myriad of young relatives, all your own grandchildren and all of Ben's brothers' grandchildren, Zeke's and Caleb's and—''

''Your point, please, darling,'' Kate teased merrily.

''With all the young Fortune lives to manage and arrange, kindly explain to me why you've branched out to meddle in Renee Riley's life? I agree that fiancé of hers, Lyle Whoever, is a repellent character, but young Renee did agree to marry him, didn't she? Sending her off to Last Resort, Wyoming, days before her scheduled wedding is a bit beyond the pale, even for you, my love.''

''But Renee is a darling girl.'' Kate smiled. ''And deep in your heart you believe I've done the right thing, don't you, Sterling? She shouldn't have to marry a man she doesn't love just to save the family business.''

''You're incorrigible, Kate. I don't suppose you mentioned to darling Renee that your great-nephew Garrett is a part-time rancher there who will be in residence when she arrives?''

"Garrett." Kate strolled along her picture wall, staring at the beloved faces framed there. "I've heard him described as a gruff loner but that's a misunderstanding. He is such a dear boy. And I know he was with Renee when they both disappeared at Kelly and Mac's New Year's Eve wedding."

"Oh, I think gruff loner is an apt description of the dear boy. And if he and Renee Riley—who is fleeing one fiancé and certainly not looking for another—happen to cross paths in Wyoming, odds are great that nothing at all will result."

"Oh, ye of little faith," quoted Kate jovially. "It seems to me—" The telephone rang, interrupting her.

"It's your private line," said Sterling, a frown already creasing his face. Only close family members had that particular number, and a call at ten o'clock at night did not bode well.

He moved to answer the phone but Kate beat him to it.

"Mom, it's me." Brandon's voice came over the line.

"Brandon, how are you, dear?" Kate watched Sterling heave an exasperated sigh and head for the desk where he kept a supply of his trusty antacid tablets. She sat down.

"I saw my daughter tonight. We went to this club. She's—she's—beautiful, Mom!"

"Oh, Brandon, my dear, what an evening this must have been for you! Brandon, are you crying?"

"If he is, it's undoubtedly a crying jag," Sterling injected sourly. "Ask him how much he's had to drink tonight."

"I think I might've acted like a jerk, Mom. I was so shook...and when I saw the picture of Romina...I felt this cosmic connection to Romina. I mean, we made this kid...but I don't know her, Mom. I don't know my very own kid. It's too weird."

"It makes perfect sense to me, Brandon," Kate said softly.

She thought of the lost years without her youngest son, of being introduced to him as an adult stranger. How ironic that very son should face the same situation with his own child. "Now, why do you think you acted like a, um, jerk with Angelica tonight?"

She ignored Sterling's exaggerated groan.

"I played it as cool as I could, but I had to get away and kind of get myself together, you know?" Brandon paused and took a deep breath. "So I went to the men's room and when I came back, I saw her—Angelica in a hot, hot clinch with Flynt."

"Angelica was kissing Flynt Corrigan?" Kate was intrigued. Sterling's eyebrows shot up questioningly.

"I wanted to stay and talk to her, but I figured she wanted to be alone with Flynt. I mean their lips were...locked. They were really into each other. I didn't want to intrude, so I caught a cab back to my suite. They're still out together, but I can't stop thinking about my kid and about Romina and—and I *am* crying, Mom. I feel like—I don't know." Brandon broke into sobs.

Kate did her best to console him. But her mind was racing, over the past nine years with Brandon. He'd said he had wanted to stay and talk to Angelica but didn't because he "figured she wanted to be alone with Flynt."

As far as Kate could recall, this was the first time that Brandon had ever considered someone else's feelings and placed them above his own. The Brandon who had left Minneapolis yesterday would've stayed in that club and monopolized the conversation without a second thought, because he wanted to and he always did what he wanted.

But this post-Angelica Brandon had assessed his daughter's feelings and acted accordingly. Contrary to his own wishes. A small thing, perhaps, yet Kate was enormously encouraged.

"Mom, do you think I should—oh, wait, someone's at the door. Guess I better get it, huh?"

"Go right ahead, dear. Call me back, if you want."

Brandon opened the door to a uniformed bellhop who handed him a sealed envelope. He tore it open with one hand while fumbling with his money clip for a tip.

A piece of paper fell out and fluttered to the floor. The bellhop snatched it up and gave it to Brandon. It was another threat spelled out in cut-and-pasted letters, just like the previous one: Angelica would be killed and Brandon framed for murder if he didn't pay up. One more letter would follow, with directions about the required cash payment.

"Where did this come from?" Brandon demanded. "Who gave it to you?"

The bellhop grinned. "Sorry, I swore I wouldn't tell."

"You better. Here, read this." Brandon shoved the note in front of him.

"It's a threat?" The bellhop was clearly astonished.

"This has gotta be some kind of joke. While you were out, a geeky little kid gave me that envelope along with a dollar bill and a bag of cookies. He said to bring it to you but not tell where it came from. I told him to keep his money, but I'd take the cookies."

"A geeky kid?" echoed Brandon.

"Skinny, thick glasses, about eleven or twelve years old. Sound like anyone you know?"

Brandon shook his head and then his face grew worried. "Listen, uh, I'd better call my people and get on this right away." He peeled a fifty-dollar bill from his money clip and placed it grandly in the bellhop's hand. "Thanks for the info."

"Thank you, sir." The bellhop seemed torn between gratitude and uncertainty. "If there's anything else I can do for you, please, just ask."

"Uh, yeah. Sure."

"A baby boy," Flynt marveled, cradling the small blanket-wrapped bundle in his arms as he paced the kitchen.

The newborn liked the motion; his crying had ceased the moment Flynt began walking with him. The new mother was asleep in the bedroom upstairs, having delivered her child a little over an hour ago.

"Your very first delivery is always special." Mara smiled at Flynt from her seat at the kitchen table. "I bet you'll never forget little Sawyer and the night he was born."

"Sawyer Matthew." Flynt gazed down at the dozing infant. "At least he has a name. Unlike his mother who remains Ms. Anonymous. I wonder who she is?" The secrecy continued to nag at him.

"It doesn't really matter, does it?" Mara shrugged philosophically. "What counts is that you were a terrific big brother to her during labor and the delivery. So I guess that makes you baby Sawyer's honorary uncle."

"Some big brother!" Romina frowned her disapproval. "He searched Sugar's coat and her bag looking for ID the minute she fell asleep."

"And I didn't find a single clue to her identity. There aren't even labels in her clothes." Flynt stopped pacing and looked up as Angelica joined them in the kitchen.

She'd just returned from checking the patient again. "Sugar is fine, she's still sleeping," Angelica reported. She walked over to Flynt and stroked the baby's shock of silky black hair. "How's this little guy doing?"

"Okay, I think," Flynt said huskily. "Thanks to you."

She lifted her eyes to meet his, and he hoped she saw the admiration and respect he felt. Watching her deliver the baby had been an extraordinary experience. She'd been so confident and competent, a true professional in a far-from-professional setting. Kind and calm and thorough, right down to having diapers for the infant in her big medical black bag.

"It looks like he's really taken to you," Angelica observed. Her dark eyes glowed. "Uncle Flynt."

The sight of the baby in Flynt's big hands was having a most peculiar effect on her. For a change, the notion of a man's strength didn't unnerve her. She knew Flynt Corrigan would use it to protect, never to hurt; she didn't know how she knew this, but she'd never been more certain of anything in her life. A child would be safe with him. A woman would, too.

That renegade thought slipped through her usual defenses, and a wave of heat rushed through her. Their intimate little interlude in the Martini Lounge flashed vividly to mind, leaving her dazed and unsteady. And very, very nervous.

She thought she was safe with a man who affected her like none other? A man who held an entirely different set of values and principles from her own? She'd seen him rummaging through Sugar's things, looking for some sort of identification information. What if he'd found some? What would he have done then, called the cops? He was an ex-cop himself, an ex-FBI agent, which was even worse!

Angelica backed slowly away from him. That he'd been able to make her feel safe around him paradoxically proved that Flynt Corrigan was a dangerous man, indeed.

"What do we do now?" Flynt asked.

Ostensibly, he was asking about the baby, but if she were to interpret his question to be What should they do about the burgeoning attraction between them? she would be right on the mark.

"Now you go back to wherever you're staying or go look for Brandon or do whatever you want," Angelica replied tersely. "Mama is going home, and Mara and I will stay here with Sugar and the baby."

Flynt felt frustration roil through him. Not only was she dismissing him, she was inching away from him as if he were radioactive. He wanted her closer, where he could touch her, where he could inhale the clean scent of her hair....

But he knew it wasn't going to happen, because she intended to keep her distance from him. Somehow he was so attuned to her that he could pinpoint the exact moment when the nascent bond between them had snapped, the moment she'd emotionally frozen.

What he didn't know was why.

"Oh, yikes! Angel, there was so much going on I forgot to ask you about Brandon!" Romina suddenly interjected. "You saw him tonight! Tell me everything! What did you think of your daddy? How did he look? Did he ask about me?"

Angelica met Flynt's eyes for a long, silent moment. She felt that innate connection between them and quickly looked away, wanting to break it. Needing to.

"Tell me *something* about him!" Romina persisted impatiently.

Angelica folded her arms in front of her chest and stared at her mother's flushed face and glittering eyes. It was not a good thing when her mother showed signs of excited interest in a man. They'd been down that road too many times before, and Angelica wasn't up for yet another perilous journey.

"Because he's my father, I'll be kind and just say that he's a few cans short of a six-pack," she said dampeningly.

"What's that supposed to mean?" Romina snapped.

Flynt stiffened. He'd seen Romina turn her temper on the cops and wanted to protect Angelica from it. "Brandon is a Hollywood player wanna-be, Romina. He isn't anyone's idea of a father, not even his."

"Well, what do you expect? Brandon was given away to that witch Monica Malone by his very own father!" Romina's defense of Brandon surprised them all. "At the time, he wasn't much older than the little baby you're holding right now, Flynt. After a trauma like that, how can you blame poor Bran for being the way he is?"

Flynt's grasp tightened on the warm little bundle snoozing in his arms. Put in that perspective, Ben Fortune's deed seemed uncompromisingly evil, yet it was almost impossible to compare the adult Brandon of today with this helpless infant.

Bran? Angelica felt her blood chill. The nickname had slipped so easily off her mother's tongue, she was sure it was a long-ago term of endearment. Well, it was definitely time to end this nostalgiafest!

"Mama, Brandon Fortune gives off vibes that would give Count Dracula the creeps! Getting reinvolved with him would be a horrible mistake and—"

"Don't use that tone with me, Angelica Alina *Fortune*!" Romina's voice rose. "And don't you dare try to tell me what to do! You might think you know everything, but I'm still your mother!"

"I'm sure she never forgets that for a moment, Romina," Flynt inserted smoothly.

"More coffee, anyone?" Mara had jumped to her feet and was circling the table with the coffeepot.

"I've had enough." Romina stood up. "I have to get home. Casper will sit up and watch TV all night unless I'm there to order him into bed. I'll be in touch with you girls." She paused. "In the morning. Oh, and would you feed the parrot and the dogs before you leave for work?"

"Of course, Mama," agreed Angelica. "Drive safely."

"I packed a few things for us 'cause I figured we'd be staying over tonight, Angel," said Mara. "I'll run out to my car and get the bag." She followed Romina out the door.

Left alone in the kitchen, Angelica and Flynt faced each other.

"Your mother is going to contact Nancy Portland tonight and plug little Sawyer and his mother into the underground, isn't she?"

"Mama doesn't even know who Sawyer's father is, Flynt."

"Nice dodge, Angelica." A mirthless smile curved the corners of Flynt's mouth. "You adroitly manage to sidestep every question posed about Nancy Portland and the underground." He took a step toward her. "Angelica, this child belongs to someone. He and his mother have a family somewhere who care about them, who are crazy with grief and worry and want them back."

Angelica looked at him askance. "You don't know that. It's more likely that nobody cares about Sugar, and the best move she ever made was to go to Mama for help. Because my mother comes through for people, she never hesitates to get involved."

"Well, it sounds like she's considering getting involved with your father again." Flynt felt a perverse streak of satisfaction at the hot pink color that stained her cheeks. "She's already thinking of you with the Fortune name."

"No, she isn't, she just said that to rile me," Angelica retorted. "Just like you're deliberately trying to rile me by implying that Mama wants to take up with Brandon again.''

''I wasn't *implying* anything, I said it flat-out,'' Flynt corrected. ''And why would I want to rile you, Angelica?''

''Because—'' She looked at him. Because the unresolved sexual tension between them was so thick it was practically a tangible force, and arguing somehow made it easier to deal with, she thought, but didn't dare say. She wasn't ready to deal with the ramifications of such candor.

''Because you're a jerk,'' she said instead.

Instead of being insulted, Flynt laughed, as if he knew exactly what she had avoided admitting.

Angelica scowled. ''Give me the baby, Flynt. I want to take him up to his mother to nurse.''

He could hardly refuse that order. Flynt placed the child in her arms. The exchange made it necessary for them to come closer together. He towered over her, his body not quite touching hers.

Angelica clutched the baby tight. Instead of intimidating her, Flynt's masculine size and strength were exciting her. The warmth of his body heat and the musky aroma of his aftershave filled her senses. Her head began to spin.

''You have to go.'' Her voice quavered.

Flustered and aroused, she automatically backed away. The wall was four short steps behind her, and her back came up against it. Flynt moved directly in front of her, trapping her between him and the wall.

''Yeah, I guess I do.'' But instead of leaving, he leaned his lower body into her.

Angelica felt his hardness and caught her breath. The fierce, fast pounding of her heart roared in her ears. "Flynt, we can't do this, we—ohhh!"

Her voice broke on a gasp as his mouth brushed hers.

"We probably shouldn't," he agreed, nibbling on her lips between words. His hands settled on her hips and he stroked lightly with his thumbs. "But we're going to, anyway, aren't we?" He didn't lift his mouth, but kept his lips against hers as he spoke.

"No." She tried to turn her head from side to side but he kept his mouth gently, lightly against hers, tantalizing her with teasing little kisses. The baby's small warm body between them only heightened the aura of intimacy.

"No?" he repeated. He slipped his knee between her thighs. "Do you mean 'No, we can't,' 'No, we shouldn't' or 'No, we aren't going to'? Specify, please."

She felt him smile against her lips. It was so hard to resist him; she was suddenly tired of trying. When her eyelids dropped closed, she made no attempt to open them. The tip of her tongue glided over his lips before she was fully aware of what she was doing.

He didn't deepen the kiss, the baby's presence precluded that, but continued to entice her with the staccato touches of his mouth on hers. Angelica moaned as desire rippled through her.

The baby made a soft snuffling sound and for those few moments, it was all too easy for her to pretend that this was their child, created from the passion burning between them.

What would it be like to be in love with a man, to give birth to his child? Angelica had wondered about that before but always with trepidation and a certain clinical detachment. Not now. She was aroused and aching, sensually aflame.

Flynt moved his mouth from her lips to the sensitive curve of her neck and kissed her there, tasting her skin, savoring its texture and scent.

"This is crazy," he rasped, nuzzling her. "I want you so much but we—"

"Holy Mother of God!" Romina's voice resounded around them. She repeated her stunned invocation in Spanish, then in Romanian.

By then, Flynt was on the other side of the wide kitchen counter, and Angelica had sunk into a chair, holding baby Sawyer. Both kept their eyes fixed steadfastly to the floor.

"I forgot to leave the dogs their little biscuit treats," Romina said. "So I came back to—" Her voice trailed off for a moment, then she recovered enough to demand, "Do you know how shocked I am?"

"I'm sure you're about to tell us," muttered Flynt.

"I'm shocked. Shocked!" Romina exclaimed, ever louder.

Angelica hung her head. The small gesture touched Flynt; she looked so vulnerable. All his protective instincts were aroused, inspiring him to defend her.

"We were only kissing," he protested. "It's hardly the crime of the century, Romina. Lighten up!"

At that moment Mara returned to the kitchen, carrying an overnight bag. She cast a wary glance at Romina's irate face. "What's going on?"

Romina glared at Flynt, then directed her laser eyes at the visibly bewildered Mara. "Do you know what I saw when I came back to give the dogs their treats? Those two—'' she pointed her finger accusingly ''—kissing! And now *he* has the nerve to say it means nothing to him. Well, *he* might have casual flings that mean nothing, but he's not going to have one with my Angel!''

For a moment Flynt was too startled to speak. ''I never said,'' he began, and remembered what he'd said. Could he possibly have sounded a bit cavalier? Of course not! ''Romina, you've completely misinterpreted the entire situation.''

''There's nothing to misinterpret. I know what I saw and what I heard you say!'' insisted Romina.

Flynt noticed that Angelica was sitting stock-still, barely breathing. Was she mortified at being caught by her mother, or by Romina's overreaction? Probably a little of both. Poor Angelica! Life with a firecracker like Romina had to be tough.

''We'll talk later, Angel,'' Romina announced. ''I can't look at Mr. Anything Goes without wanting to burn him at the stake! Here, give these to the dogs!'' She flung the biscuits on the table and stormed out.

Without uttering a word, Angelica fled from the kitchen with little Sawyer. Flynt started to follow her.

Mara stepped in front of him, blocking his way. ''Angel's taking the baby to his mother so she'll be in total midwife mode now. It'll be better if you leave and call her tomorrow. She might be more receptive then.''

''It was embarrassing to have Romina catch us, but Angelica looked—as if she felt she *deserved* to be burned at the stake.'' Flynt frowned thoughtfully.

"Surely she doesn't think Romina was right to make such a scene over—"

"I guess you have to know Angelica pretty well to know how unbelievably out of character it is for her to be—kissing a guy she hardly knows," Mara said quietly. "That's why Romina was so freaked. Angel, too, I'm sure."

"I don't care about Romina, I—" Flynt stopped himself, cleared his throat. "I'll go up and say good night to Angelica."

"Expect her to freeze you out," Mara called after him.

Which was exactly what happened when he stepped into the bedroom where Angelica was putting the newborn to its mother's breast.

"She wouldn't speak to me, she looked right through me," he told Mara as he passed her in the hall. "You were right, she was so cold I wouldn't be surprised if she inflicted me with freezer burn."

He drove back to the hotel suites, a righteous ire growing stronger with each passing minute as he brooded over the undeserved treatment dealt him. Romina's character assassination, Angelica's shunning. Since when had kissing a woman—who'd responded ardently—become a capital offense? Romina and Angelica Carroll both needed to lighten up!

Chapter 7

There was no response when he knocked at Brandon's door, and Flynt was tempted to retire to his own suite for the night. He could definitely use a cold shower before attempting to sleep.

But his professionalism wouldn't allow him to assume that his charge was in bed and asleep until he'd seen proof with his own eyes. He knocked on Brandon's door again and again, to no avail. Had he passed out? How much had he drunk tonight anyway?

Flynt picked the lock—it was a cinch, the security in this place left a lot to be desired—and entered Brandon's suite.

Brandon wasn't there, and his bed hadn't been slept in.

There was no cause for panic, Flynt assured himself. Brandon was an adult with a taste for women and nightlife. It was reasonable to assume that he'd instructed the taxi driver to drop him at some nightspot in the city where he could seek some action.

A reasonable assumption, but he'd been trained never to assume anything, to consider and weigh all the possibilities. Automatically, he began to list the variables to his eminently plausible theory.

Brandon had been drinking and his judgment, even when sober, could be described as questionable *if* one was in a charitable frame of mind. If not, his judgment could be deemed downright atrocious.

And Brandon had been in an emotional state tonight. He'd seen his adult daughter for the first time, which meant facing his own age—certainly a difficulty for an eternal Peter Pan type like Brandon Malone Fortune.

Finally, there was that damn threat, and though every criminal-detecting instinct Flynt possessed told him that Brandon was not in danger and the blackmail note was meaningless, still, it would be foolish to dismiss it out of hand.

All of which meant he was going to start hunting for Brandon immediately.

Flynt sat down on the sofa in the suite's living room. He always began a case by trying to put himself into the head of the suspect.

So if he were Brandon, what would be a likely destination on his first night here in rain-soaked Birmingham? Especially if he were trying to prove that, father or not, he was still a hot guy. "A chick magnet" in Brandon's own words. Where would a self-described chick magnet go?

Flynt rubbed his temples and concentrated. But instead of envisioning Brandon dancing with a girl younger than his daughter to techno-pop music in some club, he found himself remembering the way Brandon had stared at the Carroll family picture that Angelica had shown him as they sat in the booth at Swank.

What had he said to Angelica? Something like, "Romina still looks damn fine for a woman her age." Could Brandon possibly have gone to see Romina, his first lover, the mother of his daughter? Seeking out a teenage sweetheart was one way of turning back the clock to one's youth, wasn't it?

Romina's surprising defense of Brandon tonight abruptly echoed in Flynt's head. *Who could blame poor Bran?* She had eagerly pressed Angelica for news of her long-ago love. Suppose both Romina and Brandon were not averse to rolling back the years?

Impulsively Flynt reached for the telephone directory, looked up Romina's number and dialed it. She answered on the second ring.

"Romina, this is Flynt Corrigan. Is Brandon there?"

"You!" Romina's tone made it clear she hadn't absolved him of the mortal sin of kissing her daughter. "As a matter of fact, Brandon is here, and he would like to speak to you."

Brandon came on the line. "Romina and I won't let you use our daughter and then throw her away, Corrigan."

Flynt's relief at having located Brandon—so easily, on the very first try!—was immediately transformed into outrage. "What the hell are you talking about?"

"I saw you all over Angelica at Swank tonight, and then Romina caught you groping her later on," Brandon said indignantly. "You leave our baby girl alone!"

"Listen to me, you ingrate," growled Flynt. "I've never forced myself on any woman and I sure as hell wouldn't start with Angelica!"

"You're saying she wanted to make out with you? Both times?"

"Yes!" Flynt could hear some background murmuring, presumably Brandon and Romina discussing their baby girl. Him, use Angelica? The accusation deeply rankled.

"It did look mutual to me, okay?" Brandon was back. "That's why I left you two alone."

"Thank you," Flynt cut in quickly, before Brandon could extrapolate further. "And kindly tell Romina I was not *groping* Angelica."

Another pause, while Flynt relayed the message. And then: "Hey, Flynt, I got another one of those threatening notes tonight. It was in my room when I came back from Swank. Must've been shoved under the door or something."

The abrupt switch from the accusations about Angelica to yet another blackmail note was dizzying. Flynt, who usually made conversational leaps easily, had a hard time following this one.

His thought processes had been derailed, and his mind was filled with images of Angelica. The way she smiled, her warmth and competence while delivering the baby, the haunting vulnerability in her dark eyes. And of course, the seductive feel of her in his arms.

He hadn't forced himself on her; she'd wanted him as much as he wanted her. He was sure of it. Wasn't he?

Preoccupied, he hardly heard Brandon. "I called my mother and she wants to talk to you, but how about if we wait till tomorrow morning? It's getting pretty late to call tonight.''

''Yeah,'' Flynt said absently. He hadn't read Angelica wrong, he hadn't groped her. *Good Lord, what if he had?*

''Romina and I are going to hang out awhile over here. Y'know, talking about the good old days at Venice Beach. Would you believe she still knows the words of all the Beach Boys songs?'' Brandon sounded exceptionally cheerful for one who'd received another diabolical threat against him.

Flynt's head was beginning to clear. ''Look, Brandon, if you received another threat right here in the city, you—''

''You don't have to worry about me, I'm handling everything, Flynt. I really am. Oh, and uh, don't wait up for me. I'll catch a taxi back to the hotel.''

Flynt phoned the Rydells' house next.

Angelica sounded shocked to hear him. ''How did you get this number? It's unlisted.''

Not a warm greeting, but at least she was speaking to him, a definite improvement. ''I didn't know it was unlisted, I copied it down from the phone while I was at the house. Just an example of my attention to detail that has served me so well in my career.''

''I'm impressed,'' Angelica said in a tone that implied the opposite. ''Why did you call?''

''Angelica, did I force myself on you tonight at any time?'' He held his breath, half expecting her to hang up on him. But he had to ask, he had to know if he'd badly misread her.

''I'd rather not talk about tonight,'' she said coolly.

"Well, your parents are talking about it, even as we speak. They seem to think—"

"My *parents?*" Angelica echoed, aghast.

Flynt was sure she wouldn't hang up on him now. "Romina and Brandon are at her place talking about old times and singing Beach Boys tunes. And sharing news, too. Brandon saw us together tonight, Angelica, and your mother told him about—"

"They're together?" Angelica sounded truly horrified. "Oh, no!"

"You never answered my question, Angelica."

"I don't remember it."

"Brandon and Romina warned me not to grope their baby girl again. Is that the way you see it, Angelica?"

"I am not their baby girl! And no, you didn't force yourself on me or grope me. Are you satisfied now?"

"No. Far from it. I'll be taking an ice-cold shower tonight." He smiled broadly. "But I am relieved. It's been such a long time since I was with a woman I'd started to second guess myself at interpreting your response."

"A long time?" Angelica sounded suspicious. "I'm sure a guy like you has women hanging all over you."

Flynt chuckled. "I suppose I'm flattered you think so, but it's not true. When your mother accused me of having lots of casual flings, she couldn't have been more wrong. The truth is, my social life has been less than zero for quite some time."

"Why?" Curiosity had replaced some of the suspicion in her tone.

"I'm a workaholic, particularly since starting my company and getting it off the ground. Dating has never held much appeal for me, anyway. The getting-to-know-you chatter, the feigned interest in each other, the whole forced scenario. I get nothing out of it and put nothing into it. I'm sure I'm the world's most boring date."

"No, you're not!" Angelica said quickly. Too quickly, she realized. She blushed and was glad he wasn't there to see. "But I—I know what you mean about dating. I feel the same way. There are so many more interesting ways to spend your free time."

"Like watching The Weather Channel with your cat?"

"Absolutely. Rascal is great company and what's more fascinating than weather?"

They both laughed.

"Angelica, your mother got something else wrong tonight, too," Flynt said slowly, "when she said that—what went on between us in the kitchen meant nothing to me. It did, Angelica. What happened, counted."

She wasn't ready to admit that it mattered to her, too. But she liked hearing him say so.

"How is Madame X and little Sawyer X?" asked Flynt, filling the brief silence.

Angelica appreciated his tact. "Both resting comfortably." She trusted him enough to ask the question that was plaguing her. "Flynt, what—what's your take on my mother and Brandon spending time together?"

"Since each of them strikes me as two of the most unpredictable people on the planet, I can't really say, Angelica. But—" he paused "—Brandon sounded sober, if that helps."

"No, that's worse because if he'd been drunk, Mama would've thrown him out. She hates drunks. Finally."

There was a wealth of meaning in that one word, Flynt mused. The more he heard, the more he understood Romina's motives for helping women escape into the underground, away from allegedly abusive men. He would bet his company that Romina had had genuinely abusive men in her life, that her kids had been subjected to them, too.

He burned at the thought of Angelica at any age at the mercy of some violent drunken bully. Her mistrust of men in regard to women and children seemed depressingly logical.

Well, whatever Brandon Fortune was or wasn't, he had never been violent toward women or children. Which made him one of Romina's worthier choices. But would Angelica ever see it that way?

"Angelica, Brandon mentioned that he'd received another of those threatening notes tonight." Flynt made a stab at engaging her concern. "I didn't see it, he must've taken it to Romina's house."

"He probably made it himself." Angelica was scornful. "If he showed it to Mama, she'd…uh-oh! This could be disastrous. Mama has a soft spot for people in trouble. If Brandon pretends he's terrified, she'll want to do whatever she can to help him."

"Well, Brandon isn't terrified and doesn't act like it. But I just don't believe he is the one behind the notes, Angelica."

"That's right, you thought it was my mother—or me."

"Not anymore, not since I met you. But I do think it might be time to go to the police with this."

"Oh sure, go to the police!" Angelica actually

laughed. "And why stop there? Why not call in Agent Weatherall too? Maybe Brandon's family could even hire Searcy to track down the evil note sender."

"Hire Searcy?" There was a smile in Flynt's voice. "That's a low blow, Angelica. They've already hired me, remember? And I intend to make sure that both you and Brandon are safe."

"Then go over to Mama's house and get those two away from each other. I can't imagine anything worse than them deciding to rekindle their old flame."

"Worse would be something happening to you or Brandon. Put the security alarm on in the house and let the dogs run loose downstairs, Angelica. I'm going over to your mother's place now to bring Brandon back to the hotel. Or would you like us to come and stay there with you?"

"No!" she exclaimed. "Absolutely not!"

"Somehow I knew you were going to say that," he murmured wryly.

Angelica swallowed. "It's not you. It's Brandon. I've seen enough of him for one night."

"Will you see him tomorrow?"

"Flynt, there's no point, I—"

"Will you see me tomorrow?" Flynt interjected.

Angelica felt trapped. Because she really wanted to see him. What was it about Flynt that stirred these feelings in her?

She was aware that it was more than physical, though she was certainly attracted to him. She liked him. There, she'd admitted it. He was honest and straightforward, intelligent with a sense of humor she could relate to. She'd observed him being kind to Sugar, gentle with the baby, patient with her mother and sister and brother—and Brandon.

He had been all three with her, too. Warmth spread through her. "I—I guess I'll see you tomorrow. If you're hanging around my mother's house baby-sitting Brandon, I won't have much choice." A lifetime of defensive reserve made her add that qualifier.

Flynt laughed, and she added another reason to the list of why she liked him. He didn't take offense easily. It was as if he *understood*.

"Maybe we can make a real evening of it," he drawled. "Put on The Weather Channel, track some storms. Will you bring the cat over for additional entertainment?"

"No, Casper's allergic to animals. Mama hasn't been able to have one in the house since he was a baby. Rascal is Mara's cat, and I'm the favorite aunt."

"Angelica." Flynt paused. "I don't want you to worry about these threats." His voice was husky and deep. "I'll find out what's going on, and I'll take care of everything."

She believed him. It was both comforting and unfamiliar to feel such confidence in someone other than herself. Angelica wasn't sure how to cope. Flippancy seemed as good a way as any. "I'm not worried at all, Flynt. After all, Brandon is the bogus blackmailer. You'll find a way to prove it."

"Brandon isn't the blackmailer," Flynt told Angelica as they pushed their trays along the cafeteria line.

He had arrived at her office in MetroHealth a few minutes before and asked to join her for lunch, cheerfully admitting that he'd called Mara earlier to get her schedule for the day.

Angelica vowed to have a word with her best friend about giving out personal information to the enemy. Except she didn't consider Flynt an enemy and Mara knew it…

"Don't let your mom ruin things for you with Flynt, Angel," Mara had said last night, as they were getting ready for bed.

"Flynt and I don't have a *thing* to ruin," Angelica had insisted, and Mara hadn't pressed it.

But she had given Flynt the information he asked for today and now here he was.

Flynt followed Angelica as she bypassed the specials of the day and crossed into the sandwich line where she ordered a ham and cheese on wheat bread. When he ordered the same thing, she looked at him quizzically.

"Deductive reasoning. I noticed that the only people in the hot entrées line are the visitors. The hospital personnel all head for the cold sandwiches. When in any institution, I always follow the regulars' lead."

"You really do pay attention to detail." She was rather impressed.

"I also have strong instincts for self-perservation, which warn me against things labeled savory stew surprise or zesty pasta casserole."

"A wise move."

He insisted on paying for both their lunches when they got to the register.

"This is not a date," she felt compelled to tell him. Because she'd spent entirely too much time last night thinking of him. Reliving every word, every nuance that had passed between them. Every kiss and touch, too. Angelica's cheeks flushed.

She was having a hard time keeping her eyes off him, a hard time trying not to look thrilled to be with him. It was as if she were on an emotional merry-go-round, going up and down and in dizzying circles whenever she saw Flynt, whenever she thought of him. As a first-timer on this ride, she felt almost disoriented.

"No, it's not a date," agreed Flynt, picking up their trays and heading to an empty table. "This meal is being expensed to the Fortune Corporation. Since they're your relatives, technically this lunch is on you."

"The Fortunes are my relatives," she murmured. No wonder she was disoriented! "How can that be true? I keep waiting to hear it's just a hoax."

"It's not a hoax, Angelica." He took a bite of his sandwich. "How are little Sawyer and his mother doing today?"

She wasn't fooled by his casual tone. His blue eyes radiated intensity. "They were fine when Mara and I left the Rydells' house this morning. We're going to stop by later, after—"

"Don't bother," he cut in. "I called there myself about an hour ago. Your mother answered."

"She gets paid to be there, remember?" Angelica bristled defensively. "She was there to take the dogs outside."

"Romina told me the mother and baby weren't there, Angelica. She claimed to have no idea where they'd gone, but she had no intention of reporting them missing."

"Why would she?" Angelica countered. "They ar-

rived out of nowhere and now they've disappeared—"
her voice faltered a little "—into nowhere."

"They're now fugitives in the underground," Flynt
said flatly. "And there's a good chance that the baby's
father, and the rest of his relatives, grandparents, everyone else, will never see him. Or maybe not until he's
grown. Your own father suffered the same fate, Angelica, and the resonance is still being felt in your life, a
generation later."

"The circumstances aren't the same, Flynt!"

"How do you know, Angelica? Nobody knows the
circumstances because the child's mother refuses to talk.
But that doesn't stop Romina from contacting her underground pal Nancy Portland to spirit both mother and
baby away."

"We don't know if that's what happened," Angelica
murmured. "And Mama will never say."

"Of course not, she's sworn to secrecy, isn't she? But
we can certainly assume the obvious."

"I try not to assume anything," Angelica said loftily,
and Flynt made an exclamation of disbelief.

She took a bite of her sandwich, determined to sit in
silence if Flynt persisted in grilling her like a hostile
witness. But she couldn't seem to keep her eyes focused
on her plate. She stole a glance at him.

He was staring at her, his blue eyes glittering with a
hunger that she knew had nothing to do with the lun-
cheon menu. The intensity of his gaze electrified her,
and she felt a sweet, tight ache in her middle that radiated a glowing heat to her very core. Angelica flushed.
And struggled to contain her fierce awareness of Flynt
Corrigan.

She cleared her throat. "Before we got—uh—side-tracked, you mentioned you were absolutely certain Brandon isn't the blackmailer. Do you have proof or are you assuming the obvious again?"

"In Brandon's case, it seems like you broke your own rule about not assuming anything, to assume that he is the guilty party," Flynt pointed out.

He reached for the salt shaker at the same moment that she did. Their hands touched. He crooked two of his fingers around hers. "I don't want to fight with you, Angelica."

Just that simple touch made her breathless.

"We weren't fighting," she countered weakly. She didn't engage in fighting with men, she froze them out, she withdrew. Fighting was too intimate. It required a personal connection and energy she didn't care to invest.

Flynt arched his brow before tightening his fingers around hers.

Angelica studied the sensual line of his mouth and shivered with evocative memory. And haltingly acknowledged that yes, she did fight with Flynt, even though fighting required intimacy, a personal connection, and invested energy. With Flynt she'd already established all three.

The realization disturbed her. She jerked her hand away. Flynt merely picked up the shaker and salted the tomato slice on his sandwich. It occurred to Angelica that she was staring at him like a starstruck teen in the presence of her celebrity crush.

"Tell me what you've learned about the threatening note Brandon got last night," she prompted, striving for a little more dignity than that.

"I called Kate this morning. She said she was on the phone with Brandon last night when someone knocked on his door. When I double-checked at the hotel desk, I learned that it was the evening bellhop who was delivering an envelope last night. Everybody knew because Brandon gave him a fifty-dollar tip. Needless to say, every employee in the hotel is vying to make the next delivery to Mr. Fortune."

"What does she—my grandmother—have to say about it?"

Imagine Kate Fortune being her grandmother! The thought floored Angelica all over again. She'd read about Kate Fortune. Who hadn't? At one time the woman had secretly arranged to pretend she was dead for nearly a year while sabotage and murder were being investigated within the Fortune Corporation! Angelica couldn't help but be fascinated. After all, outside of the soap opera world, how many people "came back from the dead" as Kate Fortune had done in a spectacular blaze of media coverage?

"Kate has always been certain that Brandon had nothing to do with the threats. But she seemed a bit distracted when I was talking to her today. Apparently, her grandchildren who run the corporation called a board meeting to discuss an attempted takeover of one of the Fortune subsidiary companies."

"Aha! Maybe *that's* who is behind the threats! The fiend who is daring to mess with a Fortune subsidiary!" Angelica laughed. "Mystery solved!"

Flynt looked into her laughing eyes and had to suppress a sigh of longing as desire ripped through him. He'd spent a long time last night trying to expunge the feelings she evoked in him. Finally, he'd fallen asleep from sheer exhaustion, but obviously he'd failed at the expunging effort. Because being near her again already had him hot and primed for sensual action.

"Does anybody know who this fiend is?" Angelica teased.

"Er, fiend?" Flynt blinked uncomprehendingly. He'd been caught in the beginning of an erotic fantasy starring Angelica and had no idea what she was talking about.

"You know, the one behind the takeover attempt."

"Ahh, that fiend!" He smiled at her. Their eyes met and held for a long moment, until Angelica averted her gaze and took a gulping bite of her sandwich. He made her nervous, Flynt noted, recognizing the signs of a primal nervousness, based on sexual awareness and urgency. Mingled excitement and delight surged through him.

He remembered that they were supposed to be having a conversation as they continued to communicate on a wholly nonverbal level. "The alleged fiend is Gray McGuire, and he would not stoop to cut-and-paste extortion threats," he felt obliged to add. "McGuire's the CEO of McGuire Enterprises."

The name meant nothing to her. "I don't read the business section or keep up with CEOs and their companies. The only one I know by name is Bill Gates because he's Casper's ultimate hero."

"That's unusual. Don't most twelve-year-old boys prefer sports figures as their heroes?"

"Gates has lots of money and plenty of computers, Casper's version of nirvana." Angelica twirled the straw in her drink. "I worry about my little brother. He's been so lonely since he started middle school. He's never had a lot of friends but now he's drifting away from the few he did have. The other kids tease him a lot, about his name and his height, about anything, I guess.''

Flynt was paying attention, but when he thrust his long legs farther under the table, they brushed against hers. She didn't withdraw. Instead, she kept talking as he felt the warmth of her shapely legs suffuse his entire body.

''I wish Danny was around. I know Casper does, too.''

''Danny's with the Marines in Bosnia,'' Flynt said.

''That's right.'' Angelica's face was suddenly wreathed in smiles. There was something incredibly seductive about a man who actually listened and remembered what she had said.

''Danny used to play ball with Casper and tell him all about sports teams. Things he could talk about with the other boys.''

''Guy stuff.'' Flynt nodded his understanding. ''As long as I'm here, I'd be willing to pitch some balls to Casper and bring him up to speed on baseball. The season is just getting underway so it's a good time to start.''

''That's kind of you, Flynt.'' Angelica was touched. ''But I don't think you'll have much luck. All Casper wants to talk about these days are computers and the internet and the games he doesn't have. He won't even go outside, he sits in the house and watches TV by the hour.''

''Which doesn't go over big with your mother.'' Flynt remembered Romina's anger. And empathized with Casper. He knew exactly how it felt to be a kid who unerringly aggravated his mother; he also knew how much having a father who cared about him had eased the situation for him. Too bad Casper didn't have a strong male presence in his life to offset the tension with Romina. Too bad Romina didn't have a man in her life who cared enough about her to want to help her with the youngest son who so clearly baffled her.

Flynt wanted to help, though he recognized he was not what the pair needed. Still, he could do *something*...

"You know, my company is always upgrading electronic equipment. I could see about having one of the models to be replaced shipped down here to Casper. Maybe having his own computer would help the kid feel like he fit in."

Angelica's eyes widened. "You would do that?"

"Sure. No trouble." Flynt decided to call the home office and arrange to have a computer sent to Casper Carroll as soon as possible.

So what if they'd only recently been upgraded? He would instruct the office manager to purchase another to replace the one to be given to Casper. It was a small price to pay for the pleasure he felt seeing the light in Angelica's eyes, the relief on her face.

Angelica immediately felt a stab of apprehension at the glow that suffused her. "I would pay you, of course," she said quickly.

She wasn't accustomed to feeling so completely in sync with a man. It was scary. Even more disturbing was the way Flynt was looking at her. As if he *treasured* her or something. An absurd observation, a hopelessly romantic one. Flynt hardly knew her and while mothers might treasure their children, a man certainly didn't treasure a woman. She would do well to remember the facts instead of spinning fantasies. That was Mara's department!

"Tell me how much we owe for the used computer, and I'll send you a payment each month," she said, eager to put the transaction on an all-business footing.

"I have no doubt that you would." Flynt smiled wryly. "But suppose I ask for something else instead of money?"

Angelica rolled her eyes. "Of course, here it comes. The inevitable proposition." What a naive idiot she'd been, even for a moment, to consider any other motive on his part. "Forget it, Flynt. Much as I love my little brother, I'm not going to bed with you to get him a computer."

"Don't worry about it, Angelica. Much as I'd like to take you to bed, I wouldn't touch you under those conditions," he returned. "If and when we go to bed, you'll be there of your own free will."

Scalded with embarrassment, she looked down at her tray. And was surprised to realize that she'd finished her lunch. When she was with Flynt Corrigan, she tended to be unaware of anything else but him.

"Then what are you asking for?" It was a real effort to sound blasé, and she didn't think she'd pulled it off.

A group of student nurses sat down at the table next to them, laughing and talking. Flynt glanced from the girls to Angelica. "I'll tell you later. Right now I'd like to talk privately with you—about your father."

She was not about to let anyone eavesdrop on a conversation about Brandon Fortune. Angelica gave a quick nod. "We can use my office. My next patient isn't scheduled until an hour from now," she said, getting up and heading for the door.

When they reached the office suite, it was completely deserted because everybody was on their lunch break. They could've talked in the brightly wallpapered waiting room, but Angelica automatically led Flynt into her small private office.

It was where she talked with patients and their labor and delivery coaches, but was barely big enough for her desk and the two comfortable armchairs across from it.

"Sit down," she invited, feeling nervous as Flynt closed the door. It suddenly occurred to her how completely alone they were.

"I was going to suggest that you do the same," said Flynt. "Because I have some news you probably ought to be sitting down for." He placed his hands on her shoulders. "Just hear me out and don't launch into a Romina-esque attack of hysteria."

"I never get hysterical." The pressure of his hands made her sink into the armchair.

"That's good to hear." Flynt took the chair next to her.

"All right, what is it?" she demanded. Anxiety swept through her like wildfire on a prairie. "What has Brandon done now?"

"Nothing, it's what I've done," Flynt said, visibly bracing himself for her reaction. "I reported last night's extortion threat to the police."

Angelica waited for some kind of feeling—rage? fear?—to strike. But she felt…nothing. Even her anxiety was dissipating. Instead of jumping to her feet in outrage, she settled back in the chair. "I bet that was an exercise in futility."

"True," Flynt said ruefully. "At my insistence, they filed a report. End of concern, end of incident. It was frustrating."

"That can't have come as a surprise. After all, there hasn't even been a crime committed," she reminded him.

"You're as nonchalant as the police and Brandon and Romina are about the threat." Flynt was exasperated. "Aren't you remotely curious as to why I decided to go to the police?"

"Maybe you miss the good old days in law enforcement and wanted to experience the atmosphere of a station house again?"

Flynt ignored her sarcasm. "There is a troubling discrepancy in Brandon's story about the note, Angelica. He told me he found it in his room, shoved under the door. He told his mother—and the hotel staff confirmed—that a bellhop delivered a note to his room. When I arrived at your mother's house last night, something seemed...odd. I felt Romina and Brandon knew something about the new note, but when I tried to question them, they both clammed up. Claimed no knowledge and refused to discuss it at all."

He shook his head and grimaced wryly. "No wonder the police didn't take me seriously. I have nothing but a hunch that something is fishy."

"Fishy, huh?" Angelica chuckled. "Did they write that down on the police report?"

"Go ahead and laugh. If you weren't involved, I probably wouldn't give it a second thought, either. But since you're the focus of the threats…''

Flynt reached over and took her hand. ''I am not going to let anything happen to you, Angelica.''

Angelica's heart seemed to come to a complete stop, then began racing at warp speed. She felt him tug lightly on her hand and knew what he wanted her to do.

She was on the verge of doing it, too. Of sliding over onto his lap and picking up where they'd left off *twice* last night, in the booth at Swank and the Rydells' kitchen.…

Chapter 8

Angelica jumped to her feet and half stumbled to the door and flung it open.

"We can't, Flynt. We've got to keep our hands off each other. We can't keep grabbing each other like oversexed, hormone-crazed adolescents every time we're alone," she heard herself breathlessly blurt out.

She leaned against the door, horrified by her candor. She waited for Flynt to say something appropriately cutting that would make her cringe at the memory for the rest of her life.

"You're right, of course." Flynt heaved a deep sigh. "It's murder on the nerves, on every system in the body. This has never happened to me before," he added, his brow furrowing in perplexity.

He looked as off guard and off balance as she felt. Which greatly heartened her. And with the threat of verbal humiliation removed, Angelica relaxed a bit. "Not to me, either. I—I'm usually very controlled."

"I have a will of steel." Flynt stared at the floor. "Except around you. It's damn disturbing, physically, mentally, in every way. I slept approximately an hour and a half last night. The rest of the time I thrashed around…" His voice trailed off.

Angelica, who'd spent a similar night but wouldn't dare admit it, felt allied with him in a whole new way. "I wonder why this is happening?"

"You have no idea?" Flynt rubbed the back of his neck.

Angelica assumed the muscles there were tense and restrained herself from massaging them. She was quite good with relaxation massage techniques, an elective course she'd taken while pursuing her midwifery certification.

Not that she intended to touch him *or* answer his provocative question. She remained still and silent.

Flynt sighed again. "Well, I have a theory. Since I was awake most of last night, I had plenty of time to think."

"What is it? And don't say because of *love at first sight* or something insipid like that," she warned.

"I wouldn't dream of insulting your intelligence that way. No, I think what's happened to us is that we're both caught in an emotional maelstrom. This—case, for lack of a better term—has stirred a lot of feelings that we don't normally access." Flynt laughed without mirth. "Listen to me, I sound like one of the agents at the Behavioral Science Unit at Quantico."

"Aren't they the ones who do the criminal profiling?

Are you going to profile our behavior?'' Angelica asked incredulously. Embarrassment hovered uncomfortably close.

"It's easy enough to do. Look, Angelica, the, er, situation we're in has undoubtedly unleashed feelings we've actively suppressed for years. Plus, we're attracted to each other. Normally, we would have no trouble handling that attraction. As two careful, mature adults, we could ignore it. Certainly resist it.''

"So why aren't we doing that now?''

"Because of the unique set of circumstances. Aroused emotions, released energy, adrenaline. Now throw in sexual attraction. A dynamite combination.''

"You mean we're kind of—sexually imploding?'' She gaped at him.

"Yes.''

Angelica was dubious. His theory of random sexual implosion struck her as unlikely, even insulting to their powers of discretion. She was absolutely certain that if, say, TJ Gibson had brought her father into her life, she would not have sexually imploded at all.

But Flynt's theory was a shade more realistic than the foolish one she couldn't accept yet couldn't seem to get out of her head—that old cliché of *love at first sight*.

"Well, what do you think?'' he pressed.

"It's a theory,'' she conceded cautiously.

Flynt took that for agreement. "Exactly. Consider what we're dealing with, Angelica. For you, it's your father and all the emotional baggage that goes with that territory, including the assorted men who've passed through your mother's life. Tell me that doesn't send you into the emotional spin cycle.''

She visualized herself spinning and trapped by forces from the past. It seemed an apt image. "What about you? Why are you affected by Brandon meeting me?"

"It's not you and Brandon, per se. It's the whole issue of lost and found. Of people missing and then recovered."

She stared at him, comprehension dawning. "Was your own father—"

"Not my father, my brother," Flynt corrected quietly. "My little brother Mark. He was six years old when he disappeared."

"Disappeared?" Angelica felt her heart clench. "How? When?" She dropped back into the chair beside him.

"Twenty-six years ago. I was ten and Mark was six, and we were at the school playground with a bunch of other kids one summer afternoon in late August," Flynt said, reciting the facts, staring straight ahead.

Angelica watched him intently. His voice, his expression gave nothing away, but she picked up clues of the terrible tension underlying his dispassionate delivery. She saw the muscle twitching in his jaw, saw him tighten his left hand into a fist, so tight that his knuckles turned white. She leaned closer.

"Go on," she urged softly.

"It was a hot day and Mark got thirsty and wanted to go home to get something to drink. We were playing ball and I didn't want to leave in the middle of the game. I told Mark to wait awhile but he didn't, he started home." Flynt swallowed hard. "And never made it."

"Oh, Flynt!" Angelica impulsively reached for his hand and clutched it tight. "Was he kidnapped?"

She knew how much effort he was exerting to maintain his steely self-control. Holding his hand, she could feel the emotions churning within him. She wished he would let himself express those emotions with her but understood why he didn't. She knew all about building walls to keep feelings in and other people out. She and Flynt were a lot alike, though she had never had a tragedy of such magnitude in her own life.

"We never knew what happened to Mark," Flynt replied tonelessly. "When I came home for dinner that day, my mother asked me where Mark was. He wasn't at the house, and she started calling around, looking for him. But nobody had seen him since he'd left the schoolyard."

Angelica found it hard to breathe. "What a nightmare!" His hand was icy cold. Instinctively she pressed it to her cheek to warm it and offer him what comfort she could.

"It's been a never-ending nightmare, Angelica." When he said her name, the careful flatness in his tone changed to one of undisguised pain.

His eyes met hers and for one searing moment, she saw what he was feeling mirrored in his bleak gaze. She gripped his hand as if she would never let it go.

Flynt lowered his eyes, and she felt his withdrawal viscerally, yet knew that for him it was necessary. He had already let his mask slip and now he had to get it back into place. Her heart ached for him.

"You've read about similar stories about missing children in the news many times, unfortunately." Flynt attempted to resume his role of stoic agent.

But Angelica could feel his pulse beneath her fingers,

and it was racing, a tangible indication of his high stress level. She gently stroked the underside of his wrist.

Flynt intended to end the conversation here, which is what he usually did when circumstances required that he reveal the sad story of Mark. After all, this was where the case ended, with Mark's fate unknown. There was no need to go into detail about what had happened next, to himself and his family.

"Every time I read one of those stories I feel sick," Angelica murmured. She used her other hand to brush a stray lock of hair off his forehead.

The tender gesture seemed to unleash Flynt's restraint. Once again, he swallowed so hard, the reflex was visible. "There was a massive search for Mark, but he had disappeared without a trace. There were never any leads, nothing. It was as if he'd dropped off the face of the earth. To this day, the case remains unsolved."

"Oh, Flynt!" Angelica felt tears sting her eyes. "I'm so sorry."

"When Gabe Devereax asked me to look into finding you, I agreed at once, though it's not the sort of case my company normally handles. We're in the business of corporate security, not locating lost relatives."

Flynt played absently with her fingers, lacing them with his. "But the very idea of Brandon Fortune intrigued me, fascinated me actually. Here was someone who'd been taken as a child—and subsequently recovered and sent home to his family. How had all that played out? How had the lost years affected relationships? I leaped at the chance to observe firsthand."

"And pictured your brother as an adult, coming back to your own family?" she asked quietly.

"I tried but I couldn't. To me Mark will always be six years old." His eyes clouded like a dismal, rainy morning.

Angelica tried to imagine what it would be like to have a ghost sibling, frozen in time. It was awful beyond imagining. She felt like crying for him and had to hold back her tears. She instinctively knew that if she were to cry, Flynt would be quick to comfort her, he would even welcome assuming the familiar role of strong-male-in-charge. And this wasn't about her; this was Flynt's tragedy. She wanted to be the strong one for him. She wanted him to know he could lean on her.

"I seldom think about what happened anymore," Flynt insisted gruffly. "I stopped dwelling on it years ago. I had to." He set his mouth in a grim line.

His defenses were intact; he wasn't ready to let go of them. Angelica understood but wished it could be different. Maybe someday, it could?

She was both buoyed and surprised by that small hope. She never thought in terms of "someday" with a man.

"Did seeing Brandon with his family stir up all those powerful feelings again?" Angelica asked, reconsidering his emotional-maelstrom theory. Now it didn't seem as far-fetched, at least not from his perspective.

"I didn't think so at the time. But possibly it did…and then coming here and learning about Nancy Portland's underground and families broken apart and kids missing really struck a nerve." His face was grim with disapproval.

Angelica shivered. "I can see where it would. I—I

understand your objections, though it's not the same as losing Mark. It really isn't, Flynt.''

"Just hearing you say Mark's name feels good." Their eyes met and held fast. "No one in my family, or in my hometown, ever mentions him. It's been that way since a few months after his disappearance. People stopped talking about Mark, stopped saying his name. It's as if he never was—except his absence left this enormous crater in all our lives.''

"You and your parents must have been devastated.'' Angelica gulped back a sob. What if Danny or Sarah or Casper had vanished at the age of six, never to be seen again?

"It tore our family apart,'' Flynt said matter-of-factly. "My mother blamed me. I was the older brother. I should've walked Mark home. She never forgave me for not doing that, and I can't blame her.''

"Flynt, you were only a child yourself," Angelica protested. "Both you and Mark might've been snatched, and then your parents would have lost both their sons.''

"That's what my dad used to say. He and I had always been close, but Mark was Mom's baby, her favorite..." Flynt shrugged resignedly. "Losing Mark, not knowing what happened to him, ruined my parents' marriage. They turned all their pain and anger against each other. They were either quarreling or not speaking a word.''

"And you didn't know what to do. To try to help smooth things over or to keep out of it.'' Angelica nodded her understanding. Over the years she herself had wondered what role to take in the countless fights between Romina and her men.

"Mostly, I tried to stay away. My refuge was school and sports. I played on every team and joined every organization. Dad finally moved out when I was fifteen. I wanted to live with him, but Mom wouldn't hear of it, solely out of spite, I'm sure, because she and I didn't get along at all. A year later, Dad was killed in a car accident."

"Flynt, I don't know what to say." There were no words, so Angelica expressed herself physically. She leaned over and wrapped her arms around his waist in a hug. "It's so sad, it's such a tragedy."

She tried to hold him tighter but their separate chairs kept her from being as close to him as she needed to be. It was the most natural thing in the world for her to move from her chair onto his lap.

"I'm sorry, I'm so sorry," she whispered, stroking his cheek, his neck with her fingertips.

Flynt closed one hand around her throat and tilted her head. "It's all right," he said softly, staring into her dark eyes that glistened with tears. "Bad as it was, I gained some invaluable lessons. I grew up fast, and I learned early on the difference between illusion and truth, which some people never do get straight."

His lips twisted into a cynical smile. "The illusion is the vow that starry-eyed couples take to stick together for better or for worse, in good times and in bad. The truth is that when atrocious things happen—like losing a child—it's likely that the couple will split because they can't stand the sight of each other. Each reminds the other of the pain and all that lost promise."

"That's what happened to your parents." Angelica tried and failed to swallow a sob.

"Don't cry," he murmured. "It happened so long ago, it's over now."

It seemed incongruous that he was attempting to comfort her, but that was Flynt, determined and strong and controlled. She traced his lips with her thumb. "Flynt, you—you don't have to be brave around me, you can let the pain show."

She wanted to share the hurt he'd felt, then and now; she didn't want to be protected from it. Instinctively she wound her arms around his neck.

Their lips met and they kissed with lingering tenderness that swiftly flared into something hotter, wilder and more demanding. The first kiss blended into a second, then a third, seamless and intimate.

Angelica whimpered and clung to him, her body surging with sheer primitive need. She felt so close to him, united in spirit in a way she'd never experienced with any other person.

Yet it wasn't enough, she wanted—needed—more. To physically express their closeness. This craving for intimacy was brand-new to her. For the first time in her life, the urge for sex finally made sense.

Moaning softly, Angelica arched against him in urgent sensual hunger. Her breasts were swollen and achy, the tips throbbing. She wanted him to touch her there so much she was trembling with it.

When his big hand closed over one breast, she shuddered with pleasure. His fingers cupped her breasts and fondled her, his thumb seeking and finding the almost painfully sensitive nipple. Angelica cried out his name.

It was the sound of that breathless feminine demand that abruptly snapped Flynt out of sweet, sensuous oblivion. He opened his eyes, saw the provocative picture they made, and realized exactly where they were—*in Angelica's office with the door not even closed!*

He was painfully aware of how inappropriate their behavior was in this setting.

Even acknowledging all that, he had to fully utilize his will of steel to make himself stop. With great effort Flynt rose, lifting Angelica along with him. He set her on her feet, keeping his arm around her.

"Easy, baby," he said softly, his lips caressing her hair. It was silky-soft and thick and smelled wonderful. "This isn't the time—and it sure isn't the place."

Angelica leaned her forehead against his chest. Her arms were around his waist, locking her to him. She felt weak and limp.

"We…imploded again, didn't we?" Common sense told her she ought to get far away from Flynt Corrigan as fast as she could. But she stayed exactly where she was.

"Seems that way." Flynt rubbed her back, the strokes becoming more sweeping, from her shoulder blades to the gentle curve of her waist and back again.

She nuzzled him, her eyes closed, pressing herself firmly to him. She could feel the tension in him, the lusty throbbing of his arousal. Angelica cuddled closer.

Flynt's hand strayed lower. His fingers closed over the rounded curve of her bottom, and a shudder of pleasure and anticipation jolted through him. He wanted to lock the door and place her down on the top of her desk; he wanted to push the skirt of her demure gray-and-yellow pin-striped dress to her waist and—

"Flynt." she breathed his name.

And snapped him back to sanity once again. This time it was even harder to summon his will of steel, but Flynt dutifully did so. He dropped his arms and moved away from her, taking the necessary steps into the small hallway connecting the rooms of her office suite.

"I have some calls to make," he said hoarsely. "To my office in Minneapolis. Business related."

Angelica nodded. She understood he needed some space. Oddly enough, she did not feel that need herself. Flynt had breached the self-protective wall around her, but instead of wanting to withdraw further, she wanted to draw him closer.

"About the computer for Casper," she said, following him into the waiting room, wanting to prolong their time together. "You said you didn't want money, but you'd ask me for something else instead?"

"That's right." As the sensual fog lifted, Flynt felt his brain begin to function again. "I'm asking you to dinner tonight."

Angelica arched one dark brow. "Isn't that kind of a pricey dinner date?"

"Well…" Flynt cleared his throat.

"Uh-oh! What's the catch? Now I'm sure there must be one."

"It depends on what you consider a catch, Angelica."

"You're stalling, Flynt."

"Maybe. But you still haven't said you'll go."

"All right, I'll go. Now what haven't you told me?"

"You and I won't be alone for dinner tonight."

She tried not to appear disappointed. "Okay."

"Don't you want to know who'll be joining us?"

"Could it be…Brandon Fortune? Just a wild guess," she added unenthusiastically.

"Smart girl." Flynt tried to coax a smile from her. "But tonight won't be a repeat of last night's awkward trio. Brandon has invited along some new friends he's made in the city. You know them extremely well—Romina, Sarah and Casper."

"Ohhh!" Angelica did not smile.

"I have to admit, I didn't exactly jump for joy either, when I first heard." Flynt reached for her hand. He couldn't be near her and not touch her. He smoothed his thumb over her palm. "Since the undercurrents at the table tonight will be more like a riptide, I decided to bring along some reinforcements. You know, the more the merrier, there's strength in numbers. Very applicable clichés."

Angelica found it difficult to concentrate; his subtle caress was making her shiver with renewed longing. "You asked somebody else to take part in this surefire fiasco? Who?"

"Your old friend TJ. I saw him at the police station this morning. He agreed to come along, but he's under the impression that Mara will also be there."

"And how did he get that impression?" Angelica tried to sound cross, but she couldn't work up any real ire.

"I guess I gave it to him. Will you convince Mara to come? Then we'll be a party of eight. Enough people to provide diversions, if need be."

"Actually, your safety-in-numbers theory isn't a bad one," she conceded. "I'll talk Mara into coming. If all else fails, I'll play on her sympathy for Sarah and Casper. The thought of two innocent kids being subjected to an evening with Brandon Fortune ought to do it.''

"You're an excellent strategist." Flynt lifted her hand to his mouth and brushed his lips across her knuckles. "I'll talk to you later." He left the office, his stride swift and purposeful.

"Later," Angelica murmured wistfully.

She stood in the doorway of the waiting room and watched him go. He didn't look back at her. It wasn't until he had turned the corner and was out of sight that Angelica realized how much she'd wanted him to.

Flynt sensed tension the moment the Carroll family, accompanied by Mara and TJ, walked into the Plantation Family Restaurant. There wasn't a smile to be seen among them, and everyone kept glancing covertly at Romina, whose face was a study in fury.

Even Brandon, not known for his astute observations, realized something was wrong. "Oh, man!" He was already seated at the table they'd reserved for their dinner party. "Romina looks ready to blow sky-high."

Flynt's eyes locked with Angelica's.

She made a slicing motion across her throat with her finger, and Flynt had a sudden image of Romina as the volatile Red Queen in *Alice in Wonderland* ordering, "Off with their heads."

"This place is stupid!" Casper announced upon joining them. "I didn't want to come but *she* made me." Her jerked his thumb toward his mother.

Flynt, always a man of action, decided to step in and head off the inevitable fight. "Romina, did Angelica mention that my company is upgrading computers? I would like to send Casper one of the—''

''You want to give Casper a computer?''

''Yes, I talked to Angelica about it at lunch,'' said Flynt. It wasn't hard to guess that his offer didn't please Romina, judging by her troubled expression.

Angelica came to stand beside Flynt. ''Mama, before you say anything—''

''Give a computer to a kid who ditches school and spends the day hanging out in a video arcade?'' Romina's voice rose on every word.

''You skipped school today, Casper?'' Brandon chuckled. ''I played hookey a time or two myself at your age.''

Apparently Romina hadn't. She ranted on about Casper's various misdeeds, before roundly rejecting Flynt's offer of a computer. Casper burst into tears.

''What's the big deal, Romi?'' Brandon looked confused. ''We used to ditch school all the time, remember?''

''Yeah, and look at us! Just take a good look at the both of us! We messed up our whole lives! You think I'd let my kids do what I did? Drop out of high school, spend the rest of their lives having to scrounge for every cent! Let my kids turn out like me? Ha! Not ever!''

Nobody said much during the decidedly tense dinner that followed.

''At least the service was fast. We got our food in record time,'' Flynt remarked to Angelica as they left the restaurant thirty minutes later. He hung back, catching her hand to keep her at his side as the others filed out.

"The staff couldn't wait to get us out here. I think they were expecting Mama to start overturning tables and throwing plates."

"Hmm, so was I."

"It wouldn't be the first plate Mama's ever thrown, although she hasn't overturned any tables."

"Not yet, anyway. It doesn't seem too far beyond the realm of possibility."

Angelica sighed. "I tried to call you to warn you not to mention the computer tonight, especially not after the school called to report Casper's truancy today. I knew it would make Mama even madder. Unfortunately, you'd already left to come here."

"You know, it's not so awful for a twelve-year-old kid to choose a video arcade over school once in a while, Angelica," Flynt said calmly.

"But he's never done it before." Angelica looked troubled. "And then he lied about where he'd been. Lately he's been lying a lot. Mama is so worried."

"I noticed." Flynt's lips quirked. "But Brandon eggs him on."

"He would!" she said, with feeling. "There is an up side to all this, though. If Mama was harboring any sweet, nostalgic pangs over Brandon Fortune, he's killed them. And since his celebrity-sized ego won't tolerate Mama calling him a loser, I don't have to worry about the two of them hooking up anymore." Angelica was visibly relieved.

"So you consider this evening a success?" Flynt rested his hands on her waist, enjoying the feel of her supple curves. "Well, I'm glad *someone* had a good time here tonight. The rest of us were holding our collective breaths, just waiting for the next round of hostilities to resume. It's hard to enjoy a meal under those circumstances.''

He happened to look up and see Romina and Brandon at the front of the restaurant. They stood apart, but both of them were staring intently at him and Angelica.

Their scrutiny made Flynt even more uncomfortable than he'd been during dinner. ''I agree with you, Angelica. It's a good thing Casper's day off put that pair on opposite sides of the abyss.''

''Definitely.'' Angelica smiled wryly. ''Look what happened the last time Romina and Brandon played on the same team—me!''

Flynt gazed down at her. She was beautiful and strong and smart. Behind her self-protective wall of cool reserve, she was funny and warm.

Which made him completely rethink his dire Romina-and-Brandon-apocalypse hypothesis. If the two of them could produce Angelica...

''Do you two want to go to the Have A Nice Day Café with Mara and me tonight?'' TJ joined them to issue the invitation. ''It just opened last week and is supposed to be cool. Everything is from the seventies, the music and raised lit dance floor with a mirrored ball hanging from the ceiling. There are posters of celebrities from back then plastered all over the walls. It could be fun.''

Angelica and Flynt looked at each other and quickly looked away, each remembering their previous evening at another nightspot, Swank. The booth. The kisses.

''We'd better not,'' Angelica said quickly.

''Ah, come on, Angel,'' TJ pleaded. ''Mara won't go

without you. She's still not over me going into your mom's house with the search warrant.''

''I know that wasn't your fault, TJ,'' Angelica said in his defense.

''Certainly not,'' Flynt agreed. ''And if going to this retro place with you will persuade Mara of that, maybe we ought to go along. Although we aren't really dressed for the seventies, are we, Angel? Nobody is wearing bell-bottoms or platform shoes.''

''I'd give a lot to see *you* in bell-bottoms and platform shoes,'' Angelica retorted. Flynt hadn't called her Angel before, and the way he said it was something of a challenge. A dare. Should she go with him?

She glanced at Mara, who had remained at the door in earnest conversation with Romina. Sarah and Casper were laughing at something Brandon had said.

''I hope your father isn't sharing tales of his Hollywood childhood with the kids,'' Flynt said, following her gaze. ''Casper's escapade at the video arcade pales in comparison to some of Brandon's preteen adventures.''

It was as if he'd read her mind! She supposed their shared confidence today had given each of them a certain insight into the other. She thought of little Mark Corrigan, snatched off the streets near his home and still missing, of Flynt's grim family life following his brother's disappearance. But Flynt hadn't used the tragedy as an excuse to fail; he'd grown into a successful, strong adult. Who could still empathize with a troubled kid like Casper.

And like her, he didn't burden himself with fantasies about love and marriage providing all the answers to life's uncertainties; he didn't kid himself that loving was a salve to soothe pain. It was a relief to find a kindred spirit.

Angelica decided then and there to extend their evening together. She wasn't ready to go home alone, she really wanted to be with Flynt.

The revelation was both scary and exhilarating.

"I'll go tonight," she said, before she could change her mind. "I'd like to see those old posters, I bet they're hilarious. And I want to persuade Mara not to hold a grudge against TJ."

She couldn't admit that she simply wanted to spend more time with Flynt. Old habits, like holding back, died hard.

"Of course," Flynt said, and tucked her hand into his pocket.

"I haven't heard from either you or Brandon in nearly two weeks, Flynt Corrigan." Kate sounded perturbed. "I was beginning to wonder if the two of you were still in Birmingham or had taken off on a lark for parts unknown. No one has called me, and any time I've tried to reach either of you, you aren't in."

"Kate, I—I am so sorry!" Flynt stammered, his face reddening.

He'd come back to his suite to change clothes for his date with Angelica tonight just in time for Kate's phone call from Minneapolis. "There is absolutely no excuse for not calling. It's, um, well—Brandon and I are seldom around the hotel, and when we come in at night, it's very late, too late to call you, and—"

"Gracious, listen to you!" Kate laughed, her sense of

humor reasserting itself. "You sound like my grand-children back in their college days, when they would forget to call their parents for weeks on end. There were apologies and excuses, and if I'm not mistaken, next come the abject regrets and fervent promises to do better."

"I really am sorry, Kate." Flynt smiled ruefully: "Consider me abjectly regretful. And I fervently promise to phone you every day."

"Heavens, no! I'm on the phone enough as it is, I don't need daily reports from you. But I have been dying to hear about my granddaughter. As you know, Brandon called me the first night he was in town and said things had gotten off to a shaky start between them. I'd like your impressions and opinions, Flynt. Tell me about Brandon and Angelica."

Flynt sat down on the bed, cradling the phone between his shoulder and his ear as he fastened the buttons of his shirt. "You're going to be very proud of your grand-daughter, Kate. Angelica is—" He paused.

How to describe Angelica to her grandmother?

It wasn't as if he didn't know her well enough to give a detailed description.

He and Angelica had spent every evening together since his arrival in Birmingham; sometimes they met for lunch in the hospital cafeteria, too.

Three nights ago, one of her patients had gone into labor and delivered the baby close to midnight. The late hour hadn't deterred Flynt from stopping by Angelica's apartment when she got home. He'd arrived with a pizza, knowing she had been in the labor-and-delivery suites for hours and missed dinner.

It was a quick visit. After eating, Angelica had been so tired he'd left so she could go to bed. But merely spending that short time with her buoyed him; letting a whole day pass without seeing her was unthinkable.

"Brandon said she was beautiful, that first night he called," Kate prompted helpfully.

"Yes, but there's so much more to Angelica than looks," Flynt countered, sounding slightly defensive. "I know how important physical appearances are to Brandon, but to simply rave on about Angelica's beauty is to, uh, to—" He broke off, aware that his heart was pounding and his entire body felt flushed with heat.

"To lessen the impact of her fine character?" Kate suggested. She smiled widely as Sterling, who was sitting in the room, chortled behind his newspaper.

"Exactly!" Flynt exclaimed, his tone almost reverential.

"Are you having any problems keeping up with your company while you're in Birmingham, Flynt?" asked Kate, ever the businesswoman.

"No, not at all. I've been on trips overseas that've lasted longer than this particular sojourn. I have an excellent staff. I call headquarters at least once a day and make good use of conference calls, e-mail and faxes, so it's been business as usual for SMS."

"Good. I'm very glad to hear that, Flynt. Now tell me what I've been longing to know. How is Brandon's relationship with his daughter developing?"

"Brandon's relationship with Angelica," Flynt repeated, stalling.

It was a tough question, because he wanted to give Kate the answer she so hoped for: that Brandon and

Angelica were getting to know each other, that they were making up for all their lost years apart.

But the truth was, Brandon's relationship with his daughter hadn't developed at all. How could it when they never saw each other?

Which was probably his fault, Flynt silently conceded, since he and Angelica were together every evening.

They'd sampled a little of everything that Birmingham had to offer. For nightlife, the clubs in the rejuvenated Southside, for culture, the Birmingham Civil Rights Institute and historic Linn Park and for all-around fun, the Alabama Spots Hall of Fame and the Birmingham Zoo.

Last weekend Mara and TJ had accompanied them to Oak Mountain State Park, thirty miles south of the city, where they'd rented canoes and paddled around the lake and sunbathed on Oak Mountain Beach.

Flynt pictured Angelica in her demure, yet incredibly tantalizing, one-piece blue swimsuit and felt his mouth grow dry. He'd been both grateful and frustrated with the other couple's presence. They had served as an effective restraint against his increasingly powerful need to—

"Oh, dear, from your long silence, I'm going to assume that Brandon and Angelica haven't—what's the popular lingo?—bonded." Kate's voice jarred Flynt from his reverie.

He cleared his throat. "No, they haven't, Kate. They haven't—er—bonded. Yet," he dared to add, feeling like a fraud. He didn't want to lie, but would a little prevarication be such a bad thing?

Otherwise, Kate would be doomed to disappointment, because Angelica was more than happy to avoid Brandon Fortune. She did not want her father in her life, she'd told Flynt too many times to count. She didn't want *any* of her mother's exes around, ever again, but especially not her own father.

After hearing some of the chilling tales about the men in Romina's past, as experienced by Angelica and her siblings, Flynt understood her opposition to fathers. She was equally opposed to the concept of husbands. She admitted she'd never seen a happy marriage firsthand— "no man ever bothered to marry Mama"—though some of the expectant couples whose babies she delivered seemed to "act" happy.

"But it's like you said, Flynt, the good times can't last forever," she'd told him earnestly during a surprisingly frank conversation they'd had about relationships one evening. "And love is the first thing to go when the bad stuff happens."

Something in Flynt urged him to recant his earlier pessimism, to argue that he'd seen people—his aunts and uncles, his grandparents, face adversity together and become stronger and closer. That his parents' particular tragedy and weaknesses weren't universal. But he hadn't contradicted Angelica because he didn't understand his own strange shift in perception.

"Do Brandon and Angelica have anything at all in common?" Kate asked a little plaintively, once again drawing Flynt out of his strange reverie.

It took a moment for him to reconnect. Yes, he was supposed to be facilitating the Fortune father-and-child reunion; the lucrative SMS contract with the Fortune Corporation depended on his efforts to at least try to establish a connection between them.

But when he was with Angelica, the last thing on his mind was Brandon—or the Fortunes or even SMS. His interest, his thoughts, were riveted to Angelica herself.

"Well, there's no common interests yet, but we'll keep looking for something, Kate," he said, feeling like a fraud.

"Thank you for being honest with me, my dear," Kate said wistfully. "And as long as you are able to remain there, I won't give up hope that somehow Brandon will...bond with his child. I know my great-nephew Jack's trying to do the same thing with his young daughter, Lilly, now that his ex-wife Sandra is dead."

Now Flynt felt acutely guilty. "I'll try to get them together again tonight, Kate," he promised. And grimaced.

How could he do that, when he didn't know where Brandon was going to be?

They seldom saw each other because, as Brandon put it, "Let's just continue doing our own thing, man."

To Flynt's amazement, Brandon Fortune, known for quickly growing bored, had yet to tire of Birmingham. While Flynt conducted his company business from his suite during the day, Brandon went out—somewhere—without ever complaining about the limitations of a city that wasn't Los Angeles.

And while Flynt spend his evenings with Angelica, Brandon spent his with...

Flynt frowned thoughtfully and remembered hearing Brandon sing enthusiastically about "a girl crazy for me." He hadn't given the lyrics much thought at the time. Brandon also sang about "little deuce coupes, funkytowns and superfreaks."

But now that he took time to consider the situation, Flynt realized that Brandon must have a girlfriend here in Birmingham. Brandon viewed himself as quite the ladies' man; typically, he would not have lasted two weeks without female companionship. Would he have lasted here two weeks without any complaints unless he was occupied by a girl crazy for him?

Girl—that was the operative word. Flynt suppressed a groan. He fervently hoped Brandon's Birmingham "girl" was at least of legal age.

"Flynt, one last thing before we hang up," said Kate. "Have there been any more threatening notes? We've been concerned that Brandon and Angelica are at risk and—"

"Angelica is safe, Kate," Flynt hastened to assure her. "There haven't been any more threats and I've— kept a close eye on her."

He actually blushed. If Kate only knew how close! But frustratingly, maddeningly, never close enough.

Flynt gulped with enough force to swallow a head of lettuce whole. His propensity for sexual implosion in Angelica's presence hadn't lessened one iota, nor had hers. Though they hadn't discussed his theory about emotional maelstrom-equals-loss-of-control since he'd outlined it that day in her office, both heeded it.

Neither was ready to risk implosion or to cede control to someone else, particularly not someone they'd known such a short time. He and Angelica were well matched when it came to caution, willpower and restraint, Flynt mused. Just as their desire and their need for each other was well matched.

And though they couldn't give in to their lust, they

couldn't ignore it, either. They had to kiss, they had to touch. The temptation, the necessity for it was too strong to be denied.

So they kissed good-night at the end of every evening; they held hands and lightly caressed each other's backs or necks or arms. That was titillating and exciting, yet safe, as long as they set very firm limits.

Which they did. They didn't spend time alone in cars, unless they were driving to and from a place; they avoided his hotel suite and her apartment unless Mara and TJ were there, too. Otherwise…

Flynt didn't dare speculate on *otherwise,* not with Angelica's grandmother on the other end of the line.

"I'm glad to hear you're so conscientious, Flynt," said Kate, "though I never doubted it. I would love to fly down there and meet Angelica, but I don't want to barge in when she's just getting used to the idea of her father. I suppose we'll have to wait until she is ready to meet the rest of her family. Do you think it'll happen soon, Flynt?"

"I don't know, Kate," replied Flynt.

Actually, he did know. It wasn't going to happen soon, if ever, because Angelica insisted she wanted nothing to do with either her father's or her mother's relatives.

Flynt guessed it was her way of proclaiming total loyalty to Romina, though whether or not Romina herself demanded such fealty, he did not know.

But he was unwilling to dash Kate's hopes with unbridled pessimism. "Maybe it'll be sooner than any of us think, Kate."

Chapter 9

Two days later, Flynt realized that the kind little white lie he'd told Kate actually had been uncannily prophetic.

Angelica was to meet the Fortune side of her family much sooner than any of them had anticipated. Especially Angelica and himself.

They were sitting at a coffeehouse when Angelica told him a reporter with the notorious and very popular *Globe Star Probe* had called her, claiming to be checking out an anonymous tip. Was Brandon Malone Fortune actually her father?

Even though Angelica had been aghast and muttered an unintelligible reply before hanging up, the reporter, Kieran Kaufman, had left repeated messages on her machine.

"Do you think Brandon has been blabbing the story in bars around the city and somebody phoned it in to the *Globe Star Probe?* Or maybe...is it possible that Brandon himself is the anonymous tipster?''

''I truly doubt it,'' replied Flynt.

''Because his paternal feelings are so strong he'd never expose me to a scandal rag?'' Angelica took refuge in deadpan, gallows humor.

''As much as I'd like to believe it, what I really think is that Brandon operates from a position of self-interest.'' Flynt was blunt. ''And he has nothing to gain by calling the *Probe.*''

''Except publicity. Maybe he developed a taste for it when he was reunited with Kate. Maybe he wants to be in the spotlight again,'' Angelica surmised darkly.

''Why is Brandon hanging around Birmingham, anyway?'' Angelica cried, anxiety making her stomach somersault. ''Haven't I made it clear that I don't want to know him? I don't even see him, except every once in a while by accident, if he happens to stop by your suite when I'm at the hotel.''

And always chaperoned by Mara and TJ, Flynt mused wryly.

''Somehow Brandon has managed to keep himself entertained while he's in town.'' Flynt refrained from adding that it was likely a young female companion who was doing the entertaining. Why upset Angelica further?

''I bet I know why he hasn't left.'' Angelica scowled. ''His mother probably made some deal with him, that if he stays here for a set number of days or weeks, supposedly spending time with me, he'll get a nice cash payoff.''

She noticed that Flynt looked uncomfortable. ''I'm

right, aren't I, Flynt? Kate Fortune is paying him to stay here on the pretext of playing daddy.''

Flynt thought of the terms of the deal he himself had struck with the Fortunes. If he were to tell her those details, she might assume he was staying because *he* was getting paid.

And nothing could be farther from the truth. The way he felt about her now, Flynt knew he would stick around even if Kate were to cancel their deal.

''Brandon's mother isn't paying him to stay here on the pretext of playing daddy, Angelica.'' He felt compelled to clear Kate of that charge. He didn't want Angelica harboring hostility toward her grandmother, who was genuinely eager to accept her as a full-fledged member of the Fortune family.

''I'm listening to what you're *not* saying, Flynt.'' Angelica stared intently at him. ''That my grandmother isn't involved but one of the Fortunes, maybe one of Brandon's brothers or sisters, is paying him to stay here in Birmingham? And they don't care if he gets to know me or not, they're just glad he's not in Minneapolis stirring things up.''

Flynt couldn't help but smile. ''It's safe to say that Brandon's sisters and brothers prefer him out of Minneapolis and out of their hair.''

He reached across the table and laid his hand over hers. ''Do you know that you just referred to Kate as your grandmother? Not Brandon's mother, not Kate Fortune, but your grandmother.''

''Don't go reading anything into it, Flynt. It doesn't mean anything,'' Angelica insisted.

''I think it does. I think you're beginning to adjust to

the idea of being related to the Fortunes, Angelica. To accepting Kate Fortune as your grandmother, rather than as some larger-than-life character who occupies a separate universe from you."

"But she does. Which brings us back to all those calls from that nosy reporter, that Kieran Kaufman creep," Angelica said grimly. "The press might be a part of the Fortune family's world but not mine. The *Globe Star Probe* wouldn't call plain old Angelica Carroll, nurse-midwife, unless maybe they wanted help concocting a story about delivering a Martian baby or something."

"They wouldn't need help concocting a Martian baby story, they could bang it out in an hour themselves. And whether it's Carroll or Fortune, you are anything but plain old Angelica."

"And you're a sweet-talking smooth operator." She smiled flirtatiously at him, feeling better for no other reason except talking things over with him...made her feel better.

Suddenly the situation didn't seem so alarming, just merely annoying. And eminently manageable.

"If I screen all my calls and that reporter keeps getting my answering machine, I bet he'll give up and go away." She shook some chocolate shavings into her cappuccino and took a sip. It was delicious.

"After all, Brandon and I are hardly a hot story that warrants a zealous pursuit. It's not like either one of us is a movie star or TV or sports star. Those are the tabloids' prime targets."

"You would definitely be superceded if a movie star should get arrested or pregnant or if a TV star throws a tantrum and walks off a hit show," Flynt agreed dryly.

"Some celebrity somewhere will be sure to fall in love or break up with another celebrity. Or get married or divorced or sick. Or die. Then awful Kieran Kaufman and the rest of the tabloid pack will be hot on that trail. Brandon and I will be forgotten."

Angelica clinked her cup to Flynt's in a cheerfully irreverent little toast.

She shouldn't have been so quick to dismiss her apprehensions, Angelica lamented in the frenzied days that followed. Deluding herself into a state of misplaced optimism not only had been naive, but downright stupid.

The *Globe Star Probe* reporter did not leave Birmingham. And though Angelica continued to avoid all his calls, Kieran Kaufman reached Brandon, who admitted the truth of her parentage.

"I'm proud to have a daughter like Angelica, even though she doesn't want anything to do with her old man. And who can blame her? I've messed up my life, I'm a loser," Brandon mournfully told the reporter, adding a hopeful, "I just hope it's not too late to change."

The *Globe Star Probe* printed the quote and the story along with pictures, one of Angelica, snapped unawares as she left the hospital. The other photo was a glamorous retouched studio portrait of Brandon—perhaps supplied by him?

Angelica was upset but since the story was buried in the middle of the *Probe* and nobody she knew would admit to reading the tabloid, she anticipated little or no troublesome aftermath.

Once again she was to be proven wrong.

A singularly slow news week followed that particular

issue of the *Globe Star Probe*. No celebrity anywhere
did anything at all to attract tabloid attention. In fact,
nothing newsworthy seemed to be happening on any
front. Quiet reigned in the entertainment industry and in
politics. Not a single intriguing crime occurred. Even the
weather remained calm, with no horrific storms to provide diverting tales of survival and loss.

The *Globe Star Probe* sought to correct the dearth of
stories by nourishing the one they'd found in Birmingham. And as Kieran Kaufman explained to Brandon who
then told Flynt, the TV tabloid shows weren't averse to
bolstering their print counterpart by pumping up a prom-
ising story.

A TV crew for *Insider*, a popular but critically scorned
tabloid news show, arrived in Birmingham to accom-
pany Kaufman as he interviewed the loquacious Brandon
and a wary, reluctant Romina. Angelica refused to deal
with any reporters at all, and except for being occasionally ambushed by cameras, she was left alone.

And then Kieran Kaufman found Ike Searcy P.I., or
maybe it was the other way around. But it was the revelation of Romina's connection to the Fortunes, as the
mother of Brandon's child, that inspired Searcy's client
Ted Carson to file a hundred-million-dollar civil suit
against the Fortune Corporation.

The lawsuit accused the Fortunes of financially en-
abling Romina Carroll to aid and abet Darlene Carson's
custody violation and flight with the Carson children.

Suddenly the mainstream media was interested in the
story, sending reporters, camera and film crews to interview whatever Fortune they could corner in Minneapolis, as well as Brandon and Romina in Birmingham. The

top-rated network magazine shows expanded the story to include "secrets of the underground," a look at the "hidden world of women and children on the run."

The Fortune family was not pleased....

"We are being accused of subsidizing an underground network for fugitive mothers and their children in flagrant violation of custody laws?" Jake Fortune yelped during an urgent phone call to Flynt and Brandon. "What in the hell have you gotten us into now, Brandon?"

"Brandon hasn't done anything," Kate, on the other line for this conference call, said, defending her youngest son to her oldest.

"If it's not too much trouble, perhaps Flynt Corrigan, our man on the scene, could explain what is going on down there and why the media jackals have been unleashed on us this time?" Jake was sarcastic.

Flynt tried to explain about Brandon's alleged connection to Nancy Portland's underground network. "Romina might be involved—well, she undoubtedly is—but there is no tangible proof linking her to it, only circumstantial evidence that will never stand up," he added, quoting Weatherall the FBI agent.

"No one has been able to nail Romina for anything, though plenty have tried," Brandon boasted proudly.

"And, of course, there is no proof that Romina has financial ties to the Fortunes or ever had. Searcy and Carson's lawsuit will be thrown out," Flynt predicted.

Jake Fortune was not appeased. "But if a judge decides to throw the case to a jury, they just might decide all that lack of proof makes her look slippery and deceptive rather than not guilty. And if *she's* found guilty, *we're* guilty simply by association. It's the law of the jungle.''

"Even if the suit is thrown out, our team of lawyers will be tied up for weeks, filing motions and scheduling depositions," growled his brother Nate, on another extension.

"Meanwhile, we're faced with a barrage of negative publicity, not to mention the possibility of inspiring a horde of paranoid greedy crackpots to file their own lawsuits against us for whatever absurd reasons," Sterling Foster, on yet another extension, intoned glumly.

"So what should I do?" Brandon sounded downcast. "Come back to Minneapolis?"

"No!" Jake, Nate and Sterling all chorused so loudly that Flynt's ears rang.

"You stay down there with Angelica, Brandon, dear," Kate interjected diplomatically. "Getting to know your daughter is the most important thing."

"I didn't have the heart to tell your grandmother that Brandon isn't getting to know you at all," Flynt told Angelica later that afternoon, after the fractious phone call.

They were strolling in the rose garden next to the city library, enjoying the warm May sunshine. Angelica had a break between patient appointments, and Flynt was always ready to rework his own business-by-proxy schedule to take the opportunity to see her.

"Brandon isn't, but *you're* getting to know me pretty well," teased Angelica.

In spite of the media storm swirling, she felt almost

recklessly happy. Just being with Flynt affected her that way.

Besides, to her heartfelt relief, she seemingly had been relegated to footnote status in this latest Brandon saga.

"Yeah, I am," Flynt said huskily. He took both Angelica's hands and drew her toward him. "But not well enough."

He was feeling bold enough, hungry and desperate enough to kiss her right there, in a public place, in full view of anyone who happened to come along. He still wasn't sleeping very well, and when he finally did fall into a restless slumber, he experienced incredibly erotic dreams, all starring Angelica.

The risk of losing control and giving in to sexual implosion no longer seemed so threatening, so foolhardy. Flynt tried to remember why he'd thought holding back was the wise, safe course for them to follow.

He didn't want to be wise or safe, he wanted Angelica. More with every passing day.

Abandoning restraint, he touched his lips to hers, half expecting her to pull away. He knew she was uncomfortable with public displays of affection; she still blushed at any reference to their totally uninhibited PDA in Swank that first night.

To his surprise Angelica stretched up on tiptoe and leaned into him, letting her mouth linger lightly against his. Flynt's response was instantaneous. With a soft muffled groan, he crushed her to him, thrusting his tongue into the moist heat of her mouth.

She clung to him, her tongue meeting his stroke for stroke, wriggling to get closer. She couldn't seem to get close enough.

Flynt wove his fingers through her hair, pulling it away from her face to expose her neck. He began to nibble on the smooth, creamy skin.

"I want to be alone with you," he said huskily,

"We are alone…sort of." Angelica's heart was thundering in her ears. She touched the tingling spot on her neck. It felt moist and ultra-sensitive. She swayed a little, her legs weak and unsteady. "The park is practically deserted this time of day."

"You know what I mean, Angelica."

She knew. Shivering, she pulled away, turning her back to him.

Flynt closed his hands over her shoulders and kneaded. "I'm sorry, Angel. Not for kissing you, but for doing it here."

"Flynt, I—I didn't want to stop," she whispered, her voice taut and breathless.

It was a disturbing admission, one she'd never expected to make to any man. But Flynt wasn't just any man. Until she'd gotten to know him, she hadn't thought a man like him existed.

Flynt Corrigan was honest and direct and didn't resort to lies and deception to get what he wanted. He was a man who got angry but never went crazy with temper, a passionate man with control over his emotions. He was reliable and dependable, but understood fear and pain. Perhaps even better than she did, for she'd never had to deal with a loss as profound as a missing brother.

And for the first time in her life, Angelica could say with certainty that she knew a man who would never hit a woman or child. Why, Flynt would clobber any other man who did such a thing. She gazed at him, her dark eyes rapt.

Flynt smiled at her. "I didn't want to stop, either, Angelica."

"But you did…and—and you didn't whine about it, either."

He laughed at that. "I hope my whining days are over, Angelica." He glanced around the garden. "Thank God those sleazy snoops aren't here."

"When do you think they'll go away and leave us alone?"

"It should be soon, very soon." His hand glided to her nape and began a sensuous massage. "After all, there's nothing new to report here in Birmingham. It's already been revealed you're Brandon's daughter, and the link was made to Romina and the underground. Now Ted Carson and Nancy Portland and the fugitive mothers and children are the main story. What's left to say about you or Brandon?"

Flynt tried to remember the last time one of his predictions had turned out to be so totally wrong. It seemed his once-infallible instincts, so valuable to him in his career, were no longer sufficiently attuned.

At least not when it came to gauging media ability to extend and recreate a story, which in turn extended and recreated interest in the newer version of the original event.

There was, it seemed, plenty left to say about Angelica and Brandon.

Flynt had not anticipated the furor caused by young Casper Carroll's TV interview with an *Insider* reporter.

Nobody did, just as no one had thought to warn Angelica's little brother away from friendly reporters asking questions.

Kieran Kaufman had waylaid Casper on his way home from middle school, treated him to many quarters' worth of video games at the local arcade plus snacks, and the boy repaid his new friend by telling him all about the extortion notes threatening Angelica.

Casper was eager and willing to retell the whole story in front of the TV camera, supplying details with relish: the pasted-letters spelling out Angelica's possible grisly fate, the additional threat to frame Brandon for murdering his daughter unless "big bucks" were paid. The boy explained that the Fortunes had taken the threat seriously enough to send a bodyguard for Angelica—some ex-FBI agent—but no money had been paid.

Whether done deliberately or not, the story was ultimately transformed into a tale of the wealthy Fortunes disregarding the safety and well-being of poor, hapless Brandon's only child. The bodyguard Casper so briefly mentioned was dismissed, and Brandon's life story was rehashed again in histrionic detail.

The latest chapter had the powerful-but-heartless Fortunes willing to ignore the threat to Brandon's daughter, the child he had only recently been reunited with after years of not knowing she existed. Somehow the Fortunes ended up being blamed for that separation, too.

And there was more publicity to come. The day after the Casper interview aired, Sugar and her baby, Sawyer, surfaced on the local evening magazine show, PM Birmingham. Sugar—also known as Debra Dawn

Springer—related a melodramatic tale of the clandestine delivery of little Sawyer.

"Your role as midwife was mentioned, but the real hero of Sugar's story was Brandon," Flynt told Angelica who had missed the broadcast. "And by the way, Debra Dawn wasn't on the run from an abusive husband."

Flynt wished he hadn't tuned the show in either. His memories of Sugar—aka Debra Dawn—had been fond ones inspired by their time together during the delivery of baby Sawyer. It was disappointing to see the young mother attempt to interject herself into the current Fortune media circus.

"Brandon?" Angelica was incredulous. "The rest of the story doesn't make sense either. Who was Sugar, uh, Debra, running from? And why wouldn't she tell us her name that night?"

"She ran off because she'd had a fight with her boyfriend, Sawyer's father, because she wanted to date another man."

"She was nine months pregnant and she wanted to *date?*"

"I'm only repeating what she said on the program. Debra also explained that she wouldn't give her name because she sensed that Romina didn't want to know it. Of course Romina wouldn't want to know it, she makes a point of not knowing the names of women who are going underground."

Angelica shrugged. "I wouldn't know about that."

"Naturally not," Flynt murmured drolly. "But in this case, Debra Dawn had no intention of going underground. She took Sawyer and returned to her boyfriend. They're now living together, and the boyfriend is so understanding that he's agreed to baby-sit if she still wants to date other guys. And do you know who talked our Sugar into reconciling with her boyfriend for the sake of their child?''

''Not Brandon,'' Angelica guessed hopefully, though Flynt's description of him as the hero of the story was certainly inauspicious.

''Bingo.''

''That's impossible!'' spluttered Angelica. ''Brandon wasn't there that night, he doesn't even know the woman!''

''Of course not, but she recognized you and Romina and heard about your connection to Brandon and decided she'd been close enough to go for her own fifteen minutes of fame. Think about it, Angelica, it happens all the time. The nuts come out of the woodwork to bask in the spotlight, no matter how tenuous their link to the person starring in the current media circus.''

''So she just made up a story about Brandon to get on TV?'' Angelica groaned.

''You have to admit, she tied her story into the ongoing one fairly well. She has Brandon, the kid who was separated from his family as a child, the man whose child was separated from him, earnestly pleading not to keep a child away from its blood kin.''

''I can't believe the TV people fell for—for such a hoax!''

''Look at it from their point of view, Angelica. They have program hours to fill, nothing much of interest is happening anywhere, and this woman comes to them to talk about the only major news story going on at the moment. Of course they were receptive.''

"Do you think there will be others?" Angelica was appalled by the prospect.

Flynt didn't sugarcoat reality. "There is always that possibility as long as Brandon is in the news."

Two days later, as if to swing attention back to the extortion threat, which had been temporarily displaced by Debra Dawn and her son and Brandon's surprising role as the couples' therapist, Angelica received another note with the same pasted letters, the same ugly threats.

It had been shoved under her apartment door, and the implications were clear. Whoever intended to harm Angelica and frame Brandon had easy access to her residence.

With the alluring threat of murder and extortion to report, the national mainstream press reentered the story in full force. The Fortune family was again under siege, and Kate called Flynt to tell him that she'd just sent the corporate jet to Birmingham to fly Brandon, Flynt and Angelica to Minneapolis, where they'd stay with her and Sterling at the estate.

"I don't want to go to Minneapolis! I can't go! I won't!" Angelica wailed the moment Flynt told her of her grandmother's edict.

She offered a plethora of reasons. Her patients—one was due to deliver within the next two weeks and she couldn't possibly leave at such a crucial time. Her family—she couldn't abandon Romina and the kids to the media hoopla currently surrounding them. Her lack of fear—if Flynt would kindly return the gun he'd confiscated on his first visit to Romina's house, Angelica could protect herself against any letter-pasting jerk who made stupid threats.

And last but certainly not least, there was her unwillingness to meet the Fortunes.

"I don't even know them, but already I don't like them!" Angelica declared to Flynt and her mother, to her youngest sister and brother. To Mara and TJ. Even to Brandon on one of the rare times she encountered him at her mother's house.

"I kind of felt that way about them, too, at first," Brandon confessed. "But now I get along great with all of them. It'll be that way for you, too, Angel."

Nothing she said dissuaded anyone from the stand they'd uniformly taken. The Fortune corporation jet was arriving in Birmingham, and she was supposed to be on it for its return flight to Minneapolis.

"It's as if the whole world is conspiring to get me out of town!" Angelica told Flynt, and recounted how she'd been summoned into the office of the chief hospital administrator.

She was informed that two highly respected physicians in Minneapolis, Dr. Frank Todd and Dr. Stephen Hunter, had placed calls to the powers that be at MetroHealth. Angelica's patients were to be reassigned to obstetricians who assured her they were only stepping in on an emergency basis, that when it was deemed safe for her to return to the city, she could resume her midwifery practice.

"How dare those Minneapolis doctors interfere with me and my patients!" raged Angelica. "What are they, Fortune lackeys? Why would—"

"They're not lackeys, they're, uh, your relatives, Angelica," Flynt said. "Frank Todd is married to your aunt Lindsay, Brandon's twin, and Stephen Hunter is married to Jessica who is—well, she's sort of a fringe Fortune. Ben Fortune, your grandfather, had an affair while he was in England during World War II that produced Jessica's mother."

Angelica gaped at him, nonplussed. "This would be the same man who gave my father away to that deranged witch? He also had a child with another woman while he was married to my grandmother?"

"From what I've heard, those war years were pretty much an anything-goes time, Angelica."

"It seems like Ben Fortune was pretty much an anything-goes type no matter what the times were! My poor grandmother!" Angelica was irate on her behalf. "She and my mother could share their own war stories about their rotten luck with bad men."

Flynt tried to picture Kate Fortune sitting down with Romina Carroll to deplore their rotten luck with bad men. It was a mind-boggling scenario.

"Well, Kate is now married to a great guy named Sterling Foster," Flynt assured Angelica. "He was her longtime friend and the Fortune family's personal lawyer. The two of them are very happy. Of course, they'd be even happier if they knew you and Brandon were safe. You'd do that for them, wouldn't you, Angelica? Give an elderly couple peace of mind by—"

"Oh, stop! All that's missing is the violin music." She regarded him sternly. "Don't manipulate me, Flynt."

"Then don't make me have to resort to it, Angelica. Pack a bag and get on that jet."

She caught her lower lip between her teeth. "It's just that I don't feel like I'm in danger, Flynt. And I really don't want to go to Minneapolis."

He cupped her face in his big hand. "I know, sweetheart. But we can't take any chances with your safety. And I'll be with you, Angelica. I'm invited to fly back on the jet with you."

"You are?" For the first time, her voice, along with her defiance, wavered.

Flynt nodded. "You, Brandon and I are supposed to take off tonight."

"Tonight," Angelica repeated. She could tell by the determination in his eyes, by the set of his jaw that Flynt was prepared to continue reasoning or arguing with her, whatever it took to get her on that plane to Minneapolis tonight. Odd, but suddenly she wasn't prepared to rebut every statement he made.

Then again, maybe it wasn't so odd. From the moment Flynt said he was coming with her, her opposition to making the trip had begun to dissolve like sugar in a cup of hot tea. She had a feeling that if Flynt were with her, she would go anywhere, Angelica mused. Even to meet the Fortunes.

That gave her pause. "I'll have to discuss this with my mother. And Mara."

"By all means." He smiled and she tried to keep from melting. It wasn't easy. "I hope you'll decide that a temporary respite from Birmingham might not be such a bad idea."

"I'm not making any promises," she warned.

"Duly noted," said Flynt.

Chapter 10

Angelica had never been on a private jet before. She'd never been on any type of plane. The Carroll family's travels across the Southwest to Alabama had been by either bus or car. This was her first flight, and her pulses raced with excitement, despite her reluctance to leave Birmingham.

But after her talk with Flynt, followed by another with her mother, Mara and a few other friends at the hospital, she decided that a temporary respite from the city might not be such a bad idea. After all, her patients were in good hands, assigned to well-respected obstetricians; she'd personally called and spoken to each expectant mother, explaining the circumstances.

Flynt was on board the Fortune jet with her, watching her as she walked around the spacious cabin. It was furnished like a luxurious living room with supple-leather oversize chairs and thick carpeting. There was an entertainment center with a movie screen and VCR and an elaborate compact disc player with a storage tower of CDs and videotapes.

An opaque dark curtain separated a small bedroom and a bathroom from the living room area. At the other end was a galley complete with stocked cabinets, a refrigerator and microwave oven and a few other small kitchen appliances.

"You could live on this plane," Angelica marveled. "It's roomier and better decorated than my apartment."

"It's sure beats flying coach," Flynt said dryly.

A uniformed steward, who'd been busy in the galley when they boarded, came in to offer them wine and an assortment of hot snacks.

"Where is Brandon?" asked Flynt. "He left a message back at the hotel telling me to bring Angelica to the airport. He said he would join us on the plane." Flynt glanced at his watch. "He was supposed to be here fifteen minutes ago."

The steward chuckled. "We've learned that Mr. Brandon's sense of time doesn't necessarily jibe with the clock."

"In that case we might as well indulge." Flynt accepted a plate of food and a glass of chilled Chardonnay from the steward.

Angelica refused the refreshments. "How long do you suppose we'll have to wait for him?"

The steward shrugged. "I have no idea, Miss Angelica." He departed, leaving the snacks, the bottle of wine and an extra goblet for Angelica.

"No idea?" She knelt on one big chair and peered out the oval-shaped window. "It's starting to get dark.

Where do you think Brandon is, Flynt? What is he doing?''

"I have no idea, Miss Angelica." Flynt did a passable imitation of the laconic steward and reached for another mushroom cap stuffed with crab meat.

Angelica tried to divert herself with the selection of magazines in the tall oaken rack built into the wall. She should've been able to find something. Magazines covering every possible area of interest were available, from news to entertainment to business to fashion and health, and all the issues were current. But she couldn't concentrate on reading.

"Now he's over half an hour late." She stared from her watch to the window. "And there isn't a sign of him."

"This probably isn't a good time to tell you about the time Brandon was so late meeting me for lunch one day in Minneapolis, we ended up having to discuss the threatening note he'd just received at dinner instead."

Her dark eyes flashed. "If he doesn't arrive within the next half hour—"

"Why don't you find a movie we can watch?" Flynt cut in, before she could issue her threat to leave. "It'll help pass the time while we're waiting."

He poured himself another glass of Chardonnay and one for her, as well, handing it to her.

Angelica absently drank every drop. She was thirsty; the air felt dry in here.

"I don't feel like watching a movie." She flopped down onto the roomy leather armchair beside Flynt. "I'm sorry. I sound as fractious as Casper on one of his moody days. I'm just…"

She searched for the words to describe how she felt. Anxious? That would work. Disgusted with Brandon? Definitely. Scared to death because she was leaving home and flying to a northern city to meet a wealthy clan who lived in a world light-years removed from her own?

She thought about the Fortunes, who happened to be related to her but undoubtedly wished they weren't and wondered exactly how much they would resent her—a little or a great deal?

"I think I'll have some more wine." Angelica reached for the bottle and filled her crystal goblet to the top.

"This seat is more comfortable than any furniture I own." Flynt sighed appreciatively and settled more fully back in the wide chair. "I feel like kicking off my shoes."

"Let's." Angelica's dark eyes were glowing as she set down her empty wineglass. She removed her sandals and flexed her toes in the plush carpet.

Flynt slipped out of his well-worn boat shoes that he'd worn without socks in deference to the warm Alabama weather.

He looked at her toenails, neatly manicured and painted a rather stunning aqua shade. He smiled, amused. "Sarah's been giving pedicures again. She's still set on her future career as a nail technician?"

Angelica nodded. "I don't now how long it'll last. Sarah's past career choices have been a princess, a rock star, an astronaut and a marine biologist. Her nail career is the first one she's been able to practice for. And you should see the color she used on Mara! A hideous purplish black. Sarah called it 'goth.'"

"A shade favored by Dracula, no doubt. Thank God I didn't let Little Miss Sarah work on my feet. I can't believe TJ did." Flynt shook his head. "The poor guy will go to any lengths to make up for that search-and-seizure raid."

"But I think letting Sarah practice her skills on his toes actually did win TJ some points with Mama." Angelica laughed at the memory.

A short while later the steward appeared and asked them to fasten their seat belts, that the Fortune jet had to be moved from this particular gate. It was time for another plane that had been assigned to the gate to pull up for boarding.

The steward left them with an uncorked bottle of chilled Chardonnay, the same label as the one they'd just finished.

Angelica and Flynt complied and buckled themselves into their seats. The jet was already in motion.

"When Brandon finally gets here, he'll have to run all over the airport looking for the new gate." Angelica sighed. "That means an even longer wait because he'll have trouble finding it."

"True. Brandon is not the sharpest knife in the drawer," Flynt said resignedly. He poured each another glass of wine.

They clinked glasses as the plane backed up and made a turn. Angelica nearly spilled her wine. She laughed, then hiccuped. And laughed again.

"How many glasses have you had? And with no food." Flynt arched his brows. "I think you're about to be cut off, Angelica."

"I've had three glasses—or four? Now that you mention it, I do feel a bit of a buzz." She tilted her head. "Do you hear that whirring sound or am I *hearing* a buzz too?"

"I hear it." Flynt's eyes widened. The plane began to move faster. "I think...we're getting ready to take off?"

"What?" The seat belt restrained her from jumping to her feet. Angelica fumbled with the clasp, but Flynt reached over and took her hand.

"Leave it fastened, Angelica. We are taking off."

The plane sped down the runway.

"We can't take off. Brandon isn't on board!" cried Angelica, trying again to free herself from the seat belt.

Flynt's fingers closed over hers, preventing her from unclasping the buckle. "Honey, I've flown enough to know when we're about to take off, and we are. Right now."

At that moment the plane lifted off the ground and began to climb.

Angelica was stunned. "We left without Brandon?"

"It looks that way. Unless he stowed away in the cockpit. Or maybe he stuffed himself in the refrigerator."

"It's not funny, Flynt. What's going on?"

She posed that same question to the steward who reappeared a few moments later. Since he was walking around unrestricted, Angelica pushed Flynt's hand away and unbuckled herself.

She got up and went to peer out the window at the night sky and the lights sparkling on the ground below. They were in the air, all right, and were going higher.

"Why didn't we wait for Brandon?" she demanded. "Where are we going?"

"We're flying to Minneapolis, as planned, Miss Angelica," the steward said calmly. "As for leaving without Mr. Brandon—well, he called to say that he intended to remain in Birmingham and for us to take off without him."

"Brandon is staying in Birmingham?" Angelica's voice rose in a squeak. Her unexpected panic on hearing this news thoroughly confused her. She despised Brandon, so why would his non-appearance upset her so much? Bewildered and alarmed, she stared at Flynt.

Who was looking none too pleased with the steward's announcement.

"He told you he wasn't coming, and you listened to him?" growled Flynt. "I didn't think anyone employed by the Fortune Corporation took orders from Brandon."

The steward cleared his throat. "Well, the pilot did check with Mrs. Kate before taking off. She'd apparently already talked with Brandon and agreed that he should stay in Birmingham and Miss Angelica should go on to Minneapolis. May I get you anything right now or—"

"I want a parachute," Angelica said grimly. "Something weird is going on and I want off this plane."

"I think we're fine for now," Flynt assured the steward who swiftly departed back to his own small area.

Flynt stood up and joined Angelica at the window. He put his arms around her waist, clasping his hands to rest on her belly. "Don't be afraid, Angelica. You—"

"I've been hoodwinked!" She tried to wriggle away from him but he held firm and didn't release her. "And I'm not afraid, I'm furious!"

"At me?" Flynt nuzzled her neck.

Her eyelids drooped as she drew a shuddery breath as ribbons of sensual heat streaked through her. She forced her eyes open and tried to stiffen her already too-pliant body.

"Should I be, Flynt?"

"Absolutely not. I swear I expected Brandon to join us." Flynt ran his hands over her hips. She was wearing a neatly pressed khaki jumpsuit that fit her slender but curvy figure well. Very well.

"Then I'm not mad at you."

She gave up her half-hearted struggle against leaning into him and did exactly that, relaxing her body against his, her head lolling back against his chest, her bottom nestled in the hard cradle of his thighs. He was big and strong and he seemed to surround her completely.

But instead of feeling at risk and overwhelmed, she felt safe, protected. Flynt was the only man she had ever met who could comfort her, soothe away her anxiety. And right now he was her only ally in this strange new place she was being whisked away to.

She reached her hand up to stroke his cheek. "I'm glad you didn't decide to blow off the trip and leave me to face the Fortunes alone."

"Never, Angelica."

Flynt turned her around to face him. He gazed intently at her, his eyes drinking in the lovely features of her face. Her ivory-smooth complexion. Her luxuriant, almost ebony-black hair.

"You're so beautiful," he blurted, his voice suddenly hoarse with emotion.

"The Fortunes are going to think I'm trash."

Only to Flynt would she confess to feeling dread; she knew he wouldn't use her apprehensions against her. Her lower lip trembled a little, and she caught it between her teeth to still it.

Flynt stared, so turned on by the simple gesture that almost instantly his body was taut and straining.

"They can't, they won't, because you aren't, Angelica. You're as classy and elegant and smart as any Fortune anywhere."

"When you say it," she swallowed hard, her breathing quickening, "I can almost believe it."

"Believe it, Angelica. I wouldn't lie to you."

His hands were moving over her possessively, touching her everywhere, her breasts, her hips, her buttocks. She felt tension build inside her, swirling through her belly, making her nipples harden into tight little beads.

His erection surged against her, so male and foreign to her own body. So powerful. Yet no longer threatening but tempting instead.

Angelica felt oddly disoriented, as if her words, her actions—even her feelings—were being scripted, and she had been cast to play the assigned role. Which she did, with passionate urgency. Running her hands over his hard frame. Melting with sheer pleasure, quivering with excitement.

He covered her mouth with his and kissed her thoroughly. Angelica responded hotly, hungrily, need bursting within her like a flame swept by a gust of pure oxygen. All at once she was burning and shivering at the same time.

Her control faltered and then she willingly abandoned it, giving herself permission to tug at his blue chambray shirt, pulling it from the waistband of his jeans so she could slide her hands under to touch his skin. She was emboldened as she'd never been before, driven by her need to feel him, flesh on flesh.

When he lifted his mouth from hers, she nearly collapsed with frustration. She held on to the front of his shirt.

"No, Flynt." She hardly recognized her own voice. It was husky and velvety thick with desire. "This time we aren't stopping."

He ran his fingers through her hair, tousling it even more. "Angelica, you know how much I want you."

"I think I hear a 'but.'" Her heart jackhammered in her chest. She pressed her mouth to his throat and flicked her tongue against his skin, tasting him. "I hope not. I'd better not, Flynt." She looked up at him, her dark eyes fierce and desperate.

Holding her, Flynt slumped back against the wall of the plane, taking her weight against him.

"I just need to know that you know what you're doing, Angel. The wine…are you drunk? Because if you are…" His voice trailed off and he touched his forehead to hers. "I'd never hurt you, Angelica."

"Don't you think I know that?"

"Then tell me, Angel. Are you—"

"Drunk?" She moved sinuously against him. "No, Flynt, I'm not."

"Not even a little dizzy?"

His lips feathered hers in a series of light little kisses that were both stimulating and maddening because he wouldn't kiss her the way she wanted him to, deep and slow and intimate.

She did feel a little woozy, Angelica silently conceded, but she was sure it wasn't the result of the wine. If she was drunk, it was with desire.

"I'm dizzy because you're making my head spin, Flynt," she said.

At that moment, the plane encountered a patch of turbulence. Angelica clutched him for balance. They stood pressed together, holding on to each other until the plane was once again cruising smoothly.

She looked up at Flynt, laughter bubbling within her. Her head felt as if it was going to float right off her body. "That was exciting, like a ride at the county fair. Think it'll jump up and down like that some more?"

"I sincerely hope not. I make it a point to avoid rides that shake up your insides."

His eyes bored into hers. "But if it's excitement you're looking for… Ever hear of the Mile-High Club, Angelica?"

She could smell the wine on his breath as he spoke, and his intense, focused-solely-on-her gaze was as enthralling as the feel of his body against hers.

"I've heard of it." A rush of unexpected jealousy assailed her. "Are you a member in good standing, Flynt?"

"I've never been a member." His expression was challenging her now. Daring her, tempting her.

"Ever think of joining, Flynt?" She was deliberately baiting him and was pleased when he exhaled harshly.

"Not until this particular flight." His lips nipped playfully at hers. "What about you, Angel?" He unbuttoned her jumpsuit to the waist as he spoke, his fingers deft and quick. "Care to attain membership?"

She gasped as his hand brushed the smooth satin of her bra, then reached inside the cup to take her nipple and squeeze, his fingers, his touch exquisitely gentle.

A moan of quiet desperation sounded, and Angelica realized it had come from her. "Yes, Flynt." She heard a faraway voice, her own voice, whisper, "Please."

Her arms were around his neck, and he smoothed his hand over her hip, over the curve of her bottom and lifted her high, draping it over his hip. She'd barely had time to adjust to this provocative angle when he boosted her up.

Instinctively she wrapped both her legs around his waist.

"That's it," he said, his voice softly, sexily encouraging.

Savoring the intimacy of their position, craving even more, they kissed greedily, frantically.

Angelica felt her insides soften and melt in hot liquid waves. She felt heavy and tight. Confined by too many clothes. She wanted something she'd never before experienced, the sensation and the freedom of bare skin against skin.

Sensing her need, attuned to it, Flynt pushed aside the dark curtain and carried her into the small bedroom.

Once inside, he set her on her feet beside the bed. Her hands went to the buttons of his shirt and she began to unfasten them, her hands trembling. Flynt helped her after she'd fumbled with the first two. Working together, they managed to discard his shirt swiftly.

Angelica allowed herself the luxury of pressing her palms against the hard smoothness of his chest, running her hands over his heated skin. She traced the contours of his ribs, the shape of his nipples; her fingers followed the path of crisp dark hair arrowing down into his jeans.

Daringly she slipped her fingertips beneath the waistband.

Flynt inhaled sharply and went still. And then he trembled, uttering a deep groan. Angelica was enthralled with her power. She needed only to touch him, to hint at the possibility of more, and he went weak.

And then Flynt caught her nape and pulled her to him, kissing her with a demanding possessive urgency, and she realized that she was the weak one. The needy one. Wanting him in a way she had never experienced, but somehow intuitively knowing that she needed him inside her, to be a part of her.

He slipped the bodice of her jumpsuit off her shoulders, her arms, letting it fall to her waist. His hands cupped her breasts through her bra, holding them, testing their shape. The satiny fabric shifted and tightened, rubbing against her taut nipples, increasing their sensitivity even more.

Flynt brushed his thumbs lightly over them, and she whimpered as sensual electricity bolted through her. He continued to draw slow, almost leisurely circles, barely touching her, and Angelica arched forward, needing more.

His expression grew more intent and he traced the shadowy cleft between her breasts before unclasping the front clip of her bra. He quickly removed the soft snowy white garment and dropped it on the bed.

Her breasts were free and bared to him and he closed his hands over them, caressing and massaging as fire coursed through her. They kissed, and her breasts rubbed his naked chest, the erotic friction sending her higher.

She felt his lower body throbbing against her, and a powerful curiosity drove her to lay her hand against his belly. Her face was flushed with embarrassment mingled with need.

Her hesitancy cued Flynt to clasp her wrist and guide her hand lower.

Through the denim of his jeans, she felt him, his heat, his hardness. She impulsively flattened her hand against him and her fingers learned the shape of him, the weight and thickness.

Inspired, she tried to unbutton the top metal button of his fly. She couldn't do it and moved to the zipper. The same bad luck plagued her there.

"They're both stuck," she mumbled, exasperated.

Flynt gave a rumble of laughter. "Let me help you out here."

He rid himself of his jeans and navy cotton knit boxers in what seemed like a millisecond.

"You're good at this," she observed, feeing suddenly shy.

"At undressing myself? Well, I started early. I was about two, I guess."

"You know what I mean." Her temper flared. "You have no trouble at all undressing in—with—" She paused and heaved a sigh, unable to sustain that indignant flash. "You know what I mean, Flynt."

"I'm no bedroom Olympian, if that's what you mean, Angelica." He took her hand. "And I've never wanted a woman as much as I want you."

She wrapped her fingers around his rigid sex and felt the hot flesh pulsing.

Dazed, she was hardly aware as he slipped her jumpsuit over her hips, taking her underwear with it. They pooled around her feet, and he picked her up and deposited her on the bed.

Lying beside her, he took his time with her, exploring her curves, the hollows, the rounded softness, his hands tracing a path of heat that conversely made her shiver.

He splayed his fingers as his palm glided over her belly, his fingertips brushing the lush tangle of dark curls at the apex of her thighs. Their eyes locked.

She knew he was seeking her permission to continue, and she loved him for his consideration, for his willingness even now, at this crucial stage, to put her wishes before the powerful urge driving him.

She knew she would never have to be afraid of him using his strength against her, she loved the way he—

It took a moment for Angelica to catch up with her own thoughts.

She loved him!

She drew a swift, gasping breath. She'd said it in her mind yet the realization hadn't fully registered until this moment. She loved Flynt for his consideration, true, but for so much more as well.

She loved being with him, no matter where or when. She would've never thought it possible to actually enjoy a man's company—her beloved brother Danny excepted, of course—but she would rather be with Flynt than with anyone else.

Because they could talk about anything, even terrible things, and reach an understanding, because they shared the same sense of the ridiculous and could laugh together.

He was fun and intelligent and ambitious; she admired him. She didn't think it immodest to believe that he valued similar traits in her.

She had never thought of herself as looking for a man—that fabled female search for Mr. Right had always struck her as misguided—but Flynt had come into her life, anyway. And turned out to be the man she hadn't known she was waiting for.

I love you, Flynt, she thought. The words pounded in her head in rhythm with her heartbeat. She thrust her hips against him, and his probing fingers stroked her, finding her center.

She moaned as his touch became more insistent, bolder, exciting her beyond reason. Something shimmered and beckoned, something wild and fiery, and she closed her eyes, her head moving back and forth, reaching, reaching…

"Just go with it, Angel," he said. His voice urged her on, encouraging her. "I've got you. Let it happen."

She moved with him in counterpoint and her entire existence narrowed to pure sensation. Her body twisted and arched, in his control, out of hers, and she didn't care.

"Come on, sweetheart," he ordered, his voice a deep and sexy command. "I want you to."

She felt herself soaring, she felt wild and primal and free. She cried his name as she shattered, overpowered by rapturous release.

Angelica clung to him until the final fluttering contractions faded into a sweet glowing warmth.

She lay curled against him, feeling languid and liquid and utterly amazed.

He slowly withdrew his fingers and kissed her lips tenderly, lingeringly. Angelica opened her eyes and found him watching her.

She blushed. And felt a stunning urge to burst into tears.

"Angelica?" He stared at her more intently.

"I want you, Flynt." Her voice was raw and trembled with emotion.

She tangled her fingers in his hair and drew his mouth to hers. He rolled on top of her, and they kissed, lips parting, tongues teasing, tasting each other, relishing the flavor, the intimacy.

Lying beneath him, her thighs shifted and opened, making a place for him. Flynt felt the wet heat of her against him, and thought he would explode right then and there.

With a deep sigh, summoning up his considerable self-control, he moved away from her and sat up.

"Flynt!" She called his name, sounding confused and urgent and frustrated as hell.

He smiled. "Don't worry, honey, I'll be right back."

She lay still, too dazed to move. "Where are you going?" Her voice was tight with need as she watched him stand and reach for the dark privacy curtain.

"I have—something—in my bag. And I left the bag beside the chair in the cabin." He shook his head wryly. "And I damn well hope our friendly flight attendant doesn't make an appearance to offer us food or drink or he'll get an eyeful."

Angelica started to giggle, which shocked her. She

never giggled, not even back in her adolescence when girls were expected to giggle. She had always been too serious for giddiness. But she was giddy and giggling now, at the thought of the Fortune steward encountering a buck-naked Flynt.

Flynt disappeared for an instant and then returned with a small cardboard box.

"Did he—" she began, dissolving into laughter again.

"No, he didn't. Thank God!" Flynt's relief was heartfelt.

He sat down on the bed and opened the box of condoms.

She watched him lazily. "You came prepared for this, huh?"

"In answer to your *unspoken* question, no, I don't routinely travel with condoms in case I happen to get lucky." He arched his brows, watching her as he removed the small foil packet. And tore it open. "But I bought this box the day after I met you because I *knew* we would be together, it was inevitable at some point, and I wasn't going to take any risks with you."

He slipped on the latex sheath. "I care too much about you, Angelica. I hope you know that. I want you to know it."

She reached up and pulled him down to her. "Thank you, Flynt."

Her heart was in her eyes. She compared Flynt to those men who'd taken risks with her mother and then left her to face the consequences alone. There was no comparison. Before, she'd never believed that a man could care enough about a woman to want to protect her.

But now, loving Flynt, she believed it.

Flynt entered her slowly, sinking into her heat with a groan of pure pleasure. She was hot, tight, her body clenching around him.

"We fit together perfectly," he rasped, his mouth against her neck. "It's good, Angel, so good. I knew it would be."

Angelica kept her eyes tightly closed as her body adjusted to his. He'd described a perfect fit, but she felt stretched and painfully full....

He was kissing her and slowly, gradually, the discomfort began to fade. It was starting to feel good, being filled by him. A sigh escaped from her throat.

She smoothed her hands over the long expanse of his back and imagined telling Mara, "I'm in love with Flynt Corrigan." Mara would scream with glee; she'd always maintained that someday Angelica would fall in love. Angelica had been equally adamant that it would never happen.

"Sweetheart?" Flynt seemed aware that her mind was drifting. "Are you okay?"

She smiled and shifted a little. "I'm a lot better than okay."

He was right, it was so good. She loved the feeling of him deep inside her, taking pleasure in her body.

He slipped his hand between their bodies and touched her intimately. A spark shot through her, sending heat and pleasure to every nerve ending. She moaned.

Still stroking her, Flynt began to move, easing in and out of her in a slow sensual rhythm. She felt vibrations begin to pulse within her. He was taking pleasure from her body but giving it to her, too. More and more. She felt infused with fire, a torrid heat so intense, it glowed deep in her center.

Erotic, voluptuous sensations overwhelmed her. Her body sheathing his, the delicious friction as he thrust in and out of her. His lips against her skin. His muscular shoulders that she clung to. The smell of his aftershave mingled with his sweat, mixed with the heady aroma of sex.

He seemed to intuitively know when she needed more speed, more pressure, and gave her what she craved. He was right, she thought before her thoughts splintered into rapturous incoherence. They were perfect together.

She arched her back as wild spasms of pleasure rocked her; she felt his body coil as he emitted a low groan of harmony with her own muffled cries. His release came in a deep fast series of thrusts as her body melted and convulsed around his. Time seemed to crystallize as they surrendered to the sweet oblivion.

They drifted slowly back to reality, lying together on the bed, the drone of the plane's engine an oddly soothing background noise. Her arms and legs were wrapped around him, and she lifted her head to trail a path of delicate kisses along his jawline.

She loved the sensation of the two of them joined, forming one whole, intertwined and inseparable. She loved him.

''Wow.'' He cradled the back of her head with his hand.

Her eyes met his. He looked satiated and sexy and he grinned at her, sending a flush of heat straight to her core.

"Can I take that as a compliment?" She felt satiated and sexy.

"You know you can." He pulled her hair back in a ponytail, playing idly with it.

"Angelica..." All of a sudden, he sounded serious, as if he wanted to have a *discussion,* which undoubtedly meant something about Brandon.

Angelica pouted a little. "Flynt, I'm not in the mood for a serious discussion, particularly about my father."

She felt supremely content and wanted only to savor these intimate moments. Their bodies merged, their limbs tangled, the exquisite exhaustion of spent passion.

Flynt wondered if she'd realized that she referred to Brandon as her father more and more, signaling her own subconscious acceptance of his paternity. He decided this wasn't the time or place to make that point. She wasn't in the mood for a serious discussion.

"Does this mean you don't want to talk about the Fortunes? Because there are things you should know, Angelica."

He slowly withdrew himself from her body.

"I'm sure there are." She sat up and caught his hand, drawing him back to her. "And it won't be long before I'll know more about the Fortunes than I ever wanted to, I'm sure of that, too. But right now let's have a moratorium on anything Fortune."

He put aside his intention to tell her about his pending-and-certain-to-be-activated SMS contract with the Fortune Corporation. Did it really matter, anyway?

"Anyway, discussing business pales in comparison to making love with you." He pulled her into his arms and kissed her.

It was a long time and many kisses and caresses later before they briefly resurfaced.

"I like making love with you, too," she confided breathlessly. She groped in the darkness for the box of condoms that had been dropped somewhere on the bed. She couldn't find it, and when he pulled her on top of him, she completely forgot to search again.

She forgot everything but the incredible pleasure of Flynt's body beneath her own. "I want you to make love to me again, Flynt." She trailed biting little kisses along his jawline, her hands stroking him.

Flynt's head was spinning; his body taut with need. But his primary concern was for her. "Are you sure you feel up to it, sweetheart?"

She laughed wickedly. "I think that's more applicable to you." And caressed him intimately. "And you are most definitely up to it."

She felt his hands on her breasts, his long fingers stroking her, and gave herself up to the incredible sensations rolling through her. Her legs flexed deeply and waited, open and vulnerable, for his body to merge with hers.

They made love more leisurely this time, playfully, almost light-heartedly. It was passionate and thrilling and wonderful in a new and different way. They moved together slowly, easily, until the fiery currents of pleasure built and burned hotter, and they climaxed together in an incandescent explosion of pleasure.

"For a novice, I'm pretty good at this," Angelica murmured later, as she cuddled against him, feeling such bliss.

"How much of a novice?" Flynt's hand, which had

been caressing her back, stilled. "Never mind, you don't have to answer that. I shouldn't have asked."

"I'm so much of a novice I don't mind the question. I—I was—I hadn't—" She swallowed, suddenly nervous.

What if her virginity upset him? There was a chance of that, she knew, because Danny had once confided to her that he avoided virgins; they scared him. It was a little late now to find out if Flynt shared her brother's anathema. She shouldn't have brought the subject up, and berated herself as very much a novice for doing so.

"You're my first lover, Flynt." Angelica tensed, waiting for the possible repercussions. "I know that's probably unwelcome news but—"

"Sweetheart, it's welcome news," he said quickly. He kissed her tenderly, lingeringly, then held her close and tried not to dwell on the enormous implications of being Angelica's first lover.

It was a first for him too, being someone's first lover, and that the woman should be Angelica was all the more overwhelming to him because he cared so much about her. Right now they were so close, so attuned he couldn't imagine it ever being otherwise.

But just like a soundtrack in a movie, every doubt he'd ever had about permanency in relationships played in the background of his mind. How many other couples had experienced harmony, only to set about destroying it? He had watched it happen with his own parents.

"Some men don't want to deal with the responsibility of a woman's virginity." Angelica sighed softly as Flynt stroked her hair. "But I should've known you would be understanding, Flynt."

"I'm not some anonymous man and you're not some anonymous woman," he chided her gently. "This is you and me, Angelica." He was not about to inflict his doubts on her; she didn't deserve that. Not now. She needed reassurance and tenderness and he could provide that for her. He wanted to.

"I needed to be reminded of that." She nuzzled his neck. "Sometimes I tend to generalize."

"You?" he joked drolly. "Never!"

"Okay, I admit it. Generalizing is a habit of mine." She laughed a little, feeling languid and mellow and so very close to him. "But it's not fair to you, Flynt, because you are unique." Her voice grew thick with emotion. "I've never known a man like you."

"And I never dreamed there could be a woman like you, Angelica." Flynt shifted her in his arms, tilting her chin upward to brush her mouth with his. He ran his hands over her, loving the feel of her supple curves, the warmth of her smooth skin.

"I'm proud to be your first lover, sweetheart. So proud and so happy. The way I feel about you…" He tried to find the words but it was difficult to speak when Angelica was moving so sinuously against him.

She thrust her hands into his thick hair and molded herself to him, kissing him with unreserved passion. The kiss went on and on until they were both breathless.

Flynt tucked Angelica into his side, spoon-fashion, and they lay together, savoring the quiet peace. He made another attempt to describe the feelings welling within him.

"Angelica, I want you to know what I feel for you…the way I feel about you…" Flynt heaved a sigh

"I'm trying to be eloquent and original, and all I can come up with is that—I've never felt this way about any other woman, Angelica."

Angelica treasured his halting declaration. "That sounds eloquent and original and—and beautiful to me, Flynt."

She instinctively knew what he meant: that he was in love with her. She even understood why he didn't say "I love you" to her, because she shared the same inhibitions about saying it to him.

It didn't matter. When the time was right, they would say the words aloud to each other. For now, they would remain unspoken.

Chapter 11

A limousine was waiting at the airport to take Angelica and Flynt to the Fortune mansion, bordering on Lake Travis. As the chauffeur drove the limo slowly along the long driveway, Angelica stared at the huge white colonial-style house ahead, with its verandas and French doors and expanse of meticulously landscaped lawns and gardens. Even in the dark, the place looked impressive.

"Kind of takes your breath away, huh?" Flynt murmured.

Angelica made no response.

His arm was around her. She was very quiet, resting her head on his shoulder, her hand on his thigh, so silent and still that at times Flynt thought she had fallen asleep.

But a swift glance at her face revealed her big dark eyes, open and taking in everything around her: the lush upholstery of the Fortune Corporation limousine, its wet bar, small television set and music console.

But Angelica and Flynt had passed on the offer of liquid refreshment. He'd made a small joke about wine and she flashed a sly grin, the only time she had smiled since the jet touched down in Minnesota.

They traveled through the city, then into the tree-lined suburbs, finally entering a visibly exclusive enclave of gated grounds whose houses were out of sight from the road.

Angelica reached for Flynt's hand and gripped it tight, her fingers icy, a tangible sign of how nervous she was.

"It's going to be okay, Angel," he said softly, caressing the top of her head with his lips. Her hair felt soft and silky and smelled of an alluring, fresh-scented shampoo. "You'll like your grandmother Kate, I know you will, and she is going to love you."

"This place is an *estate,* and I don't like elitist palaces," Angelica said disparagingly. "I don't want to stay here. Only a couple months ago I would've been arrested if I'd dared to set foot on this property—or worse. That guard probably has orders to shoot intruders on sight."

"Look, Angelica, I know what's going on with you, you're covering anxiety with attitude. But you don't have to do that with me, honey, you—"

"Flynt, save the psych stuff for the FBI profilers, okay?"

He thought of her unguarded moments, when she'd been totally candid with him on the plane and doubted he would be seeing any more of that. She'd reverted to being Romina's daughter, in full attack mode.

Flynt heaved a sigh. "Does this mean you're going

to hate the Fortunes on sight, so they can't hate you first?''

She stiffened but made no reply.

''Keep in mind that if you arrive with chips on both your shoulders, you will also be denying them the chance of liking you, Angelica.''

''I'll keep that in mind, Flynt.''

She sounded sarcastic and bratty, and Flynt felt a pang of sympathy for Kate and the Fortunes awaiting her. First Brandon, now Angelica. It seemed the clan was in for another rocky ride, as far as reunions went.

The limousine pulled to a stop in front of the house. In her current mood, Angelica reached for the door handle to open it and hop out. Flynt held her firm, making her wait for the driver to perform the task.

''Don't make things worse, Angelica,'' Flynt muttered, boldly nipping her neck.

''Things can't get any worse!'' she wailed and went limp against him.

But only for a second. By the time the driver had opened the door and announced their arrival, she was holding her head high, in complete command. She permitted the driver to assist her from the limousine.

Flynt stared at her, amused. She looked as regal as a princess on a royal tour. He stood beside her, taking her elbow, unable to suppress a smile. Was this the way a commoner-consort felt?

''Angelica!'' Kate Fortune, elegant in blue, hurried toward them.

She stopped in front of the pair, and tears filled her eyes. ''Brandon's child! My own granddaughter! How

I've been longing to meet you, my dear." She threw her arms around Angelica in a spontaneous hug of welcome.

Angelica didn't pull away. Despite her avowal to reject anything Fortune, it struck her as churlish to physically repel her own grandmother. Slowly she raised her arms to tentatively embrace the older woman.

"I'm so glad you could come to visit us, darling." Kate draped her arm around Angelica's shoulders and started walking her toward the open door of the house.

Lights blazed within.

Angelica threw a panicked glance over her shoulder at Flynt. She might be decades younger, but her grandmother was taller and had a grip that felt strong as steel. Suddenly, vividly, Angelica recalled feeling this same apprehensive helplessness as a very small child, when Romina was dropping her off at day care.

"Come on, Flynt." Turning, Angelica called to him. The moment he took her hand in his, that sickening anxiety lessened. And almost completely dissolved.

Kate watched the couple with interest. "How was the flight? I hope everything was convenient and comfortable for you."

Angelica and Flynt exchanged glances. She quickly looked at the ceiling of the overhang that extended down to protect the front porch from the outside elements. Her dark eyes sparkled. He stared at the ground, a flush spreading across his cheekbones.

"Yes, um, the flight went well, Kate." Flynt managed to choke out the words.

"Everything was convenient. And comfortable," Angelica added in a good-little-schoolgirl tone that made him want to laugh and to strangle her at the same time.

He shot her a warning look; she gave him a provocative one.

"I'm delighted to hear it." Kate's interest turned to fascination as she observed the two. "I do hope you don't mind that Brandon canceled at the last minute. He called to say he had some personal matters to attend to, and we agreed that the plane should leave as planned."

"Personal matters," Angelica repeated, looking at Flynt. "I wonder what personal matters would keep *Dad* in Birmingham?"

"Behave yourself, Angelica," Flynt growled in her ear as Kate stepped ahead of them to enter the house.

Angelica responded with a try-to-make-me challenge in her eyes.

Flynt was both aroused and annoyed. He didn't dare do what he most wanted, to pick her up and haul her off to ravish her. Angelica ran her thumb seductively over his palm, and he knew they were on the same wavelength. Too bad they were in her grandmother's house, a most prohibitive factor.

"Welcome home, Angelica, darling," Kate said happily as Angelica and Flynt stepped inside the spacious vestibule. "I want you to always consider this your home and to come and stay as often and as long as you like."

Despite her intention to remain guarded and cynical, Angelica was touched by the sincerity in her grandmother's voice, by the warmth in her eyes and smile. She didn't doubt for a moment that Kate's offer was genuine. "Thank you," she said quietly.

"The whole family is eager to meet you, but I persuaded them not to come over tonight," continued Kate.

"After all, it's late and you've had a busy day, including the long flight here. I'm sure you would prefer to simply relax, without any further demands tonight."

Angelica breathed a sigh of relief. "I am tired."

Taking on the entire Fortune tribe tonight would've consumed an excess abundance of energy and confidence, and she was already reeling from the events of this monumental day. She needed time to process what she'd experienced tonight, from making love with Flynt to acknowledging her love for him.

And then there was the perplexing, monumental question of where did they go from here? What happened to people in love? A chill ran through her. She'd always believed she knew the answer to that one: a couple inevitably parted because love was an illusion that didn't last. But what she felt for Flynt was no illusion; it was real, and she couldn't imagine herself changing her mind about loving him.

She remembered what Flynt had said about love—that he didn't believe in it, either. His mother and father had stopped loving each other after they had suffered the unbearable tragedy of losing their small son and had pushed each other away, choosing to grieve alone.

But when she and Flynt were hurting, they had come together, not pushed each other away, Angelica mused. She thought of her many years with her mother, through all the men and the babies and the abandonments. She and Mama had chosen to stick together; she and her brother Danny had never turned on each other when things got hard, either.

Mama said it was because they were blood kin, that blood was the strongest bond, but Angelica knew that wasn't always true. Her own grandparents were a case in point. One set had turned their backs on their teenage daughter forever; her Fortune grandfather had betrayed his wife and given away their child. Hardly sterling examples of blood kin loyalty!

With her lifelong tenets turned inside out, Angelica allowed herself to consider the most radical concept of all. Wasn't it possible that a man and a woman could choose to stay together instead of going their separate ways when trouble struck, just as some blood kin chose family loyalty in adversity? That loving and not loving were *choices* that couples made. What if she and Flynt were to choose to keep on loving each other?

The insight resonated within her. She could do it, she decided, she could choose to keep loving Flynt, just as she'd chosen to love her mom even through the most exasperating times. The big question was this: would Flynt choose to keep loving her? She remembered what he had said the first time he'd told her about his parents' reaction to the loss of poor little Mark, that they'd split because the couple reminded each other of pain and loss. Angelica winced.

"Would you like to see the house or go directly to your room, dear?" asked Kate.

Angelica saw her grandmother studying her intently, almost knowingly. It was oddly comforting and somehow made her feel accepted.

Quite suddenly she revived, her curiosity trumping her confusion and fatigue. "I can't be in such an amazing place without seeing it. I would like to take the tour, please."

"The tour?" Kate laughed. "Gracious, that sounds like we're on a visit to Mount Vernon."

"I've been to Mount Vernon," said Flynt. "George Washington aside, this place is nicer."

Still clutching Flynt's hand, Angelica followed Kate through the wide hall, gazing around her. She'd seen historical mansions on TV that paled in comparison to this place. Antique furniture, Oriental rugs, beautiful paintings, vases that were works of art themselves, filled with fresh flowers in every room. Some rooms were devoted to special interests: the sizable library, the music room, the billiard room, among others.

"This could be a setting for a real-life game of *Clue*," Angelica whispered giddily to Flynt. "Can't you see Colonel Mustard whacking Professor Plum over the head with the candlestick in the study?"

"In the Fortune version of the game, the culprit could be Sheila Fortune, your uncle Nate's ex-wife, using a poisoned jeweled dagger at a costume ball in the ballroom. I only met the woman once, but she had a real flair for drama and vindictiveness," Flynt murmured dryly.

Angelica was overwhelmed by it all. "I just can't imagine living in a place like this."

"Well, unless you plan to move in with your grandmother, you won't be, Angelica. You're still Romina's daughter who lives and works in Birmingham, Alabama."

Flynt glanced at Kate, saw her attention was directed to adjusting the blooms in a flower arrangement, and seized the moment to kiss the delicate underside of Angelica's wrist.

Arousal and affection surged through her. Flynt had said exactly what she needed to hear. He understood her in a way nobody else ever had, and she loved him for it. Really loved him.

The tour completed, Kate looped her arm through her granddaughter's. "Before I take you to your room, you must meet Sterling."

Kate led the way up the grand staircase to the master bedroom suite where Sterling Foster sat smoking his pipe and reading.

Introductions were polite and swift, then Kate took Angelica to a well-appointed bedroom with an adjoining bathroom. The room was a veritable garden of violets and ivy, the wallpaper perfectly coordinated with the quilt and pillow shams, the curtains and armchair-and-ottoman set. Long-stemmed fresh flowers in a decorative vase scented the room with their subtle fragrance.

Angelica stared around admiringly. Despite the decorator perfection, the room had a homey feel. She felt comfortable rather than intimidated in it. Her luggage had already been placed in the room, and she noticed Flynt's bag among hers.

She was still holding tightly onto his hand. She didn't want him to leave her, Angelica acknowledged achingly. Not only because he was a comfortably familiar presence in the alien Fortune mansion, but because he *belonged* with her.

They were a team. And after their intimacy on the plane earlier, she couldn't imagine spending tonight alone in that big king-size bed. The prospect was simply intolerable. She knew what she would be missing without Flynt. Beside her, inside her.

Angelica blushed at her own lusty imagination. But it inspired her to blurt out, "Uh, Grandmother, would you mind if Flynt stayed a little while to—to explain the home security system my mother is thinking of buying for her house?"

Her blush deepened. "We were discussing the pros and cons of the different systems on the plane but didn't have a chance to, um, well, go into specific details. You and Sterling don't have to wait up or anything. Flynt can let himself out. Can't you, Flynt?"

Flynt glanced from Angelica who appeared embarrassed but determined, to Kate who looked ready to burst into laughter.

Kate spoke up before he could reply. "Of course Flynt can let himself out. Yes, you must certainly finish your discussion. And now Sterling and I shall retire for the night. Our suite is on the other side of the house, so Flynt needn't worry about disturbing us. We can't hear a thing over there." Her eyes danced.

She patted Flynt's arm and leaned over to kiss Angelica's cheek. "I'm so glad you are here, my darling. And thank you for calling me Grandmother. It means more to me than you'll ever know. I'll leave you to your discussion now."

Kate left the room, closing the door behind her.

"Did I call her Grandmother?" Angelica looked quizzical.

"Yes, you did. In the same sentence that you demoted me to security alarm salesman. Tell me, do I sell my product door-to-door or do I rely on telemarketing to make a sale?"

Angelica tilted her chin and held it high. "You don't. have to stay if you don't want to."

"Do you really think I'd pass up a chance to discuss home alarm systems with you? Especially after our stimulating discussion on the plane?" Flynt scooped her up in his arms.

Angelica gasped, then laughed and linked her arms around his neck.

He carried her to the bed and placed her on top of it. "Now where were we?"

She was already unbuttoning his shirt. "I don't remember. We'll have to start all over again."

"With pleasure, my Angel." He kissed her deeply, intimately and primitively, as if she belonged to him.

Her every feminine instinct gloried in his strength, and her submission was sensuous and sweet and totally fulfilling.

Immediately after saying good-night to Angelica, Kate returned to the master bedroom suite and called her son.

"Angelica has arrived safely, Brandon. She's such a lovely girl. You must be very proud of your daughter."

"I am."

Romina's voice sounded over the phone. "Hi, Kate, I'm on the upstairs extension."

"Hello, Romina dear," Kate greeted her. "I simply can't say enough wonderful things about the darling daughter you've raised."

Sterling dropped the paperback he'd been reading and gaped at Kate. He mouthed the name "Romina?" but Kate merely gave him a small wave and continued singing Angelica's praises over the phone.

"I've noticed that Angelica is...quite close to Flynt Corrigan," Kate said, directing a meaningful look Sterling's way.

"That has me worried," said Romina. "They've been inseparable since he came to town. Angelica's never been like that with any man. If he dares to hurt my Angel—"

"He'd better not!" Brandon chimed in. "What if he does, Mom?" he added, his certainty dimming somewhat.

"I don't know why Flynt would want to hurt Angelica," said Kate, attempting to reassure the pair on the other end of the line. "He seems equally besotted with her."

"So that's what they're calling it these days?" Brandon laughed, but it was his cynical, jaded, seen-and-done-it-all laugh, the one that depressed Kate because it underscored the corrupt life-style Brandon had been raised to lead.

"My Angel doesn't sleep around," Romina snapped, instantly defensive.

"Romina, my dear, nobody was insinuating such a thing," Kate reassured her.

"Brandon was!" gritted Romina.

"Angelica is *my* kid, too," Brandon said, a bit more forcefully. "So I decided I'd better look out for her like a dad should. And she *is* sleeping with Flynt, if that's what you want to call it. 'Course, neither of them got any *sleep* on that flight tonight."

There was a speaking silence from both Kate and Romina.

"I know for sure that Angelica and Flynt are, er,

sleeping together because the steward told me about the evidence he found in the bedroom on the plane.'' Brandon's voice rang with triumph as he told them what the steward had found while tidying up after the flight. ''A box of condoms under the bed.''

''That creep called you and told tales about my baby?'' Romina was incensed.

''I'm appalled by such indiscretion!'' Kate said, coldly disapproving. ''The steward shall be fired immediately. I am going to personally place the call the moment we hang up.''

''No, no, don't do that!'' cried Brandon. ''It's not his fault, Mother. I gave him a big tip in advance to check up on Angelica and Flynt, to tell me—you know, whatever he could about them. Romina and I both know how unreliable men can be, and if Corrigan's messing with my kid, I wanna know about it so I can—I can—''

''So you can what, Brandon?'' Kate demanded.

''Can't I get his legs broken or something like that?'' Brandon muttered sheepishly.

''Of course not!'' Romina shouted. ''And you didn't tip that steward, you *bribed* him! You bribed him to spy on our own daughter, Brandon Malone!''

''Romina is right, Brandon,'' Kate interjected. ''It was a reprehensible invasion of Angelica's privacy.''

''I am Brandon *Fortune* now, Romina,'' Brandon said, an unaccustomed note of dignity in his voice. ''And I'm trying to get the father bit down right. You said not to force my company on Angel, and I didn't. I hardly ever saw her! And I've been good with Casper, you said so yourself. Remember, Romi?''

''Well, yeah,'' agreed Romina, suddenly, headspinningly amiable. "Kate, he's been great with my twelve-year-old. In fact, I don't know what I'd've done without him because Angel's been so busy, and I really couldn't tell her, anyway, because what he did was so awful that I was just sick about it. Thank God, he was here. And thank you too, Kate, for sending him down to me."

"I wasn't any use to my own kid, but I could relate to Casper, Mom," said Brandon. "If anybody knows what it's like to be messed up and twelve, it's me. I think I've been acting messed up and twelve for twenty years."

"I'm afraid I'm not following, my dears," Kate said gamely. "When you reach my age, you need to have things clearly spelled out for you. It is so very tedious. So, if you wouldn't mind telling me everything, from the beginning, and—not use any pronouns?"

"We'll be glad, too, Kate," Romina said eagerly. "And then, maybe you could sort of help us figure out what to do?"

"I'll do anything I possibly can to help," Kate promised.

"'When you reach your age, you have to have things clearly spelled out for you'?" Sterling repeated later, after the phone call had ended. "Your mental acuity is as sharp as ever, Kate. On the other hand, a linguistics scholar would have difficulty deciphering Brandon at times. And am I suffering from a spell of dementia or did I hear you having a conversation with *Romina,* while you were on the phone with Brandon?"

"You are not suffering from dementia any more than I have to have things clearly spelled out for me—that is,

unless it's a conversation with Brandon and Romina."
Kate smiled. "It's true, Sterling, Romina and I have established a rapport over the telephone. Brandon has been spending almost all of his time with her, and during one of his phone calls to me, he asked if I would like to talk to Romina. Naturally, I said yes."

"You've always been inordinately brave, Kate," Sterling said drolly. "On the proverbial scale from one to ten, just how bad is she?"

"Romina can be…volatile…and opinionated, but she's tried to be a good mother. Actually, she's quite concerned with all children, which led to her controversial involvement in that fugitive underground in the first place."

"Controversial? Kate, my love, when one interferes with custody laws, the word to use is *criminal*. And she's dragged us into the mire of liability along with her. Our legal team is hard at work filing motions to dismiss that excessive civil suit brought against us by the vengeful Mr. Carson. Keep in mind it was Romina's tie to Brandon that made the Fortune Corporation a target in the first place."

"*You* must keep in mind that Romina's tie to Brandon happens to be their daughter, my precious grandchild. Besides, I think that Romina is good for Brandon."

Kate gazed thoughtfully out the window, staring at the now-tranquil waters of Lake Travis. "Brandon is thinking of someone other than himself. I believe he genuinely cares for her and her children."

"Are you sure Brandon went to Alabama and not Lourdes? That's supposed to be the place for miracles." Sterling chuckled at his own joke.

Kate did not. "Unfortunately, there is also some…less pleasant news." She turned to face her husband. "You see, Brandon has run into something of a problem while—"

"Forget a miracle personality change, Brandon remains the same, after all." Sighing, Sterling closed his book and stood up. "That's what all the whispering at the end of your call was about, am I right, Kate? Well, what's Brandon done this time?"

"Calm down, darling. It's not what Brandon has done. This time the problem involves Romina's youngest son, Casper. He's something of a troubled child who—"

"Now Brandon is bringing a troubled child into our midst? His former girlfriend's troubled child?" Sterling searched for his antacid tablets. "Wait until Jake and Nate and the others hear this. The squawking will be unparalleled." He quickly chewed two tablets and offered some to Kate.

She accepted.

Sunlight filtered into the violet and ivy bedroom through a small gap in the curtains. It was angled in such a way as to bathe Angelica's face in light bright enough to wake her up.

Her eyes snapped open, and she was instantly alert. She never hovered in the groggy realm between sleep and wakefulness, and this morning was no exception. She knew where she was—and who she was with—the moment she awakened.

She was lying in Flynt's arms in the middle of the king-size bed in her grandmother's house. Kate Fortune's mansion, Angelica quickly corrected herself.

A glance at the bedside clock caused her to bolt upright and gasp aloud. "It's nine o'clock! I never sleep this late."

Flynt's eyes flew open. "Uh-oh!"

He threw back the covers and sprang from the bed, snatching up his clothes that had been strewn around the room last night when he and Angelica had playfully, lovingly, undressed each other.

"I can't believe it!" He heaved a groan, pulling on his shirt, a sock, shoving one leg into his jeans. "We were just lying there talking, we must've fallen asleep."

Angelica watched him. He was upset enough for both of them, freeing her to view the situation—and his frantic attempts to get dressed—with humor.

"That's just what we can tell my grandmother—that we fell asleep during our home security alarm system discussion. It sounds plausible, the subject is boring enough to induce a coma. And then we can add, 'much to our surprise, when we woke up it was morning'."

"I'd only planned to stay until you fell asleep last night." Flynt was dressed now, albeit rather sloppily put together. "Then I was going to call a taxi and leave."

Angelica stretched her arms over her head, causing the sheet to slip below her breasts, baring them. "I'm glad you didn't go, Flynt. I liked sleeping with you. Literally and figuratively."

Flynt's hands stilled on the buttons of his shirt and he stared at the alluring picture she presented. It took great effort to resume buttoning. "Angelica, I respect you and your grandmother too much to—well—to—"

She rolled onto her side, propping her head on her hand. "Too much to make love to me?"

Flynt frowned. "Honey, we're under Kate's own roof, and we shouldn't have—" Heat flashed through him. "Oh hell, I might as well be honest, I wouldn't have passed up last night with you for anything."

She smiled seductively, nodding. "I feel exactly the same way."

"But I should've stayed awake and left here last night," Flynt reproved himself. "Instead of putting you in an awkward position by being here this morning."

"There is nothing awkward about any position you put me in, Flynt," she teased.

"Let me rephrase." He was smiling despite his consternation. "I don't want to embarrass you or your grandmother by being here this morning. So I'll try to slip out of the house undetected. I can hike to the nearest phone booth and call a taxi or catch a bus or something."

"Well, this place is big enough to be a hotel, so you probably can sneak out without being seen. But not yet." Angelica extended her arm, holding out her hand to him. "Why don't you kiss me good morning, Flynt?"

Flynt was unable to resist her. He sat back down on the edge of the bed. "Good morning, Angel." He took her into his arms and they kissed, a long passionate lovers' kiss.

Reluctantly he moved away from her, and she shivered at the loss of his body heat. "Cold?" he asked huskily.

"A little." She rubbed her arms with her hands. "It's chilly up north, especially compared to Birmingham this time of year."

Flynt wrapped the sheet around her and pulled her

close again, enfolding her in his arms. "Is this better?" His lips nibbled hers.

She nodded dreamily. "Much better."

The nibbling led to more kissing. Both were so absorbed in each other that neither heard the footsteps in the hall or the doorknob turn or the bedroom door open.

But Romina's scream, which seemed to reverberate through the entire house, was too loud and too shrill to disregard. Flynt and Angelica jumped apart.

She lay back in bed and pulled the covers over her head; he crossed the room to stand in front of the window. He considered leaping out. It wasn't all that far from the second story to the ground.

"You seduced my baby!" Romina shrieked.

Angelica lowered the covers to her chin. "Mama, it isn't like that at all. We—"

"And you!" Romina directed her wrath at her firstborn. "You hop into bed with—with some guy in your grandmother's house on the very first night that you met her! She must think you're a little tramp who wasn't raised to know any better."

"I am not 'some guy,' Romina," Flynt spoke up. "Angelica and I are—"

"I know Angelica isn't a tramp," Kate cut in. "I understand how compelling passion can be when a couple is young and in love, and it is obvious to me that Angelica and Flynt are very much in love."

"In love or not, they're getting married before the baby arrives," cried Romina, "I refuse to let one of my children ever have an illegitimate baby."

"Baby?" Flynt was flummoxed. "What baby?"

"There's no baby," Angelica said quickly.

"That's what *I* said in the beginning, all four times that I was pregnant." Romina's dark eyes were blazing as she paced the room. "What about last night on that plane?"

Angelica and Flynt looked at each other, too stunned to speak. A shocked awareness hit them at the same moment, as they each remembered that second shattering time they'd made love on the plane.

Angelica recalled looking for the condom box... which she'd never found. Flynt realized that he hadn't given a thought to protection that time, he had been agog with the knowledge that he was Angelica's first lover.

His jaw dropped. But how did Romina know what had happened between them last night?

Both his face and Angelica's reflected that crucial question. That Romina proceeded to answer. "What I know is that if you have sex, there's a chance for a baby, Angelica!" Romina proclaimed. "And you're going to be married well before that child is born."

"Since when have you become such a staunch advocate of marriage, Mama?" Angelica was shaking with fury and fear, a combination so potent that she was emboldened to challenge her mother in a way she never had before. "You've had *four* children and never been married once."

"You think I'm proud of that? You think I want my daughters to follow in my footsteps?" Romina raged. "Never, Angelica. You and Sarah are not going to make my mistakes, I won't let you."

"And now she has the Fortune fortune to back her up," Brandon said cheerfully. "Looks like there's going to be a wedding around here."

Chapter 12

‘‘Mollie dear, how quickly can you put together a wedding?’’ Kate asked Mollie Shaw, the pretty, red-haired, young wedding consultant who was owner and operator of a fledgling wedding planning business.

Back in January, Mollie had been hired to plan the wedding of her friend Kelly Sinclair, Kate’s former social secretary, to Mac Fortune, Kate’s grandnephew and the vice-president of finance with the Fortune Corporation.

Mollie smiled, obviously pleased to have been summoned. Planning a Fortune wedding was a boon for any wedding consultant; it was a bonanza for a newcomer in the business. ‘‘You know how quickly we put Mac and Kelly’s together,’’ she reminded Kate.

‘‘And you did a fine job.’’ Kate made her decision. ‘‘Mollie, would you make the arrangements for the wedding of my granddaughter Angelica to her—er—fiancé, Flynt Corrigan?''

"Oh yes, Mrs. Fortune, uh, Foster!" breathed Mollie.

"Kate will do, my dear." Kate grinned mischievously. "Now, would two days be enough time to plan a nice little wedding and reception?"

"Two days?" Mollie gaped at her. "The wedding is only two days away?"

"We'd prefer one day but figured two will give you a sporting chance," said Kate. "This couple is an edgy pair. Both of them are too guarded and defensive and controlled. It is imperative for them to be married quickly, while still off balance, or we fear they will build walls that will never be breached, figuratively speaking, of course."

"I couldn't've said it better myself, Kate," Romina spoke up. She was sitting on one of the cushioned window seats in the bright, plant-filled sunroom. "Any longer than two days, and either Flynt or Angel will get over the shock of us barging in on them and beat it out of here."

"Everything will be ready in two days, I promise," Mollie said decisively, though she did look a bit panicked. And curious, though she discreetly refrained from asking any questions.

"We can have the reception here, which should help somewhat," Kate said consolingly. "That means the cake, the refreshments, the flowers and such, need to be ordered. I'll leave you here with the mother of the bride to go over the details. Come, Brandon, let's let Mollie and Romina work things out."

Brandon, who was standing beside Romina, crossed the room and took his mother's arm.

Romina advanced on Mollie. "Angelica is my oldest child, and she is very precious to me. I want her wedding to be perfect," she warned.

"Don't worry about a thing." Mollie managed a plucky smile. "We'll make sure the wedding is a bride's dream."

Kate and Brandon departed, leaving Mollie and Romina to their plans.

Angelica felt as if she were trapped in a nightmare. Her life had begun to unravel the moment her parents and her grandmother had come bursting into the bedroom like a pack of terrorists bent on seizing hostages.

She felt like a hostage, trailed every moment by someone, either Kate or Romina or a cautious little redhead named Mollie Shaw who asked her things like what flowers she preferred in her wedding bouquet, how many tiers did she want the wedding cake to have and would she like a flavored filling between the layers of cake. When Angelica looked at Mollie as if she'd lost her mind, Romina or Kate would offer their own opinions.

As the day progressed, the nightmare showed no signs of abating.

There was really going to be a wedding. Mara was flying in tomorrow with Sarah and Casper, with whom she'd been staying since Romina's flight to Minneapolis with Brandon. TJ was invited, too, but didn't have enough notice to get the time off from work.

"I'm so thrilled for you, Angel!" Mara had squealed over the phone after Romina broke the news and issued the invitations and travel arrangements. "The kids are crazy with excitement. We've never flown before, and we're flying first class! Flynt is a wonderful guy, Angel. He's perfect for you!"

Angelica knew that. She was perfect for him too…but marriage? She'd just begun to slowly accept the idea that love might not be an illusion or a delusion, she'd just faced the fact that she loved Flynt…

But he didn't love her, of course. How could he, when he didn't believe in love? And being forced to marry her would be the death knoll to any hopes of him ever coming to love her. Angelica's eyes burned with hot tears.

Mollie noticed. "This wedding is very sudden," she said hesitantly.

The two young women were alone in the library where Mollie had several flower books lying open on a long table.

"It's sudden because my paranoid mother and my crazy father and my eager-to-help grandmother are forcing us to get married!" Angelica's voice shook.

"Oh," Mollie murmured.

Angelica sensed her empathy, and for a moment she considered asking Mollie for help in escaping. But she refrained. The poor girl was trying to build a business, and if she were to alienate the Fortunes, she might just as well declare bankruptcy.

Anyway, where would she go, except back to Birmingham where she would easily be found? For a moment the fugitive underground network sprang to mind, and she clamped down on that thought, just as she shut out the possibility that she actually wanted this forced marriage to take place.

"I can't believe I'm trapped in this mess!" Angelica lamented aloud, flopping down on one of the leather-and-rosewood chairs.

Mollie's fingers brushed over a page of brilliantly colored flowers in one of the books. "Uh, we really don't have to discuss flowers for your bouquet right this minute," she said tactfully.

"Can I assume that *this mess* is a reference to me?" Flynt stood at the threshold of the library.

Angelica's heart seemed to jump into her throat and then plunge to the pit of her belly. He was wearing a tan suit, light blue shirt and he loosened his tie as he walked toward them. He looked every inch the professional, successful and very sexy business executive.

She hadn't seen him since this morning, when they'd been ambushed by the Fortune Bedroom Patrol. As Romina had continued to berate and threaten, Kate had suggested—strongly—that Flynt leave for the time being. He had willingly accepted the out she'd offered. *And left!*

The thought of his speedy exit still made Angelica seethe. He'd deserted her! "You said it, not me."

Flynt came to stand beside Angelica's chair, though he looked at Mollie as he addressed her. "Would you mind leaving us alone?"

"I want her to stay. After all, Mollie is planning our *wedding*, Flynt." Angelica gave a tight smile. And stood up. Having him tower above her chair definitely put her at a disadvantage.

"Okay, then, Mollie, plan away." Flynt picked Angelica up in his arms and sat down with her on his lap.

Unbidden, came a flash memory of her on his lap last

night in the darkened violet and ivy bedroom. They were naked and hot and wild, and he'd shown her how to straddle him while— Angelica felt her body ignite and she hopped off Flynt's lap and practically ran around to the other side of the table. He watched her and laughed quietly, as if he'd tapped into her own private memory bank, as if he knew exactly what she'd remembered. Of course, he did share those memories of last night's passion.

"Mollie must think we're the clients from hell," muttered Angelica, still blushing.

"Oh, no, I love a challenge!" Mollie succeeded in sounding sincere.

The sound of a small child's squeal of laughter sounded in the hall, accompanied by Kate's own hearty laugh. The sounds grew louder and nearer, and in a moment Kate joined them, accompanied by a cute little girl about three years old. The child's laughter ceased the moment she saw Flynt, Angelica and Mollie. She immediately hid behind Kate.

"This is Lilly," Kate said reaching around to put a comforting hand on the little girl's head. "She is visiting with me for a little while today."

The trio in the library greeted Lilly, who suddenly looked ready to burst into tears.

"Let's go into the kitchen and see if Cook is ready for us to make those Easter Bunny cookies, darling." Kate scooped the little girl up in her arms.

"Easter Bunny cookies in May?" Flynt asked, perplexed.

Lilly nodded shyly. "I like the Easter Bunny," she whispered.

"Well, of course you do!" Kate hugged the child. "And I think Easter Bunny cookies are a wonderful idea, no matter what time of year."

Lilly was smiling again, her head against Kate's shoulder as she was carried from the library.

"Do you know if little Lilly is one of my cousins?" Angelica asked Mollie. "It feels so strange to have relatives and not know who they are or how they're related to me."

"I know what you mean," Mollie said quietly. "Lilly is Jack Fortune's little girl. Jack's father is Stuart Fortune whose father was Caleb Fortune. Caleb and your grandfather Ben were brothers. Got that?" She smiled slightly.

"No. Too many names and generations. It's like having to memorize all the presidents," Angelica complained.

"How about all the kings of France?" suggested Flynt. "Ever have to do that? I failed a history test, thanks to that one."

"My worse downfall was listing the Roman emperors," admitted Angelica. "I found it impossible."

"Makes keeping track of the Fortunes seem like the proverbial piece of cake." Flynt smiled at her. Angelica smiled back.

Mollie looked heartened, now that her volatile clients appeared to have declared a truce. She tried to extend the amiable mood. "I guess I'd better not mention Ben Fortune's other brothers, and all *their* children and grandchildren."

"Not unless you want me to come down with a migraine—this would surely be the day for it.'' Angelica shot Flynt a challenging look. He arched his brows.

''You know a lot about the Fortunes, Mollie,'' Flynt observed.

''She'd have to, for her business and all,'' said Angelica. ''Since there are so many Fortunes, one of them is bound to be getting married at any given time.''

''Like you, sweetheart,'' mocked Flynt. Angelica's face grew stormy again.

''Uh, something like that.'' Mollie appeared intent on studying the colorful patterns in the Oriental carpet. ''I—I was recently hired to plan Chloe Fortune's wedding to Mason Chandler. She's another one of your cousins, Angelica.''

''Congratulations, to you and to Cousin Chloe,'' Angelica said flatly. ''So who is Lilly's mother?''

''Lilly's mother, Sandra, was killed in a car accident recently, and now she's come to live with her father.'' Mollie's face was grave. ''Jack hardly knows Lilly because he and Sandra have been divorced for two years, and she made it almost impossible for him to visit his own child.''

''That poor baby!'' cried Angelica.

''She seems happy being with Kate,'' Flynt pointed out.

Mollie nodded in agreement. ''But Kate can't take care of a three-year-old full-time, not at her age, and with everything else she has to do. Lilly is shy and scared, and I don't think things are working out too well with the nanny Jack hired. I—I'm so worried about her.''

Angelica decided that she really liked the young wedding consultant. Her compassion for Lilly Fortune, a sad little motherless child, was admirable.

"A child *needs* a mother," Angelica declared. "Is this Jack guy dating someone nice? Or will he go for some trophy bimbo who can't be bothered with children and will make Lilly's life a living hell?" She warmed to the subject. Discussing little Lilly's situation distracted her from her own. "You know, if this Jack marries a witch, we can help Lilly. We can rescue her from—"

"A father is equally important to a child, Angelica," Flynt sounded stern. "Lilly doesn't need rescuing from her own father. And stop trying to recruit Mollie for Nancy Portland's underground!"

"I wasn't! I was just—"

"I don't think Jack Fortune's a jerk," Mollie inserted hastily. "And I don't know if he's dating anyone. He seems to want to be a good father." She backed slowly toward the door, her eyes darting from Flynt to Angelica. "If you'll excuse me, I have to make some calls. Um, urgent calls. We can discuss the bouquet later, Angelica."

"Well, we scared her off," Flynt said dryly. "She thinks we're crazy." He shrugged. "Hmm, maybe we are."

Angelica hurried to the door of the library and saw Mollie scurry down the hall. "The bouquet can be dandelions and poison ivy for all I care," she called to her.

"Make it white orchids," Flynt called, even louder. He'd come to stand behind Angelica. "That's your favorite flower, right?"

He *was* right. "How did you know that?" she demanded, astonished.

"You mentioned it once. I remember what you tell me, Angelica." He put his hands on her shoulders and tried to draw her back against him.

Angelica resisted and ducked under his hands, escaping his hold. There was too much unresolved between them for her to allow her judgment to be clouded with sexual urgency. *Again!* She returned to the long table, methodically closing each flower book while she spoke.

"I remember what you said, too, Flynt. About love being an illusion. That marriage is doomed to fail because the couple will end up not being able to stand the sight of each other. But when Romina and Brandon and Kate insisted that you marry me, I didn't hear you say 'no.' And why is that, I wonder? Because you see me as a—a pipeline to all that Fortune money?"

Flynt shoved an impatient hand through his hair and looked up at her. "So this is how you've spent your day? I've been at my office, clearing my schedule and trying to keep on top of everything, while you've cast yourself in the role of pitiful heiress being forced to marry a gold-digging cad? Give me a break, Angelica!"

"You don't believe in marriage, but you're willing to marry me to please the almighty Fortunes. You're a hypocrite, Flynt!"

"No more than anybody else around here. There's your mother who had four children out of wedlock but now rivals the Puritans when it comes to the possibility of an illegitimate grandchild. And your father who—"

"Leave my parents out of this! *You* might be nonchalant about having a baby without being married but *I'm* not. I was illegitimate myself, and it's not something I want my own child to have to deal with."

"Well, who said that I did?" He caught her hand and gave a tug. She neither pulled away nor allowed herself to be drawn closer. "Is that the real reason why you're letting yourself be bullied into this wedding, Angelica? Because you're worried you might be pregnant?"

"What other reason could there be?" she asked rawly.

"Angelica, if you really *are* pregnant, I—" He broke off, frustration roiling through him as he noticed the pretty young woman, holding an infant in her arms, enter the room. This discussion was far too personal to be conducted in front of a witness.

"Oh, excuse me, I'm sorry! I was told Mollie Shaw was in here. I'm so sorry to disturb you." The young woman apologized profusely as she turned to leave.

"You aren't disturbing anything." Angelica jerked her hand away from Flynt.

She noticed that he made no attempt to regain his hold on her. She wanted him to, even though she knew she would pull away again. Angelica fought a sudden urge to weep. She'd never felt so confused and off balance in her entire carefully controlled life. Of course, she had stopped being so careful and controlled the moment Flynt Corrigan had knocked on her mother's door in Birmingham that fateful day.

She looked at Flynt who was visibly displeased by the interruption and immediately decided to lengthen it. "Hello, I'm Angelica Carroll." Angelica's eyes never left Flynt as she greeted the newcomer.

"Brandon's daughter?" The young mother stared at Angelica with interest. Her round-cheeked baby gave a gummy smile and cooed.

"It appears your reputation—and Brandon's —precede you, Angelica.'' Flynt walked toward Kelly, extending his hand to shake. "Hello, Kelly. I'm Flynt Corrigan. You may not remember, but we met here shortly before I left for Alabama.''

"Of course I remember. But you haven't met my daughter, Annie.'' Kelly proudly showed off her baby. "I was looking for Mollie Shaw. Kate wanted me to give her several lists that I'd compiled.''

"Kelly used to be your grandmother's social secretary, Angelica,'' Flynt explained. "Now she's married to Mac, one of your second cousins. Annie is their daughter.''

"Annie is an adorable child.'' Angelica surveyed the infant with a professional baby nurse's interest. "How old is she?''

"Three and half months. She was born on Valentine's Day,'' replied Kelly. "She is such a daddy's girl. He was right there when she was born, and it was love at first sight between them,'' she added warmly.

"It's a bonding experience when a father witnesses his child's birth.'' Angelica recited her trademark line by rote and then proceeded to ask Kelly all about the labor and delivery. Not only was she genuinely interested, she could think of no subject guaranteed to send Flynt Corrigan out of the room, and fast. Angelica had learned that unless the child was his own, a man quickly fled conversations centering on the gynecological aspects of childbirth.

Flynt proved to be no exception. "If you two will excuse me…I'll talk to you later, Angelica.''

He fled.

But they didn't talk later. Angelica was constantly surrounded by Fortunes, who streamed in and out of the mansion to meet Brandon's daughter. They all planned to attend the wedding, but their current interest was focused on Angelica as Brandon's child, not Flynt Corrigan's bride.

Flynt understood and made himself scarce. He went to his office and busied himself with company matters. He tried to tell himself that after they were married, he would somehow regain Angelica's affection. He would have to, because she couldn't stand him now.

And who could blame her? She'd made it quite clear all along what she thought of marriage. Very little, and certainly, never for herself. Now her family was forcing her into a marriage she didn't want because they believed there was a chance she might be pregnant. She was worried about it, too.

He was deeply sorry he'd put her at risk, though he felt it was unlikely she was pregnant from that one unprotected time…. Of course that was all it took to conceive a child; Romina was right about that. Anyway, he wouldn't mind if Angelica were pregnant. The thought of her carrying his child sent a thrill through him. The problem was it didn't thrill her.

Flynt rubbed his throbbing temples with his fingertips. He wanted to marry Angelica. He was in love with her, though he hadn't told her so. And he didn't dare say it now, not when she considered him a Fortune-hunting hypocrite who'd betrayed her by agreeing to marry her.

He couldn't pinpoint the exact moment that his feelings about love and marriage had changed, Flynt mused. It had been a gradual process, a direct result of his relationship with Angelica. If only her own views had been similarly influenced by her feelings for him!

Perhaps that might've happened, given time and space. But things were occurring at breakneck speed: they'd made love for the first time, then done it again and again, they'd spent their first night together...

And been caught in flagrante delicto by her relatives. Now they were engaged. In two days they would wed!

To try to bolster his flagging spirits, he forced himself to concentrate on the successful aspects of the trip to Minneapolis. With Angelica secured in the Fortune mansion, the press was unable to get near her; even better, there had been no more threatening notes.

Flynt knew she was physically safe. At least that was good news. But the bad news invariably filtered through to sabotage his attempt at positive thinking. Angelica hated him now and would probably prefer to be the prey of a menacing madman instead of Mrs. Flynt Corrigan.

A menacing madman. Away from the stimulating, distracting, wholly engrossing presence of Angelica, Flynt began to review the facts of the case. Certain observations and insights he had initially brushed aside flowed through his mind, raising questions and alternatives that led him further. The conclusion he drew stunned him, then seemed obvious.

Could it be? Was it possible? How had he missed it before?

He reached for the telephone to place a call....

"I thought I should bring you up to speed on the complete story of Brandon and his daughter." Kate addressed the small assembly of Fortunes gathered in the large corner office of her grandson Michael at Fortune corporate headquarters.

Sterling was there, of course, but only a few selected family members. She had promised Brandon and Romina to keep the story contained.

Kate attempted to present the facts, remaining calm and nonjudgmental about the situation. Her family was not.

"Romina's youngest child has been the one sending the notes from the beginning?" Michael was aghast. "He threatened to kill his own sister and let Brandon take the fall?"

"I honestly don't believe the boy is a criminal, my dears," said Kate. "A difficult child, it's true, but ultimately just a child."

"This twelve-year-old kid, Casper, set everything in motion when he found out that Brandon Fortune was Angelica's father? He wanted cash and figured the Fortunes were a good mark?" Gabe Devereax shook his head, both disapproving and amazed.

"Casper was going through his mother's things one day and found her old diary with all the facts," Kate said, continuing her narrative. "Angelica's birth certificate simply lists the father as John Doe. Casper swears he never would have hurt Angelica, he loves his sister dearly. He said he just wanted money for a computer and some video games."

"I promised Romina we would do everything in our power to ensure that no charges will be filed against the child," said Kate, "and I intend to keep my word."

"The boy needs counseling, not jail," Sterling agreed.

"As for punishment, well, his mother certainly won't let him go unpunished. I believe we can count on that."

"It was Brandon who figured out Casper was behind the notes," Kate proudly informed them all. "He divined it very early on, when the child delivered a threat to the hotel and offered the bellboy cookies for a tip. Brandon told Romina immediately and convinced her to agree to simply watch and wait."

"If they'd confronted the boy right away, we would have been spared all the media hoopla *and* this bothersome civil lawsuit by Carson. But then this is Brandon we're talking about," grumbled Michael. "Not exactly the poster boy for good judgment, you'll recall."

"I think Romina has behaved quite responsibly." Kate defended her youngest son yet again. "He's befriended Casper and emotionally supported Romina throughout. Oh, and this is quite important, both Brandon and Romina want to keep the knowledge of Casper's misdeeds from Angelica, at least until after the wedding. They know how hurt and upset the dear girl will be and don't want to spoil her wedding day." Kate was not quite successful in suppressing the irony in her voice.

"*Brandon* figured it out first?" Gabe Devereax was still in a state of disbelief over that news. "What about Flynt Corrigan? He never even suspected the kid? He was fooled by a twelve-year-old? What the hell was he doing down there, anyway, wearing blinders?"

"In a manner of speaking. Flynt is madly, deeply, blindly in love with our own Angelica." Kate's eyes twinkled. "And she feels the same about him, I'm pleased to say. Only I don't think they've fully realized it yet."

"They're wildly in love yet they're being forced into a quick marriage," observed Rebecca dryly. "Looks like Angelica turned out to be a true Fortune, all right. Has anyone in this family ever had a nice, long, uneventful, convenient courtship before marrying?"

"Nah, too dull," scoffed Gabe.

Chapter 13

"You're right, Flynt," Gabe said to him. "The kid is the one behind everything. Kate told us today that Brandon figured it out early on."

"I didn't pull it all together till this morning." Flynt uttered an expletive. "I messed up big-time." He was deeply disappointed in himself.

As soon as he'd put his facts in order, he had gone directly to Gabe's office, to break the news and to brainstorm on the best way to tell the Fortunes about Angelica's little brother, Casper Carroll, the media-savvy, twelve-year-old extortionist. Only to be told by Gabe that Kate already knew. She had been informed by Brandon.

Flynt groaned.

"It really wasn't all that obvious, Flynt." Gabe eyed him sympathetically. "Besides, you had Brandon and

Romina conspiring to keep the truth from you. Along with—uh—certain other distractions.''

Flynt guessed that Gabe considered him a lovesick idiot who had completely botched the assignment. It was what he himself would've thought of a colleague who had been misled by a twelve-year-old con artist and subsequently had allowed his clients to be deluged by a torrent of inconvenience and bad publicity.

''You're not the first man to be blindsided by a Fortune woman, you know,'' Gabe said dryly. ''Their appeal is way beyond potent.''

''No excuses,'' Flynt gritted through his teeth. ''I'll talk to Kate today about terminating the proposed contract for SMS and the Fortune Corporation.''

''I thought you'd want to do that.'' Gabe gave his friend an approving pat on the shoulder. ''Meanwhile, it looks like Brandon and Romina are in the midst of rekindling their old flame. According to Kate, Brandon wants to move to Birmingham to be near Romina and her kids. Guess the Fortunes will have to buy a business or something down there to keep Brandon busy, not that a single member of the family will mind a bit. Keeping Brandon occupied and away in Alabama will please everybody.''

''Did Kate mention if Angelica had been told about her little brother's scheme?'' Flynt flinched, imagining the scene. Angelica worried so about Casper; she was going to be crushed by the revelation. He wanted to go to her right away, to comfort her. She might be furious with him, she might think she hated him, but he knew she was going to need him.

''Kate said that Brandon and Romina don't want to

tell Angelica. But go with your instincts on that, Flynt. I bet *you* know her better than anyone else does.''

"Yeah." Flynt actually smiled. "Yeah, I do. And I'll talk with Angelica right after I tell Kate that I'm tearing up our contract."

"Don't be surprised if Kate has her own ideas about sticking to that contract. She is very loyal, and you are marrying Brandon's kid."

"I can't let Kate reward me with something I haven't earned," Flynt said firmly on his way out.

He was sorry to lose the potential account, but it was hardly a catastrophe, he reasoned as he walked to his car and drove to the Fortune estate. His company was doing well; they wouldn't miss a client they'd never had.

He told Kate and Sterling so, when they met in Kate's personal office on the first floor of the mansion. As Gabe had predicted, Kate insisted that SMS be given the Fortune Corporation contract as originally planned. Flynt was equally adamant that he could not accept.

"You are marrying my granddaughter, Flynt," Kate exclaimed. "Furthermore, we had a prior agreement before you even left for Alabama. It is right and fitting that your company handle all security concerns for the Future Corporation."

"I agree," Sterling seconded. "Marrying Brandon's daughter connects you to the Fortune Corporation, and the Fortunes look out for their own. Nobody will dispute that."

Standing outside the office door, listening to every word, Angelica felt a roaring in her ears as every word was seared into her brain. She had been told a little earlier that Flynt had arrived at the house, but it had taken her some time to locate where he was in this cavernous mansion.

She was desperate to talk to him, to tell him all about the shocking phone call she'd just had with Mara. What she'd told Angelica had sent her reeling. Casper was the culprit, the one who had done it all, from informing Brandon of her existence, to the extortion threats, to turning their lives into a media freak circus. *Casper!*

Shaken to the core, Angelica went in search of Flynt, who supposedly was here somewhere.

She found him just in time to hear Sterling Foster and her grandmother offering him a valuable contract because he was going to marry her. Had this prior agreement they'd mentioned hinged on a marriage between her and Flynt?

It all fit together in a fractured sort of way, Angelica decided grimly. Flynt's methods had been superb. He had pretended to be reluctant to get involved—which dovetailed neatly with her own reservations, making her feel safe, trusting him—all the while he had been actively pursuing her.

And there were the rest of his actions…making love to her on the plane where that steward could find incriminating evidence…taking the risk of impregnating her…falling asleep in her bed so they could be "discovered" together….

The pieces fell into place, and the picture was disturbing and disheartening. Was it a conspiracy between Flynt and the unlikely team of her mother and father, with her grandmother's cooperation thrown in for good measure? She really had been hoodwinked!

Angelica walked slowly down the hall, her legs so shaky she felt as if her knees were jelly. Learning about Flynt's conniving hurt even more than the disclosure of Casper's misdeeds. Casper was a child, but Flynt was the man she loved and trusted and now...

What was she going to do? She was in love with Flynt, but how did he really feel about her? Waking up in his arms this morning, she'd thought she had known, she had been sure. Now the only things she was sure of was that she loved Flynt, and her little brother was in desperate need of therapy.

Impulsively, she ran out the front door, eager to be outside. At least out here, she was safe from the parade of secrets that seemed to emanate from the Fortune mansion. She was also safely removed from the people who knew those secrets, because she was alone. There was nobody in sight, and unless people were lurking behind the trees or in the shrubbery, there could be no more conversations for her to overhear.

Which was definitely a good thing. She needed time to think, to regain control of her thought processes that all of a sudden seemed to have short-circuited.

Angelica walked around to the back of the house, the tension slowly beginning to drain from her body as she absorbed the beauty of her surroundings. Strange, but it was more helpful not to think at all. So she simply enjoyed the scenery. The flowering trees and spring flowers were breathtaking, and the rippling deep blue waters of the lake provided its own calming effect.

"Mind if I join you?"

The sound of Flynt's voice made her jump. Angelica

whirled around to face him. She had been so preoccupied she hadn't heard anyone approach.

"Do—do I have a choice?" She'd intended to sound snappish and cold and was dismayed that her voice quavered. She definitely hadn't been going for teary and tremulous. But there she was.

"I guess you don't." Flynt fell into step beside her on the pretty gravel path. "I'm here and I'm staying."

Angelica intended to remain silent and stoic, counting on him to grow bored or irritated and finally leave her alone. But her tongue seemed to have its own agenda because she heard herself speaking at the very moment she'd determined not to say a word.

"Did you know that it was Casper who set everything in motion?" she blurted out.

"Not until today." Flynt grimaced wryly. "Apparently Brandon had it figured out almost from the start. My opinion of my own deductive skills has slipped quite a few notches."

"I didn't know anything, either. Mara called and told me." For some reason Angelica was relieved that Flynt had been as unaware as she. She would've hated to think he'd been keeping such vital information from her. "I—I never would've guessed Casper would do such things. My own baby brother! I'm sure the Fortunes must hate him, and who can blame them?"

"I know you've been worried about Casper, Angelica."

She should have known she could count on Flynt not to judge or condemn a child, Angelica acknowledged achingly. He'd once been a troubled boy himself and hadn't forgotten it. Her self-protective walls began to crumble. She needed to talk things out, and who better than with Flynt? Almost from the time they'd met, she had been able to talk more openly with him than with anybody else in her life—even Mara, her best friend.

"I never dreamed Casper would go to such lengths to get the things he wanted and I—I have this feeling that money and expensive games aren't what really drove him," Angelica said softly, "but were kind of a reaction to—things."

"Like adolescence and middle school and all that stuff none of us would ever want to repeat?" Flynt took her hand, and they walked to a small wrought-iron bench under a shady tree. He drew her down next to him.

"Worse." Angelica's dark eyes were troubled. "I can't help wondering that since Casper learned Brandon was my father maybe he also learned about his own father, Jurgen Heintz. He was an iceman, Flynt. He never wanted a child and made his aversion to his own son very clear. What if Casper learned about *that* during his snooping? That kind of pain could lead to some pretty serious acting-out behavior."

"Poor Casper." Flynt put his arm around Angelica. Her head seemed to naturally find a place to rest in the hollow of his shoulder.

"Do you know what else is weird?" she rambled on. "That Mama chose Brandon to confide in instead of me."

"I think Casper's actions were the result of his desperate need for a father—or a father figure—and that your mother realized it," said Flynt. "My guess is that Romina didn't confide in you because her relationship with Brandon was turning into something she could count on. I think Romina trusts Brandon, that she believes at long last she's found a good man in him.''

Angelica listened, wide-eyed.

''Your grandmother has always hoped that if Brandon found somebody truly meaningful to him, he could get past his own troubled history. Maybe he's finally found it in your mother,'' Flynt said, continuing to expound his theory. ''Romina was his first love, after all. Maybe even his one and only love.''

''Funny, but that doesn't make me want to run screaming like it would've a short while ago,'' Angelica murmured drolly.

''You've had far more screamworthy things to deal with lately.'' Flynt lifted her chin and looked into her dark eyes. ''Would marrying me be one of them, sweetheart?''

Angelica gulped and averted her gaze. ''That brings me to something I overheard today. Have I been hoodwinked, Flynt?''

''Hoodwinked?'' Flynt repeated dryly. ''Maybe you'd like to elaborate a little on that?''

She nodded her head. ''I'm talking about that special contract for your company with the Fortune Corporation that you were supposed to get when you married me. I wasn't aware of that until today—''

''Angelica, whatever you think you know about the contract—''

''Don't pretend it doesn't exist, Flynt.'' It was Angelica's turn to interrupt. ''I overheard you talking about it to my grandmother and Sterling.'' She felt strangely calm. Somehow her initial bitterness and sense of betrayal was gone. "To be fair, who could blame you for going for it? In fact, you'd be crazy not to."

"Then I guess that means I'm a certifiable lunatic because I refused to accept the contract, Angelica. If you'd lurked a little longer, you would've overheard that part of the conversation. But since you didn't, I'll assure you that I don't expect to be rewarded for marrying you when—"

"You might've made me pregnant?" She laid her hand on his arm. It was time for complete honesty between them. "You didn't, Flynt. The timing isn't right. You're off the hook, Flynt. You don't have to marry me."

"Suppose I want to marry you, Angelica?"

A thrill of elation, of pure excitement shot through her. Being Angelica, she sought to restrain herself with a quelling dose of caution. "You never mentioned marriage before my family tried to pressure you into it."

"Well, neither did you. Does that mean you don't want to marry me, Angelica?"

She frowned. He certainly had her there! She was going to have to admit to him what she'd so recently realized herself.

"I...never said that," she hedged.

"Which means if I asked you to marry me, you would say yes?" Flynt was not unfamiliar with defensive maneuvers himself. He lifted her hand to his mouth and kissed her palm. "Angelica, I love you. I'm sure it was only a matter of time until I got around to telling you, but since the timetable has been—advanced—I want you to know now. I love you and I'd like to marry you, and you are the only woman in the world I've ever said those words to. I'll never say them to anyone else, either,'' he added, eyeing her assessingly.

She stared at him, wanting to believe him. Aching to. ''Flynt, I love you,'' she said softly. ''I've come to recognize how much.''

''I sense a 'but.''' Flynt frowned.

''You were so adamant that love ends when the bad times come.'' Her words, her fears came out in a rush. ''I'm not naive enough to believe that the rest of our lives will be trouble-free. What if—''

''I'm not that naive either, Angelica. And I can't pinpoint one blinding moment when I suddenly knew we would stay together forever. It's been a gradual process, but it's a certainty that's grown stronger.''

''It has?'' she whispered.

He nodded. ''I found myself thinking about my aunts and uncles and my cousins who've stayed married, about friends who haven't split up despite some hard times. They didn't fit into my theory of 'there are only two kinds of relationships, those that've failed and those that soon will.' We don't fit that description, Angelica,'' he added, determination burning in his eyes. ''And we never will.''

''Because we'll choose not to.'' Her voice was fierce. ''We do have choices, I've learned that much from growing up with my mom. There were so many times when she could've chosen to do things differently and then everything would've been different. She said it was simply fate but I *knew* it was choices.''

''And I choose you, Angelica. For always, which brings us back to my proposal...'' His voice lightened.

"You haven't exactly come right out and said *yes* yet, you know."

"Yes!" Half-dizzy with joy, Angelica launched herself into his arms, linking her hands behind his neck.

"I love you, Flynt, and I want to marry you, too. And you are the only man in the world I've ever said that to. I'll never say it to anyone else either."

"Seems like it's official, then." Flynt reached for her, and they kissed, a sweet long kiss of passion and possession, the kind of kiss that promised love and lasting commitment.

"I guess what it all means is that we were made for each other." Angelica sighed when they finally came up for air. She snuggled deeper in his arms.

"It does." Flynt lowered his mouth to kiss her again.

"Excuse me, my dears, I don't mean to intrude but here I am, anyway." Kate's voice ended Flynt and Angelica's kiss, just as their lips touched. "You see, you are only a foot away from the lilacs which desperately need pruning."

The couple looked up to see Kate, holding a basket half-filled with fresh-cut flowers and a pair of clippers, standing beside several burgeoning lilac trees.

Angelica and Flynt rose to their feet, still holding hands.

"That's okay, Grandmother. Prune away. Oh, and Flynt and I are getting married," Angelica added happily.

"Well, of course you are, darling. That sweet little Mollie has been working hard planning for it. Did you know that your mother was quite taken with Mollie's suggestion for the reception to be a formal high tea?

Mollie has already arranged for tea sandwiches, warm scones with Devonshire cream and jam, fruit tarts and pastries, along with the traditional wedding cake and beverages, of course.''

"Gee, and I was hoping for a big steak dinner," teased Flynt. "With ranch fries."

"You may have that for dinner tonight, my carnivorous young friend," Kate teased back. "We're having the family over for dinner about an hour from now. It's very informal, an outdoor barbecue with nice juicy steaks—and of course, fried potatoes."

"Would this be the A list family or the B list or both?" Angelica asked curiously.

"I'm not certain what you mean, dear." Kate was puzzled.

"Brandon assigns the Fortunes Hollywood-style status," explained Flynt, "and that is how he described them to Angelica and me. His brothers and sisters and their offspring are the A list. The Ben Fortune aunts and uncles and their descendants are the B list."

"Oh, my." Kate grimaced wryly. "I do hope that Brandon hasn't told the additional, extended family relatives that they're, er—"

"Relegated to the B list? Brandon said what's the point of being A list if you can't lord it over the B's? He says that's show biz." Angelica shrugged.

"Angelica, dear, I can understand that you might feel…estranged from your father, maybe even hostile toward him," Kate began tentatively, "but—"

"Grandmother, there is something I've wanted to ask you but didn't feel I had the right. Or the nerve. But after today..." Angelica stared intently at her grandmother.

"After today, you feel you have the nerve and the right to ask me anything?" Kate surmised shrewdly. "And so you do, darling. Ask me."

"Why do you even bother with the B-list relatives if they're Ben Fortune's kin?"

Kate was genuinely taken aback. "Why, Angelica, I consider Ben's brothers and their wives, and my nieces and nephews and their children, to be my own family. I'm close to them. I know them so well, many all their lives. I have watched most of the younger ones grow up and—"

"But they're related to Ben Fortune and that man was evil, Grandmother," Angelica burst out, "though nobody around here ever seems to say so. I've heard the relatives mention Ben Fortune, they talk about him normally, you know, it's 'Dad this' and 'Grandfather that.' His pictures are up on the walls along with everybody else. It's like he is a regular member of the family. How can that be?"

"Ben Fortune is the family patriarch, Angelica," Flynt pointed out.

"But Ben gave away his own baby and then he lied to you about it all those years, Grandmother," exclaimed Angelica. "He had to have known how vindictive and cruel Monica Malone was, but he let his own son be raised by her—or more likely by her servants. No matter how nice Ben was to the other Fortunes, it doesn't excuse the fact that he gave my father away like—like a puppy!"

Kate flinched.

"Angelica, I think you've said enough," Flynt said firmly.

"No, let her continue," countered Kate. "I can see you've given the matter some thought, Angelica."

"A *lot* of thought, Grandmother. Whatever Ben Fortune's motives, I bet he decided to give away Brandon because he was a twin. After all, you'd still have one baby left. It's like this friend of mine at work who has a dog that had three puppies. They gave away two pups and kept one and the family was satisfied since they got to keep the one. The others were superfluous, just like Brandon was to Ben."

Angelica's face was flushed with emotion and the words kept pouring out. "I bet he decided to keep the girl twin because you already had two other sons. Ben Fortune considered my dad expendable. Can't you just imagine him saying to himself, 'A third son, who needs him? We'd been wanting a daughter, so Monica can have the extra boy.' Grandmother, how did you ever forgive that terrible man for what he did?"

Kate blanched and swayed slightly. Flynt reached out to steady the older woman. "Angelica didn't mean to upset you, Kate," he said quietly. "But she is very, uh, passionate on the subject of mothers and babies. It's only natural, since maternal-child health is her profession. And, of course, Romina's interest in, er, domestic issues has naturally influenced Angelica. Some might say radicalized her."

"You needn't explain or try to apologize for Angelica, Flynt." Kate managed a tremulous smile. "Who said I ever forgave Ben for giving Brandon away, Angelica? As I told Sterling when the news was revealed that Brandon was my son, 'Ben is lucky to be dead already because otherwise I fear I would've killed him myself—and in the most painful way imaginable.'''

"Good!" Angelica vigorously nodded her approval.

"Angelica, do you know you are the first member of the family to use the word *evil* in describing Ben's actions?" Kate regarded her granddaughter keenly. "Or at least to say it aloud to me. Whatever the others have said, it's been among themselves, never to me. It is as if we struck some unspoken sort of collusion of silence. 'Don't talk about what Ben did, it's in the long-ago past. He is dead, and there is no purpose to be served in holding him accountable for what he did to Brandon.'''

"Well, *I* hold him accountable!" Angelica exclaimed. "What Ben Fortune did to you was unforgivable, Grandmother. Just ask Flynt, whose parents had a child taken, what kind of hell your life turns into. And Flynt's little brother was taken by a stranger. Your child was taken away by your own husband, Grandmother!"

"I know, Angelica, I know." Kate's eyes filled with tears. "I would've—and did—forgive Ben's wartime affair with Lana Simpson that resulted in Jessica, of whom I've grown quite fond. It wouldn't have been as easy to get over his Monica Malone fling, but I could have weathered that, as well. But for Ben to take our own baby, one of our twins, and give him away to Monica Malone, to let me believe that bogus kidnapping story until the day he died…"

"Kate, don't." Flynt patted her shoulder awkwardly. "It's in the past and there is no need to—"

"There is a need, Flynt." Kate's eyes met Angelica's, and the two gazed at each other, forging a bond as tangible and strong as steel. "Angelica is Brandon's child, and I'm glad she is angry on Brandon's behalf. I'm also glad she has no memories of Ben that allow her to excuse what he did. You are right, Angelica, giving Brandon away was evil. During all those years, not a single day went by when I didn't think of my missing child. I would look at my daughter, Lindsay, and wonder where her twin brother was and what he was doing—or whether he was even alive. In my darkest moments I pictured a small forgotten grave and my baby lying in it."

"Oh, Grandmother, I'm so sorry!" Angelica threw her arms around her grandmother, who dropped the flower basket and hugged her back.

Flynt began to quietly gather up the spilled blossoms while the Fortune matriarch and her long-lost granddaughter hugged and cried.

"But I think we can finally lay it to rest, Angelica," Kate said through her tears to the girl. "I have Brandon back and now I have you—and Romina, too. I'm grateful to your mother for giving you to us, and I have full confidence that we'll be seeing a completely different Brandon, with her at his side."

"At the risk of sounding glib, Brandon will definitely behave himself with Romina to answer to." Flynt smiled as he handed Kate her flower basket. "His sanity, such as it is, will depend on it."

"That came out sounding glib, anyway, Flynt," scolded Angelica, but Kate laughed.

"Now about our wedding and this high tea reception for the A- and B-list Fortune tribe," Flynt said wryly.

He caught Angelica's eye. An unspoken message passed between them.

"Would the whole Fortune gang enjoy the party, even if the bride and groom were—somewhere else?" Angelica asked obliquely.

But not obliquely enough. "Could you tell me exactly where that 'somewhere else' might be?" asked Kate. "I promise I won't tell a soul. I'll let Mollie keep planning the wedding, and all the Fortunes will arrive and have a smashingly good time, with or without the presence of the bride and groom. And that will include Brandon and Romina, too, and your little brother and sister. I shall personally make sure of that, my dear Angelica."

"We could hoodwink the whole family!" Angelica was enthused. "Do you think we can actually pull it off, Grandmother?"

"My dears, I have complete faith that the two of you will pull it off. And you have my official blessing to hoodwink the Fortunes."

Epilogue

A few hours later, the Fortune jet landed at the Las Vegas airport.

"I don't think I'll ever get used to flying in a private jet," Angelica remarked as she and Flynt headed into the terminal.

"This was a much more staid flight than the one from Birmingham to Minneapolis." His eyes gleamed. "This time we actually sat in our seats and read magazines the whole time. I think the attendant was a little disappointed we behaved so very conventionally. How dull for him."

Angelica blushed. Would she ever be able to remember her first flight and their first lovemaking—*a very literal flight into passion!*—without blushing? And now she was actually thinking in florid purple prose! Her cheeks burned scarlet.

"We behaved like a respectable, about-to-be-married couple," she said rather primly.

He grinned. "Whatever you say, Angelica."

Each of them was carrying an overnight bag. When Flynt reached for hers, Angelica hung onto it. "I can carry it, thanks."

"A symbolic gesture, proving to yourself and to me that you intend to carry your own weight in this relationship?" he asked wryly.

"You sound like a profiling agent at the Behavioral Science Unit again. And you're way off target, former-agent Corrigan. I don't want you carrying both bags because I want you to have one hand free." She slipped her hand into his. "So I can hold it."

They smiled at each other, their eyes telegraphing messages that were not at all dull or conventional and certainly not staid.

"You can gamble right here in the airport." Angelica glanced around at the slot machines whirring and clanking as travelers continuously deposited coins.

"You can do almost anything, anywhere in this city, at any time, which is why I suggested flying here. We can get married immediately."

"Wedding chapels open for business twenty-four hours a day, seven days a week." Angelica read a poster as they passed. "Oh, look at that one. We can be married by a licensed Elvis impersonator."

"It would make an interesting wedding photo, but I have something a little more traditional in mind, sweetheart…"

"The Chapel O' Love is kind of traditional," Angelica decided half an hour later as she and Flynt were ushered inside a wedding-cake-shaped chapel. Everything inside, from floor to ceiling, was dazzling white like shiny frosting on a wedding cake. "In an untraditional kind of way."

"I like to think that describes us and our relationship." Flynt's thumb caressed her palm. "Are you ready?"

She nodded her head.

"Nervous?"

Angelica gazed at the white pews, at the altar where the man in white, ready to pronounce them husband and wife by the powers invested in him by the state of Nevada, stood waiting. The Chapel O' Love was a full-service chapel, which meant everything necessary for the wedding nuptials could be purchased on the premises.

The rings. She and Flynt had selected matching plain gold bands. The flowers for the bouquet; Flynt had insisted on white orchids. She was touched again by the mere notion that he remembered her favorite flower.

Even a witness could be hired to act as a wedding attendant. And so Tiffany, a buxom, leggy blonde wearing a standard but tasteful pale pink gown, was in place at the white altar.

Angelica's own wedding dress was a white silk sheath given to her by her grandmother before leaving Minneapolis. The endlessly resourceful Kate had arranged for Mollie to bring a selection of dresses to the house where Angelica chose her favorite. The elegant white silk suited her best, Kate had agreed, presenting the dress to her newfound granddaughter with much love.

A tape of "Here Comes the Bride," the Mendelssohn traditional version, Angelica's choice out of a large and extremely eclectic music collection, began to play.

Was she nervous? Angelica considered Flynt's question. Then looked up at his warm blue eyes and shook her head no. "I've never been so sure that I was doing the right thing in my whole life."

"That goes double for me, sweetheart."

Hand-in-hand, they walked to the altar. There was no father to give the bride away but since her father was a very new presence in her life, it was better this way, Angelica mused. She was giving herself to Flynt—just as he was pledging himself to her.

"Mrs. Flynt Corrigan." Angelica held out her left hand and admired the wedding ring Flynt had placed on her finger less than an hour before. "Angelica Corrigan."

"I like the sound of that." Flynt smiled as he refilled her glass from the bottle of champagne cooling in ice alongside their table.

"Mmm, I do too."

They exchanged blissful, loving newlywed smiles, oblivious to everything but each other.

They were enjoying a celebratory late supper in a dimly lit restaurant in one of the biggest, glitziest casino hotels along a long wide strip of big, glitzy casino hotels.

"We pulled it off," Angelica exulted. "Instead of being the Hoodwinked Bride—"

"You successfully hoodwinked the Fortunes." Flynt chuckled. "Which doesn't happen very often, I'm fairly sure of that."

"Well, they've never crossed paths with me before," Angelica added slyly. "Anyway, we had grandmother's official blessing, remember?"

"I certainly do. Which means if you change your

mind and decide you want to return to Minneapolis in time for the reception Mollie's been planning, nobody will dare to say a word about us skipping out of our own private wedding. Not even your mother, I'd wager. Kate has completely charmed Romina, which put me in further awe of your grandmother.''

"Do you want to go back to Minneapolis for our post-wedding reception, Flynt? Remember, you can have all the tea sandwiches and Devonshire cream with scones that you can eat there.''

"Mind if we pass on the tea sandwiches and Devonshire cream? Let's stay here and call the Fortunes at our post-wedding reception. We can accept everybody's good wishes and tell them our plans—''

"That we'll be living in Minneapolis, at least at first,'' she chimed in.

"But we might relocate to Birmingham some time in the future,'' he added. They'd agreed to remain flexible in their living arrangements.

Under the table, Angelica ran her fingers along his thigh. Her dark eyes gleamed when she felt his instantaneous response.

He leaned over to whisper something outrageously sexual in her ear. "My loving blushing bride,'' he teased, observing her reaction.

"My incredibly imaginative groom,'' she shot back, sliding her hand even higher.

He groaned. "If the waiter wasn't already headed this way with our dinner, I'd pick you up and carry you directly to our room, Mrs. Corrigan.''

The waiter arrived at their table and began to set plates in front of them. The food looked and smelled delicious.

"I have an idea, former-agent Corrigan," Angelica said brightly, reaching for her fork. "The minute we're finished eating—"

"I'll pick you up and carry you directly to our room?"

"You read my mind!" She pretended to be astonished. "Your intuitive skills are extraordinary, Flynt."

"You're very loyal, sweetheart. But don't try to tout my intuitive skills to Gabe and your Fortune uncles and cousins who probably consider me dense rather than intuitive. I don't think they'll soon forget that it was Brandon who bested me in first suspecting Casper."

Angelica shrugged, unconcerned. "You and I had other things on our minds. Like breaking down lifelong restraints and reserves and falling in love with each other."

"I do love you, Angelica."

"I love you, Flynt."

"Forever," they said at the same time, their voices and their thoughts and their hearts in perfect unison.

* * * * *

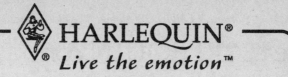

HARLEQUIN®
Live the emotion™

HARLEQUIN®
AMERICAN *Romance®*

Upbeat, All-American Romances

flipside
HARLEQUIN®

Romantic Comedy

Harlequin Historicals®
Historical Romantic Adventure!

HARLEQUIN®
INTRIGUE

Romantic Suspense

HARLEQUIN®

HARLEQUIN ROMANCE®

The essence of modern romance

HARLEQUIN®
Presents

Seduction and Passion Guaranteed!

HARLEQUIN *Super*ROMANCE®

Emotional, Exciting, Unexpected

Temptation

Sassy, Sexy, Seductive!

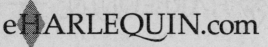

e HARLEQUIN.com

The Ultimate Destination for Women's Fiction

For **FREE online reading,** visit
www.eHarlequin.com now and enjoy:

Online Reads
Read **Daily** and **Weekly** chapters from
our Internet-exclusive stories by your
favorite authors.

Interactive Novels
Cast your vote to help decide how these
stories unfold...then stay tuned!

Quick Reads
For shorter romantic reads, try our
collection of Poems, Toasts, & More!

Online Read Library
Miss one of our online reads?
Come here to catch up!

Reading Groups
Discuss, share and rave with other
community members!

For great reading online,
visit www.eHarlequin.com today!

INTONL04R

SILHOUETTE *Romance*

Escape to a place where a kiss is still a kiss...

Feel the breathless connection...

Fall in love as though it were the very first time...

Experience the power of love!

Come to where favorite authors—such as

Diana Palmer, Stella Bagwell, Marie Ferrarella

and many more—deliver modern fairy tale romances and genuine emotion, time after time after time....

Silhouette Romance— from today to forever.

Silhouette

Live the possibilities

Visit Silhouette Books at www.eHarlequin.com.   SRDIN104

eHARLEQUIN.com

The Ultimate Destination for Women's Fiction

Becoming an eHarlequin.com member is easy, fun and **FREE!** Join today to enjoy great benefits:

- **Super savings** on all our books, including members-only discounts and offers!

- Enjoy **exclusive online reads**—FREE!

- Info, tips and **expert advice** on writing your own romance novel.

- FREE romance **newsletters**, customized by you!

- Find out the latest on your **favorite authors.**

- Enter to win exciting **contests and promotions!**

- Chat with other members in our **community message boards!**

To become a member,
visit www.eHarlequin.com today!

INTMEMB04R

Harlequin Historicals®
Historical Romantic Adventure!

From rugged lawmen and valiant knights to defiant heiresses and spirited frontierswomen, Harlequin Historicals will capture your imagination with their dramatic scope, passion and adventure.

Harlequin Historicals . . . they're too good to miss!

www.eHarlequin.com
HHDIR104

HARLEQUIN®
INTRIGUE®

WE'LL LEAVE YOU BREATHLESS!

If you've been looking for thrilling tales of
contemporary passion and sensuous love stories
with taut, edge-of-the-seat suspense—then
you'll love Harlequin Intrigue!

Every month, you'll meet six new heroes
who are guaranteed to make your spine tingle
and your pulse pound. With them you'll enter
into the exciting world of Harlequin Intrigue—
where your life is on the line
and so is your heart!

THAT'S INTRIGUE— ROMANTIC SUSPENSE AT ITS BEST!

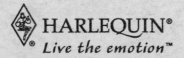

HARLEQUIN®
Live the emotion™

www.eHarlequin.com

INTDIR104

passionate powerful provocative love stories

**Silhouette Desire delivers
strong heroes, spirited heroines
and compelling love stories.**

Desire features your favorite authors,
including

Annette Broadrick,
Ann Major,
Anne McAllister
and Cait London.

**Passionate, powerful and provocative
romances *guaranteed!***

For superlative authors, sensual stories
and sexy heroes, choose Silhouette Desire.

passionate powerful provocative love stories

Visit Silhouette Books at www.eHarlequin.com   SDGEN04

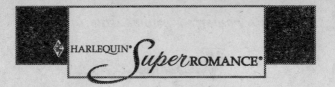

...there's more to the story!

Superromance.
A *big* satisfying read about unforgettable characters. Each month we offer *six* very different stories that range from family drama to adventure and mystery, from highly emotional stories to romantic comedies—and much more! Stories about people you'll believe in and care about. Stories too compelling to put down....

Our authors are among today's *best* romance writers. You'll find familiar names and talented newcomers. Many of them are award winners— and you'll see why!

If you want the biggest and best in romance fiction, you'll get it from Superromance!

Emotional, Exciting, Unexpected...

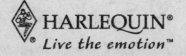

HARLEQUIN®
Live the emotion™

www.eHarlequin.com

HSDIR104